Also available from Roan Parrish

BETTER THAN PEOPLE

ROAN PARRISH

carina
press

carina
press®

Recycling programs
for this product may
not exist in your area.

ISBN-13: 978-1-335-54282-3

Better Than People

Copyright © 2020 by Roan Parrish

This edition published by arrangement with Harlequin Books S.A.

For questions and comments about the quality of this book, please contact us at CustomerService@Harlequin.com.

Carina Press
22 Adelaide St. West, 40th Floor
Toronto, Ontario M5H 4E3, Canada
www.CarinaPress.com

Printed in U.S.A.

For our beloved companions, past, present and future.

BETTER THAN PEOPLE

Chapter One

Jack

If you had told Jack Matheson when he woke up this morning that he'd end the day at the bottom of a ditch, he wouldn't have been terribly surprised. After all, his whole life *felt* like it was spent at the bottoms of ditches these days—what was one more literal one?

The nightly walk had begun as they usually did. As soon as he finished dinner and placed his plate and fork in the sink, the dogs had clustered around him, eyes hopeful and tongues out, ready to prowl. Bernard butted his huge head against Jack's thighs in encouragement while Puddles hung back, waiting to follow the group out. Dandelion pawed at the ground excitedly, and Rat vibrated in place, tiny body taut with anticipation.

The cats cleaned themselves or snoozed on various surfaces, watching with disinterest, except for Pirate. Pirate twined her way through the forest of legs and paws and tails, back arched, sleek and ready.

"Let's head out," Jack said, clipping on leashes and straightening harnesses as he shoved his feet into worn boots and plastic bags in his back pocket.

Pirate led the way, trotting light-footed ahead of them, then doubling back like a scout. Huge, snuggly Bernard—a St. Bernard who'd been with him the longest—took turns walking next to each of the others, nipping and licking at his friends enthusiastically, and drawing back when he accidentally shoved them off their feet. Bernard didn't know his own strength.

Dandelion pranced along, happy as always to snap at the breeze or a puff of dust, or simply to be outside.

Puddles walked carefully, his soft golden face swinging back and forth, alert for danger, and he jumped at every sound. Twice, Jack had to scoop him up and carry him over the puddles he refused to step in or walk around.

Rat took the lead, just behind Pirate, her tiny legs going hummingbird fast to keep ahead of the others. She kept her nose to the ground, and if she scented a threat, she'd be the first to take it on.

Their leashes crisscrossed throughout the walk, and Jack untangled them absently as he kept one eye on the animals and the other on the sky.

Summer had settled into autumn, and the leaves of Garnet Run, Wyoming, were tipped with red and gold. The air held the first promises of winter, and Jack found himself sighing deeply. Winter was beautiful here. His little cottage was cozy, his fireplace warm, and the woods peaceful.

But this year, for the first time in nearly a decade, he wouldn't have work to occupy him as the snow fell outside.

Jack growled and clenched his fists against the fury that roared in his ears as he anticipated yet another night without a notebook in his hand.

Bernard snuffled against his thigh and Puddles whined. This—this right here was why animals beat people, paws down.

They were sensitive. They cared. They wanted to be loved and they gave love back. Animals never betrayed you the way people did. They were loyal.

"It's okay," Jack murmured. He scratched Bernard's massive head and ran gentle fingers over Puddles' tense ears. "I'll be okay."

Bernard gave his elbow an enthusiastic lick.

"I'll be okay," Jack repeated firmly, to himself this time, as a squirrel's over-enthusiastic labors dislodged an acorn from an overhanging branch. The acorn rustled through the leaves and fell directly onto the soft fur between Puddles' ears, where Jack's fingers had stroked a moment before.

Puddles, skittish at the best of times, reared into the air, fur bristling, and took off into the trees, his leash slipping through Jack's fingers.

"Dammit, Puddles, no!"

Jack tried to follow, but Bernard had plopped down on the soft grass at the tree line and was currently rolling himself in evening smells. It was useless to attempt to move Bernard once he was on the ground, even for a man of Jack's size.

"Stay!" Jack commanded. Bernard woofed, Dandelion flopped down beside him, Rat clawed at the ground, teeth bared. "Pirate, watch them," he called to the cat, even though Pirate had never given him any indication that she understood orders, much less took them.

Jack took off after Puddles. The thought of the dog afraid made Jack's heart pound and he ran full-out.

Puddles had been a trembling mess when Jack found him by the side of the road two years before, and it had taken a month before the Lab would even eat the food Jack offered from his hand. Slowly, painstakingly, he had gained Puddles' trust, and the dog had joined the rest of his pack.

"Puddles!" Jack called into the twilight. He heard a whine ahead and sped up, muscles burning, glad for his afternoon runs. Leaves crunched up ahead to his left and Jack zagged. "Puddles?"

Dark was closing in on the woods and Jack narrowed his eyes, hoping to avoid running smack into a tree. When he heard Puddles' soft bark from up ahead he threw himself forward again.

"I'm here!" he shouted, and was answered with another bark. Then, the sound of crackling branches split the quiet and a whine and thud stopped Jack's heart. He barreled forward to see what had happened, and heard the sound again as his legs broke through what he'd thought was underbrush, and found no solid ground on the other side.

His legs windmilled and his hands caught at the air for a

second that seemed like forever. Then he landed hard and rolled down an embankment, stones and branches pummeling him on the way down.

Jack came to a sudden stop with a head-rattling lurch and a gut-churning snap. For a single heavenly moment, there was no pain, just the relief of stillness. Then the world righted itself, and with clarity came agony.

"Oh, fuck," Jack gasped. "Oh, fuck, fuck, fuck."

He bit his lip and lifted his swimming head just enough to peer down at his right leg, where the pain ripped into him with steely teeth. Nausea flooded him as he saw the unnatural angle of his leg and he wrenched his gaze away.

For three breaths, Jack did nothing but try not to puke. Then a wet, trembling nose nudged his hand, and he opened his eyes to Puddles' warm brown gaze.

"Thank god." Jack sucked in a breath and lifted a shaky hand to the dog's side. "You okay, bud?"

Puddles sat down beside him and rested his chin on Jack's shoulder, a loyal sentinel.

For some reason, it brought tears to Jack's eyes.

"I'm fine, Charlie. Jesus, back off." Jack growled at his older brother, who was hovering over him, one large, rough hand nervously stroking his beard, the other catching on the over-starched hospital sheets as he tucked them around Jack.

After hours of pain, insurance forms, and answering the same questions for every nurse and doctor that came along, Jack's habitual brusqueness had morphed into exhausted annoyance.

"Yeah. When I got the phone call to meet you at the

hospital after you'd been found crumpled at the bottom of a hill with your bones sticking out I definitely thought, 'He's totally fine,'" Charlie said flatly.

They looked alike—the same reddish-blond hair and hazel eyes; the same large, solid builds, though Charlie was bigger, muscles honed from his constant physical labor—and despite his brother's droll reply, Jack could see a familiar fear in his expression, and in the way he stood close, as if he wanted to be able to touch Jack and check that he was all right.

Charlie had looked after him his whole life, worried about him his whole life. It would be useless to expect him to stop now. Not that Jack really wanted him to.

"Sorry." Jack fisted his hands at his sides and closed his eyes.

Charlie eased his bulk down onto the side of the bed.

"I know I've been saying I wanted to see you more," Charlie said, making his voice lighter. "But this isn't exactly what I meant."

Jack snorted and punched his brother a glancing blow to the shoulder. He hadn't actually meant for it to be glancing, but it seemed his strength had left him.

On the table next to his bed something familiar had appeared: his sketchbook and three pens. His gut clenched.

"Where did those come from?"

"I brought them from your place. Boring in here."

"I don't want 'em."

Charlie's sincere and puzzled expression deepened.

"What? You've never gone a day without drawing in your life. I thought especially in here you'd want—"

"Well, I don't," Jack bit off. He closed his eyes. He hadn't told his brother that he hadn't drawn in eight months. Not since Davis...

Clearly confused, Charlie picked up the sketchbook and pens, huge hand dwarfing them.

Jack swallowed down his rage and fear and disappointment. He felt like every shitty moment of the last eight months had somehow been leading up to this: concussion, broken leg, cracked ribs, lying in a cramped hospital bed, with absolutely nothing to look forward to.

Darkness swallowed him as he realized that now the one thing he'd taken pleasure in since his life went to shit— walking with the animals—was off the table for the fore-seeable future.

"Fuck." Jack sighed, and he felt it in his whole body. Charlie leaned closer. "What'm I gonna do?"

The app was called PetShare and one of the nurses had rec-ommended it after a failed attempt to have Charlie smug-gle the dogs into Jack's hospital room had led the nurse to enquire about Jack's situation. She'd taken his phone from his hand, downloaded it for him, then returned the phone and said sternly, "No dogs in a hospital. Obviously."

Now, home and settled on the couch with a pillow and blanket after basically being tucked in by Charlie and prom-ising he'd call if he needed anything, Jack fumbled out his phone and made a profile.

Username? He hated usernames.

JackOfAllDogs, he typed. Then, with a guilty glance at the cats, he changed it to *JackOfAllPets*. Then he decided that looked too much like *Jack off* and changed it to *JMatheson*.

At the app's prompting he uploaded a photo of Bernard for his profile picture. Then on to the questions. He hated answering questions. When he got to the final box, which asked him to explain what he was looking for, he grumbled to himself as he thumbed too-small keys, wishing he could draw instead of type. He'd always been better with images than with words anyway. Somehow, people always took his words the wrong way.

That's why it had felt so fortuitous when he'd met Davis, who seemed to pluck the words he intended from his drawings and put them on the page. A perfect partnership. Or so he'd thought.

He banished all thoughts of Davis from his mind and mashed the Submit Profile button, then shoved his phone back into his pocket.

PetShare matched pet owners with animal enthusiasts who didn't have pets of their own. Some of the users were people like Jack who needed help with animal care. Others were just willing to let animal lovers spend time with their pets. But with four dogs (and a cat) who needed twice-daily walks, Jack wasn't optimistic about his chances of being matched with someone, no matter how enthusiastic they were. He imagined he might need three or four interested parties to meet his animals' needs.

Charlie had volunteered to walk them until he found someone, and he didn't want to burden his brother any longer than he had to. Charlie had the hardware store to run, and he spent long hours there and on construction sites.

Jack flicked on the television. He'd never watched much TV before the Davis debacle. The worlds he dreamt up in his head and the world outside his door had always been preferable to any he'd found on the screen. But over the past eight months he'd learned the numbing power of flickering lights and voices that required no response.

Wanting something mindless and distracting, Jack selected *Secaucus Psychic*. Maybe seeing people who'd lost family members to actual death would put a broken leg in perspective.

Hell, who was he kidding. He didn't want perspective. He wanted to sink into the couch and into his bad mood and sulk for just a little longer.

He'd banned Bernard from the couch because, though fully grown, the St. Bernard behaved like a puppy, flopping on top of Jack despite weighing nearly as much as him, and with a leg held together with pins and casting, and ribs and head aching, Jack didn't think he could take a careless flop. So instead, Bernard had piled himself on the floor in front of the couch, as close to Jack as he could get, and lolled his massive head back every few minutes to check if he was allowed on the couch yet.

Pirate curled delicately in the crook of his elbow, though, and he stroked her back, making her rumble.

An unfamiliar ding from his pocket startled both Jack and Pirate. It was the notification sound for PetShare. Jack thumbed the app open and saw that he'd matched. Someone whose username was *SimpleSimon* and lived 6.78 miles away from him had checked the *I'd love to!* option next to Jack's description of what he was looking for.

"I'll be damned," Jack said to the animals. "Either this dude is a saint or he's got no life at all."

Pirate yawned and stretched out a paw to lazily dig her claws into his shoulder.

"Fine, jeez, I know. I don't have one either," Jack grumbled, and resentfully clicked *Accept*.

It was a horrible night. One of Jack's worst.

Because of his concussion, he couldn't take a strong enough painkiller to touch the ache in his ribs and the screaming in his leg. He tossed and turned, and finally gave up on sleep, searching the darkness for the familiar reflective eyes watching him. After a moment, he lurched upright. The sudden movement shot pain through his head and chest and leg and left him gasping and nauseated, clutching the edge of the mattress until the worst of it passed.

Fuck, fuck, fuck.

Finally, having learned his lesson, Jack gingerly pushed himself off the bed and shoved the crutches under his arms. The pull of the muscles across his chest as he used his arms to propel him forward left his ribs in agony. By the time he got to the bathroom, usually just ten quick steps away, he was sweating and swearing, teeth clenched hard.

Then, the drama of lowering his pants.

"Can't even take a damn piss without fucking something up," Jack muttered. At least, that's what he'd intended to mutter before the pain and exhaustion stole the luxury of indulging in self-deprecating commentary.

Humbled and infuriated in equal measure, Jack gave up

on sleep entirely. Coffee. That's what he needed. Coffee was the opposite of sleep. Coffee was a choice he could make when apparently he couldn't control a single other goddamn thing in his pathetic, broken life.

The trip to the kitchen was suddenly rife with unexpected hazards. A squeaky dog toy sent him lurching to one side, groaning at his wrenched ribs and the shock of pain that shot through his leg. When he could move again, his crutch clipped the edge of a pile of unopened mail that had sat for weeks, which cascaded across the floorboards like a croupier's expert spread of cards.

Naturally, that got the attention of several animals and Jack stood very still while the envelopes were swatted at, swept by tails, and finally, in the case of the largest envelope, flopped upon by Pickles, the smallest of his cats.

Mayonnaise, a sweet white cat with one green eye missing, slunk up to him on the counter and butted her little head against his arm.

"Hi," he said, and kissed her fuzzy head. She gave him a happy chirp, then darted out the window cat door above the sink.

Everything took four times as long as usual and required ten times the energy. The crutches dug into his underarms with every touch, bruising and chafing the skin there and catching on his armpit hair. His leg hurt horribly and the longer he stayed upright the worse it ached as the blood rushed downward. His head throbbed and throbbed and throbbed.

Though he'd gotten up while it was still dark, the sun had risen during the rigamarole of making coffee and eggs.

Jack scarfed the eggs directly from the pan, afraid if he tried to sit down at the kitchen table he wouldn't be able to get back up.

He realized too late that he couldn't bend down to put food and water in the animals' bowls and began a messy process of attempting it from his full height.

His first try slopped water all over the floor. Swearing, he dropped towels over the spills, moving them with the tip of his crutch to soak up the water. Next came the dog food, and Jack practically cheered when most of it went in the bowls.

The cat food, smaller, skidded everywhere, and Pirate and Pickles looked up at him for a moment as if offended. Then they had great fun chasing the food all over the floor. When the dogs joined the chase it resulted in the knocking over of bowls of water, the soaking of food, the scarfing of said food by the dogs and a counter full of hissing cats.

Jack opened a tin of tuna and let them at it, staring at his ravaged kitchen. It looked like the forest floor on a muddy day and it stank of wet dog food. The prospect of trying to clean it up left him short of breath and exhausted.

Bernard, always one to lurk until the end of mealtimes, hoping to scarf a stray mouthful, shoved his face in the mess.

"Good dog," Jack said. He'd meant to say it wryly, but it came out with relieved sincerity.

Louis, the least social of his cats—he only liked Puddles—poked his gray and black head out of the bedroom, sniffed the air, and decided that whatever he smelled didn't portend well. He eschewed breakfast with a flick of his tail and retreated back inside the bedroom. Jack made a mental note to leave a bowl out for him later.

Just as Jack sank onto the couch, the dogs started shuffling to the front door the way they only did on the rare occasions when someone was approaching. Jack groaned. He hauled himself back up and pretended not to hear his own pathetic whimper as he made his way to the door.

"Back up, come on," Jack wheezed at the animals. Then, in a whisper, "Be extremely cute so this guy likes you." Then he yanked the door open.

There, with one hand half-raised to knock, stood a man made of contrasts.

He was tall—only an inch or two shorter than Jack's six foot three—but his shoulders were hunched and his head hung low, like he was trying to disappear. His clothes were mismatched and worn—soft jeans, a faded green shirt, a peach and yellow sweater, and a red knit scarf—but every line of his body was frozen and hard.

Then he lifted his chin and glanced up at Jack for just an instant, and Jack couldn't pay attention to anything but his eyes. A burning turquoise blue that shocked him because after years of drawing he'd always thought blue was a cool color. But not this blue. This was the blue of neon and molten glass and the inside of a planet. This was the blue of fire.

As quickly as he'd looked up, the man dropped his gaze again, and Jack immediately missed that blue.

"Uh, hey. You *SimpleSimon*?"

His head jerked up again and this time there was anger in his eyes.

"On the app, I mean? I'm Jack."

Jack held out his hand and Simon inched forward slowly, then shoved his hands in his pockets and scuffed his heel on the ground. He had messy dark hair that, from Jack's view of the top of his head, was mostly swirls of cowlicks.

"You wanna come in and meet the pack?" Jack tried again, attempting to infuse geniality into his voice instead of the exhausted, pained, irritation he felt at every dimension of his current situation.

Simon tensed and scuffed his heel again.

"I won't bite," Jack said, shuffling backward to make room. "Can't say the same for Pirate, though. She's a little monster."

Good. A dad joke. Great first impression, Matheson.

But Simon gave a jerky nod and followed him inside. When Jack reached to close the door behind him one of his crutches caught and slid to the ground. Jack swore and grabbed for it, avoiding wrenching his ribs at the last moment by deviating to grab the doorknob instead, knocking into the man's shoulder in the process. Jack wanted to scream.

Simon immediately moved away and Jack had a moment of resentment until his crutch was retrieved from the floor and held up for him.

"Thanks. Damn things. Mind if we sit down?"

Jack dropped onto the couch with a groan but Simon didn't sit. He hovered near the doorway to the kitchen and crossed his arms over his stomach.

Jack saw his nostrils twitch and begged the universe that

Simon wouldn't turn around and see the utter shambolic trough that was his kitchen floor.

They'd messaged last night to set up this meeting and their exchange had been perfectly friendly. All Jack could imagine was that his bad mood was so palpable that he'd put this guy off.

"So, uh. I'm Jack," he tried again.

The man's arms tightened around himself.

"Simon," he said, voice low and very quiet.

When nothing else seemed forthcoming, Jack launched into introductions to the animals and watched Simon unfold.

When Jack gave the signal to allow Bernard to approach, the dog cuddled Simon so aggressively that Simon ended up sitting on the floor. Bernard licked his face and snuffled into his armpit and Simon huffed out a sound that might've been a laugh. Jack caught a flash of fire blue through his dark hair.

"This is Puddles," Jack went on. "He's a neurotic dude. Hates puddles. Seriously, you'll have to pick him up and carry him over them."

Simon held out his hand, head still bowed. Puddles placed his chin into Simon's hand and then sat down right next to him, pressing himself against Simon's hip.

"Hey, Puddles." It was so soft Jack almost didn't hear it. Puddles kept leaning into Simon.

"That's Rat." Jack pointed to the tiny dog whose hairless tail whipped across the floor. Rat jumped over to Simon, then bounded away after something only she saw. "And

Dandelion." The cheerful mutt wriggled happily when Simon pet her.

Simon was bookended by Bernard and Puddles, petting them both at once. His scarf had come loose and Pickles, who was one of Jack's newer arrivals, made a beeline for it, batting at it until her claws tangled in the yarn.

"Shit, sorry. Pickles, no!"

Jack moved to stand, forgot about his leg, and groaned, falling back onto the couch.

"Fuuuck my life."

Pirate slunk single-mindedly from her perch on top of the easy chair, making her way through the room to Simon.

He reached out a hand for her to smell and she gave him a dainty lick on the knuckle. Jack thought he saw a smile behind all that hair, but before he could warn Simon, Pirate pounced on his scarf too, wrestling with Pickles over it and nearly garroting Simon in the process.

"Jesus, it's pandemonium," Jack muttered.

A creaky laugh came from the man currently buried under animals on his floor.

Simon unwound his scarf and wrapped it around Pickles and Pirate, hugging the cats to his chest with one arm. Then he got to his knees and slowly stood, patting Bernard and Puddles with his other hand. Jack could hear Pickles and Pirate purring in their swaddle.

"You okay?" he asked Simon.

"Mhmm."

"Okay, well... Still up for it? I know they're a lot, but..."

Simon shook his head and Jack's stomach lurched at the

thought of finding someone else who could help. But then Simon said, softly, "It's fine."

"Yeah?"

Simon nodded, all shoulders and dark hair and flash of blue eyes and slash of pale jaw.

"Oh, great, amazing, wonderful." Relief let loose a torrent of words, and Jack hauled himself off the couch to take Simon through whose leash was whose and where they could and couldn't go, what Puddles was afraid of in addition to puddles (sticks shaped like lightning bolts, grasshoppers, bicycles, plastic bags), which dogs they might meet that Bernard would try to cuddle to death and Rat would try to attack, what intersection to avoid because there was a fire ant hill, and why never, ever to grab Pirate if she tried to climb trees.

Simon nodded and made soft listening sounds, and every once in a while he'd jerk his head up and meet Jack's eyes for just a moment. When Jack passed the leashes, treats, and plastic bags over to him, Simon paused like he was going to say something. Then he put the treats and bags in his pocket, wrapped his unraveling scarf around his neck, and backed out of the door, head down and dogs in tow. Pirate leapt after them.

"Okay, then," Jack called from the door as Simon walked away, not wanting the animals out of his sight. "You have my number if you need anything, right?"

Simon held up his phone in answer, but didn't turn around.

"Okay, bye," Jack said, but there was no one left to hear him.

Chapter Two

Simon

Simon's heart fluttered like a wild thing and he sucked in air through his nose and slowly blew it out through his mouth, concentrating on the smells of the autumn morning. Pine and dew and fresh asphalt and the warm, intoxicating scent that seemed to cling to him after only ten minutes spent in Jack Matheson's chaotic house.

He rounded the corner so he knew he was out of sight, then led the dogs to the tree line and pressed his back to the rough trunk of a silver fir. He squeezed his eyes shut tight to banish the static swimming at the edges of his vision and willed his heart to slow after the encounter with Jack.

Shy. It was the word people had used to describe Simon

Burke since he was a child. A tiny, retiring word that was itself little more than a whisper.

But what Simon felt was not a whisper. It was a freight train bearing down on him, whistle blowing and wheels grinding, passengers staring and ground shaking with the ineluctable approach.

It was a swimming head and a pounding heart. A furious heat and a numbness in his fingers. It was sweating and choking and the curiously violent sensation of silence, pulled like a hood over his entire body, but concentrated at the tiny node of his throat.

Shy was the word for a child's fear, shed like a light spring jacket when summer came.

What Simon had was knitted to his very bones, spliced in his blood, so cleverly prehensile that it clung to every beat of his physical being.

The huge St. Bernard called Bernard—apparently this Jack guy wasn't exactly the creative type—bumped Simon's hip and he opened his eyes. The cautious yellow Lab, Puddles, was looking up at him with concern in his warm brown eyes; tiny Rat was scanning the road looking for threats; easygoing Dandelion was happily yipping at birds; and Pirate the cat was daintily cleaning her paws as her tail swished back and forth.

Simon's breath came easier. He was right where he wanted to be: outside, spending time with animals. He dropped to a crouch and murmured to the little pack, letting them smell him, letting his heart rate return to normal.

"Hi," he said, trying out his voice. It tended to go scratchy from disuse. "Thanks for walking with me." Bernard smiled a sweet doggy smile and Simon couldn't help but smile back. Animals didn't make him feel self-conscious. They didn't make him feel like he was drowning. They gave and never required anything of him except kindness.

He'd discovered this as a child, around the same time he'd discovered that other children could not be counted on to be kind. Not to him, anyway.

Pirate meowed and took off down the road and all the dogs mobilized to follow her, tugging Simon back onto the lane. As they walked, he basked in their quiet joy and the peace of simply being in the fresh air. In that peace, his thoughts drifted to Jack Matheson.

Simon had gotten himself to Jack's front door by sheer, knuckle-clenching force of will.

For the past two years, Simon had been saving up to get a bigger apartment so that he'd have space for a dog. He'd planned the walks they'd take and the parks they'd go to together.

When his grandfather died six months ago and Simon saw his grandmother's face—brow pinched with grief and eyes wide with fear—Simon knew what he had to do. He moved in the next week. His grandmother was his best friend and he didn't want her to be alone. But the cost of her company was the plans he'd made: she was terribly allergic to animals.

He'd made his profile on PetShare the week he moved in with his grandmother and for the last six months, he'd waited. He'd matched several times, usually with people who needed someone to stop by and feed their pets while they were at work, but that wasn't what he wanted. He wanted to spend time with animals, bask in their easy companionship.

So when he saw *JMatheson*'s profile pop up, with its picture of a huge, adorable St. Bernard and its description of his rather extensive needs, which managed to be both terse and self-deprecating, Simon's heart had leapt.

But when he stood outside his door, he hadn't been able to make himself ring the bell. It was like his hand ran up against a physical force when he tried. He stood there, trying to break out of the paralyzing fog.

And then the door had opened.

Stocking feet, worn sweatpants, a bulky cast on one leg—his eyes had traveled slowly up from the ground. A faded Penn State hoodie, broad shoulders, and biceps that bulged as they wielded crutches.

But it was the first glimpse of the man's face that had frozen Simon in place. He had hair the color of copper and gold, a strong jaw etched with copper stubble, a straight nose, and hazel eyes beneath frowning reddish-brown eyebrows. His full mouth was fixed in a scowl.

He was beautiful and angry and it was a combination so potent that it flushed through Simon with the heat of an intoxicant, then set his head spinning with fear.

He'd clutched his arms around himself in a futile attempt to keep all his molecules contained, dreading the sensation of flying apart, diffusing into the atmosphere in a nebula of dissolution.

Simon had been consumed by the conviction he'd held as a child: if he could squeeze his eyes shut tightly enough to block out the world then it would cease to see him too. But when he'd opened his eyes again, there was Jack Matheson, still beautiful, but now looking at him with his most hated expression.

Pity.

Simon shook his head to clear the image of Jack's pitying gaze and picked up the pace, as if he might be able to outrun the moment when he'd have to drop off the animals and interact with Jack again.

"Grandma, I'm home," Simon called as he shouldered open the door, arms full of groceries.

"In the kitchen, dear!"

He deposited the bags on the counter, but backed off when his grandmother moved to kiss his cheek.

"You'll be allergic to me. One sec."

He jogged downstairs to his basement room and changed his clothes, giving a fond look at the fur of his new friends clinging to the wool of his sweater.

"How did it go?" his grandmother asked, sliding a cup of tea toward him on the counter. The smell of lavender perfume and chamomile tea would forever remind him of her.

"As well as can be expected?" Simon hedged, sipping the hot tea too quickly. She raised an eyebrow and he sighed. "He was fine. I just… Whatever. You know." Simon raked a hand through his hair.

His grandmother knew better than anyone how hard it was for him and how angry he got at himself for the hardship. She'd been the one he came to, red-faced and sweaty, when he'd nailed varsity soccer tryouts his sophomore year and then fled the field, never to return, when the coach noticed he hadn't shouted the team shout with the other boys and forced him to stand on his own and yell it with everyone looking.

She'd been the one who found him in the basement he now lived in, tear-streaked and reeking of vomit after his eleventh-grade history teacher had forced him to give his presentation in front of the rest of the class despite his promise to do any amount of extra credit instead.

Simon swallowed, overcome with affection for her.

"The dogs are great, though. There's this really big St. Bernard who's a cuddly baby and throws himself around even though he's probably two hundred pounds. And he has cats too, and one of them comes on the walks. Her name's Pirate—she's a calico with a black spot over one eye—and she leads the group like a little cat tour guide."

Simon's grandmother squeezed his hand.

"It's so good to see you happy," she said wistfully. Simon ducked his head, but a nice, comfortable kind of warmth accompanied his grandmother's touches. She didn't rush him the way his father did, didn't try and finish his sentences the way his mother did, didn't try and convince him to *just try* and be social the way his sister, Kylie, did. The way his teachers and school counselors had.

"Yeah," he said. He gulped the last of the tea and put his cup in the dishwasher. "I'm gonna go get started on work. You need anything before I do?"

"I'm fine, dear. I'll be in the garden, I think."

Simon hesitated. His grandfather's rose garden was the place Simon still felt his presence most strongly, and it was where his grandmother went when she wanted to think of him.

"Is it bad today?" he asked softly. He wasn't sure if *bad* was the right word, precisely. After all, it wasn't bad to miss the man you'd spent your life with, was it? It was merely... inevitable. But it was the shorthand he'd used the first time he'd asked, when he'd found her at the fence, one swollen-knuckled hand pressed flat to the wood and the other clutching the locket with her late husband's picture in it, and it had stuck.

She smiled gently at him. "Medium." With a pat to his arm, she left him to make his way down to the basement.

After a year, the graphic design business that Simon ran from home had become sustainable. The ability to make a living had been a relief, but the bigger relief had been the opportunity to quit his job working for the company where he'd dreaded going every morning and the cubicle that had left him open to social incursion from all directions.

Now, he conducted all his communications via email. He made his own schedule, which meant he could take long lunches to spend time with his grandmother—or, more recently, take time to walk Jack's dogs. He didn't mind working on the weekends to make up for it if necessary. It wasn't as if he had anywhere he wanted to go. In the quiet of his basement office, without the anxiety of the company work environment, Simon could lose himself in color, shape, font, and balance.

Today, however, Simon was distracted. He'd get to see the animals again tonight and already his skin tingled with the promise of contact. After the third time he found himself staring off into space, he pinched his arm, hard.

"Stop it."

He told himself that it was pathetic to be this excited about getting to hug some dogs or cuddle a cat. He told himself that he was an adult and taking a walk should not be the highlight of his day.

He told himself a lot of things, but it still took him longer than usual to finish his work.

That evening, back in the clothes he'd worn to walk the dogs earlier, Simon stood once more before Jack's door. This time, he was able to ring the doorbell and the sound was met with yipping and barking from within. After a minute, he heard a groan that could only be Jack and then a stream of swearing.

When the door finally opened, Jack's hair was flattened on one side and sticking straight up at the crown.

"Hey," he said, voice rough. "Sorry. Fell asleep."

Simon glanced at his face and took in the shadows under his eyes, like someone had pressed thumbs there hard enough to bruise. He took in the creases on one cheek and the tightness around his mouth that might have been pain, and wondered what had happened to his leg.

He opened his mouth to say it was fine, but the words inflated in his throat until they were a balloon choking off his breath. There was the itch of panic and then he swallowed the words down and could breathe again. He nodded.

Suddenly, exhaustion hit him. He should've anticipated it, what with the effort it had taken to drag himself here this morning, the effort it had taken to go inside, and now the effort of doing it all over again. It was an exhaustion that sapped all his reserves and put a certain end to any chance of conversation that might have existed.

The anger rose and with it Simon could feel his chest get hot. The heat crept up his neck and his ears blazed. Before his face could turn red he clenched his hand into a fist and gritted his teeth. Then he closed his eyes, held out his other hand, and prayed that Jack would understand.

"Listen," Jack said, not understanding. "It's probably too much to ask. Twice a day. Maybe—"

Frustration consumed Simon and he drove his fist into the doorjamb. It hurt. He held out his other hand without looking at Jack and, after a minute of shuffling noises and barks, felt the leashes placed on his palm.

Simon closed his fingers around them and nodded. Then he headed out into the cooling dusk without a backward glance, cursing himself silently all the way.

Away from the house he sucked in deep breaths. Again. Damn it.

"Your dad makes me nervous," Simon told the animals. He could hear the misery in his shaky voice.

Bernard woofed gently in reply and Dandelion trotted excitedly at his side.

"I'm kind of crap with people," he told them.

Rat snarled at nothing.

"It doesn't help that your dad's, uh…pretty hot. Even if he is kind of intimidating. But I'd be grumpy too if I broke my leg and couldn't walk you. Wish you could tell me how he broke it."

Simon went on chatting to the animals until Puddles stopped short. Simon peered at the ground, keeping Jack's list of the dog's fears in mind. It was a stick shaped like a lightning bolt.

He tried to guide Puddles to give the stick a wide berth, but the dog wouldn't budge. Simon studied the stick, trying to intuit what it was about it that made Puddles so afraid.

After a minute he snorted at himself. Who knew better than him that fear didn't have to have a reason?

"It's okay, sweetheart. I'll take care of it."

He picked up the stick and threw it deep into the trees. Puddles let out a yip of relief while the other three dogs surged forward in an attempt to chase the stick.

"Whoa, whoa!" He pulled on the leashes, and managed to corral the dogs back onto the lane, even though it was clear that Bernard could've dragged them wherever he wanted if he'd chosen to do so.

Puddles nuzzled Simon and he rested his hand on the dog's head, appreciating the softness of his fur and the warm press of his body.

"Maybe tomorrow I'll be able to talk to your dad," Simon told him softly.

Puddles barked.

"Yeah. Maybe tomorrow will be better."

Chapter Three

Jack

Every day had dilated to a month, every night to a year, and Jack found himself wishing for anything—*anything*—to break the monotony of lying on the couch all day long and in bed all night. He wasn't precisely incapable of doing things, but the effort it took to do something as simple as taking a shower left him hollow and trembling, every instinct of movement and muscle thrown into chaos.

He'd thought the last eight months were bad, but now he was a prisoner of his own body. A prisoner in his own house. A prisoner without even the mental escape into the worlds he drew.

When the sound of snapping branches outside caught his

attention, boredom won out over comfort and Jack hauled himself to his feet, fished his binoculars from the windowsill, and lurched to the back door.

Jack put the binoculars to his eyes, breath catching for just a moment, as it always did in that first second of extended sight. Who could ever know what such sight might reveal? What bit of the world it would alight on? First, the dizzying whoosh of dislocation and then the view steadied and he was projected yards and yards beyond himself.

Once, he'd lifted binoculars casually and they'd revealed a boreal owl nestled in the crotch of a branch, wide yellow eyes fixed directly on him. For years after, every time he walked outside, Jack had thought about all the creatures that watched him unawares.

Now, though, there was no such magic. It was an overcast, grayish day, and fog lay close to the ground. When nothing of interest revealed itself in the woods behind the house, Jack scanned farther afield. He'd never paid much attention to his nearest neighbor, who lived a quarter mile or so north, but now he found himself lingering on the smoke rising from the chimney just over the rise.

Had he seen smoke coming from the chimney in the morning before? He didn't think so. But he'd likely never looked, either. The smoke crawled into the sky and Jack wondered. The man who lived there was old and kept to himself, and the law of binoculars was that you minded your own business if you happened to catch sight of humans while observing animals. But Jack allowed himself a brief scan.

The house itself lay invisible over a swell of land, but

he could make out the chimney and a bit of the roof, and just to the east, the drive to the house that snaked back to the main road.

Why had his neighbor changed his habits? Was he suddenly home during the days? Was someone else staying with him? *What if,* the voice that was usually linked to his drawing hand whispered, *someone broke in and took Mr. Whatshisname hostage? What if they're still there and have him tied to a chair or stuffed in a suitcase? What if they're robbing him or torturing him or taking revenge for an act of cruelty he committed long ago? They've just now tracked him down, thirty years later, and although he's an old man, they believe he must pay for the pain he's inflicted.*

Jack strained to see more but short of climbing on the roof—impossible in his current condition—there was nothing he could do. Gradually, the smoke lessened, then disappeared, and though he watched for as long as his leg would allow, he didn't see anything more.

Sighing as his one wisp of potential excitement disappeared along with the smoke, Jack dragged himself back inside, leg aching, armpits aching, ribs aching, and collapsed onto the couch with an *oof* that made him feel ninety years old.

With nothing else to break the monotony of the day until Simon arrived for the evening walk, Jack watched the animals until his eyes swam. He counted the beams in the ceiling. Made lists of tasks he should do once he was back on his feet—the windows could use washing; there was a loose board in the entryway; maybe he should get some plants to liven the place up.

Every crack, smudge, stain, and loose thread within his kingdom revealed itself, never to be unseen. He pet every animal that came near him until they bored of it and found a place on Mayonnaise's fur that didn't quite grow in all the way.

Then, when all of that had taken only the smallest chunk of only one day, Jack turned the television on and resigned himself to numbing distraction.

There was a quiet to the house when the dogs weren't there that Jack hadn't experienced in years. He didn't like it.

Mayonnaise and Pickles snoozed on the easy chair and windowsill respectively, and Louis was in the bedroom, but cats had their own quiet.

Jack was intimately acquainted with quiet. He'd grown up with it. The quiet of long, snow-choked Wyoming winters, of long, sleepless nights. The quiet of parents who had little to say to one another; the quiet of their absence.

His menagerie had been an antidote to the silences he hadn't chosen, and now that he was used to living with the soundtrack of their snuffles and thumps, their snores and yips and scuffles, the absence of sound echoed with deprivation.

It would be dark soon and Jack found himself hoping Simon would be back by then. He wasn't afraid of the dark; he just…didn't want to be alone in it. Not tonight.

Pickles' small form oozed into a stretch that became a yawn, the black cat shifting from languid sleep to complete alertness in one graceful gesture.

"I know. I'm not actually alone," he told her.

Finally, unable to lie on the couch for one more minute, Jack made his way slowly into the kitchen and rummaged through the cupboards for something he could throw together for dinner. With a sigh of resignation he texted Charlie to ask if he could drive him to the store tomorrow.

Right away his brother wrote back, Send me a list and I'll deliver.

Annoyance burned in Jack's stomach. It had been years since he'd felt like a burden to his brother and now, a single moment having rendered him infantile, here he was, once again depending on Charlie for everything.

Twenty minutes into laboriously cooking a horror of egg noodles, tuna, and cream soup (throughout which he had to stop every two minutes to catch his breath and give his armpits a break from the crutches) he heard the familiar sounds of his pack returning.

He'd told Simon not to bother ringing the bell anymore, so this time the sounds were just the happy yips of the animals' return.

"In the kitchen," he called, though it was hardly necessary since the dogs were already padding toward him. Toward their food bowls most likely, but still.

When Charlie had come over on his lunch break, he'd taken one look at the defiled floor and promised he'd solve the problem. He'd returned two hours later with a metal chute roughly welded, through which Jack could pour dog food and water into the bowls from a standing position without spilling anything. Charlie had always been a big one for solving problems.

Bernard barreled in and panted up at him, mouth open, and the others followed less patiently. All except Puddles.

A minute later, Simon stood in the door to the kitchen, Puddles tight at his side.

"Hey," Jack said. "Go okay?"

Simon nodded jerkily, eyes on the animals. Mayonnaise shot past him and up onto the counter. Pickles had been there since he opened the tin of tuna. And, fine, he'd fed her a few bites of it.

"You eating here tonight?" he asked Mayonnaise. She rubbed her cheek on his fist, then darted out the window cat door. "Guess not."

The pan on the stove bubbled threateningly and Jack turned the burner down, sniffing suspiciously.

"Ugh," he declared, and slumped against the counter.

Simon picked his way across the kitchen as delicately as a cat and peered at the food.

He raised one eyebrow at Jack and the look managed to convey amusement, derision, and empathy all at once. With a gentle movement, he shouldered Jack aside.

Jack sank gratefully into a kitchen chair and watched as Simon stirred, salted, and stirred some more. His movements became more relaxed the longer he cooked.

He opened a few cupboards, pulled out a casserole dish, and poured the contents of the pans into it. Top sprinkled with cheese, salted, and peppered, he slid the dish into the oven.

"You know a lot about—" *casseroles* was what he'd begun to say but, awkward as this whole situation was, that wasn't a sentence he could quite bring himself to utter "—cook-ing?"

Simon shook his head and shrugged, then nodded, as if he couldn't quite decide which was true.

With a bit of distance between them, Jack realized again that Simon wasn't particularly small. He seemed diminu-tive because of the way he stood—hunched shoulders and lowered head—and the way he moved, as if slinking silently from place to place might allow him to escape notice. But his shoulders were fairly broad and his hands sizable. Why did he make himself smaller?

Watching Simon at the stove, the night of empty bore-dom stretching in front of him, Jack asked, "Do you want to stay and have some?"

Simon snorted and shook his head quickly.

"It's no trouble," Jack said, losing hope.

Simon raised those startling blue eyes to Jack's and made a face.

"No," he said, and though his voice was soft it had an edge to it Jack hadn't expected. "It's gross."

Jack barked out a laugh. "Yeah, it really is."

"Casseroles," Simon said, shaking his head.

"Yeah. Casseroles," Jack echoed.

The silence sat between them easily and it was a silence Jack enjoyed. Then, inevitably, the demands for dinner came.

Chapter Four

Jack

There was definitely more smoke coming from the chimney of the house over the hill. Jack was keeping a list of when he saw the first tendrils and when they stopped because maybe if he could figure out the schedule he could figure out why this change had occurred. *Was* it a change, though? Or had he simply never noticed before? He couldn't be quite sure.

What he needed was some sort of periscope so that he could see more than just the roof and the chimney. Maybe if he got a ladder...?

No. No, that was a terrible idea.

Do you know who lives in the place over the hill from me? Jack texted Charlie.

Nope, Charlie replied. Did you google it?

Jack rolled his eyes. Charlie thought it was hilarious to suggest googling everything, even un-googleable things, as if he were eighty years old and it was a revelation. Or had Charlie genuinely meant to suggest it because he'd thought Jack hadn't known? It was always so hard to tell with Charlie.

Then Jack realized he actually *could* google it because real estate sales were public records. But he didn't know the address and it turned out that Google Maps hadn't taken much care to capture the fringes of Garnet Run.

He typed, Could you drive over there and see who lives there??? and deleted it. He typed, Can we take a quick drive by it? and made himself delete that too. Finally he wrote, If you happen to drive past and see anything strange will you tell me?

Charlie didn't answer. Probably busy at work.

He thought about texting his best friend, Vanessa. She did impulsive things all the time and might not question him wanting her to surveil a stranger to slake his burning curiosity. But he hadn't responded to her last few texts or picked up the phone the last couple times she'd called and he didn't want to deal with having a conversation about why. Hell, he hardly knew himself.

"Thanks," Jack said as Charlie put the last of the bags of groceries on the counter.

"Course," Charlie said and began putting the groceries away.

"You don't have to do that," Jack said.

"It's no problem," Charlie said automatically.

"Charlie, I can *do* it."

To prove the point, Jack shoved himself upright and grabbed for his crutches. He leaned one against the counter and tried to open the cabinet door above the refrigerator but the movement jarred his ribs and he hissed, recoiling. His recoil sent the crutch sliding to the floor and Jack panting.

Charlie sighed and picked up the crutch.

"Sit down before you break your other leg," he said wearily. His jaw tightened and he shoved his hands in his pockets.

Jack sighed. "Sorry, I just…"

Hate being helpless. Hate being a burden. Again.

Charlie waved him off and put the groceries away. He rolled his shoulders when he was through.

"So what's your fascination with the neighbors?"

"No fascination," Jack lied.

Charlie peered at him.

"You having a *Rear Window* moment or what?"

Jack always got a kick out of Charlie's Hitchcock obsession. Those who didn't know him well thought it was out of character, but the meticulous planning and the patience of a long game suited Charlie perfectly. At this particular moment, however, Jack glared.

"No." Jack had shot for a casual tone, but Charlie kept looking at him. Jack didn't do casual well. "Just curious."

Charlie raised an eyebrow and Jack followed his gaze to the binoculars sitting on the coffee table.

"You want me to—"

"No, it's fine," Jack interrupted. It came out sharper than

he'd intended. He wasn't sure why he was embarrassed that Charlie knew what his boredom had driven him to.

"Guess I'll take off, then."

Jack nodded.

"Unless you want me to hang out? Watch a movie or something?"

Sometimes Jack couldn't tell if Charlie made offers like this out of genuine desire for his company, out of obligation, or out of habit. Jack wasn't sure Charlie knew himself.

They got along well, enjoyed each other's company, but there was always something between them that only time would clear away. Or it wouldn't.

Charlie still saw Jack as the thirteen-year-old kid he'd gotten saddled with at seventeen when their parents' deaths had changed everything, and Jack still saw Charlie as the fierce authority figure who'd cared for him at the expense of his own desires. Not that Charlie would ever admit it. That, too, Jack wasn't sure Charlie knew.

Jack was desperate for the distraction Charlie offered. He'd only been couch- and bed-bound for three days and he was already climbing the walls. But he'd probably snapped at Charlie enough for one day.

"No, that's okay. Another time."

Charlie nodded and stroked his beard—a clear indicator that he was concerned—but just dropped a hand on Jack's shoulder.

"Let's get you back to the couch."

Jack wanted to scream. Also to burn the couch.

"Take care, bro," Charlie said when Jack was settled, and as he walked out the door darkness closed over Jack again.

★ ★ ★

That night, when Simon returned with the dogs, he lingered in the doorway instead of coming inside. Jack accepted the licks and headbutts of the returning animals and felt his stomach lurch as Simon edged out the door.

He didn't want Simon to go, leaving him all alone again to stare at the ceiling or the TV or a book or the animals.

"Um. Hey. Simon?" Simon turned. "Could you help me? With something." Jack gestured to his cast. "Damn thing."

Simon nodded and Jack wracked his brain, having spoken without thinking this through.

"Uh, in the kitchen."

They walked to the kitchen. Jack's crutches made every step an effort, giving him plenty of time to think.

What are you doing? What exactly are you trying to do?

"There's, uh, coffee filters up there. Do you mind grabbing them?"

Jack pointed to the cabinet above the refrigerator and Simon stood on his toes to catch the edge of the cabinet. The line of his back was graceful, even beneath the oversized sweater he wore. He snagged the sheaf of filters and moved to set it on the counter next to the coffee machine, but he froze.

He turned slowly and looked at Jack, and Jack saw the neat stack of coffee filters Charlie must have placed there earlier.

Simon was looking at him like he'd played a nasty trick.

"Sorry. I thought I was out," Jack muttered. "My brother—"

But Simon was already nodding and making his way to the door.

"Sorry," Jack called after him again, but Simon didn't answer, and the loneliness of a long night engulfed the house.

Chapter Five

Simon

"Goddamn motherfucking shit!" Simon let his head fall back and knock against the doorframe of his grandmother's kitchen.

"Some of us are mothers, dear," his grandmother trilled from the pantry.

"Shit, sorry!" Simon called back.

She emerged with her arms full of flour, sugar, and other canisters that indicated baking was imminent.

"What're you making?" Simon asked at the same time as his grandmother said, "What happened?"

They both smiled.

"Snickerdoodles," she replied, and he said, "Nothing."

She raised an eyebrow and gestured for him to begin measuring the flour.

Baking was something they'd done together since Simon was a child. Kylie had never had any interest, always more excited about going fishing with their grandfather or playing soccer with the neighbors. But Simon enjoyed the way having something to do with his hands took the pressure off his mouth. He enjoyed the way his grandmother would narrate each step and all he needed to do was be with her. The fact that everything she made was delicious didn't hurt either.

Snickerdoodles meant she was feeling nostalgic. They'd been something he'd loved as a boy—the taste and the word both—but he hadn't requested them in a very long time.

As she creamed the butter and sugar, Simon felt a familiar calm settle over him.

"It was nothing, really," he said. It was always easier for him to speak unprompted. "I thought for a second that he—Jack—was… I don't know. Making fun of me. But it was just a misunderstanding."

The moment he'd seen the coffee filters and felt Jack's intense eyes on him he'd remembered others. *Just say one thing, freak! What's wrong with you? Can you even say your own name? Simple Simon, Simple Simon.*

"It was stupid."

"What's this Jack fellow like?"

"Tall," Simon said without thinking. "Um. He's nice-ish. Pissed off that he can't take the dogs out himself, I think. He seems like the kind of person who's used to being able to do anything he wants."

His grandmother nodded and looked studiously at the cookie dough. "Handsome?"

Simon shot her a look. "That casual and innocent act does not work on me."

"Who's acting?" she said, cupping her hands beneath her chin in a ludicrous nod at a Shirley Temple pose. "I'm as casual and innocent as they come."

He rolled his eyes and huffed out a sigh.

"Yeah. Yeah he really is."

"Mmm," his grandmother mused.

The next morning when Jack opened the door, his hair was rumpled and his sweatshirt was rucked up on one side, revealing a peek of muscled stomach. He blinked and gave Simon a sleepy smile.

It hit Simon like a punch in the gut. What would it feel like to step forward and be wrapped in those powerful arms, press his cheek against the softness of that sweatshirt and the firmness of the muscles beneath it? What would it be like to stroke Jack's mussed hair into place and kiss his soft, smiling lips?

A shudder shook him. That didn't happen for him. That would never happen for him.

He stuck out his hand, almost hitting Jack in the chest with the plastic container of cookies.

"These for me?" Jack asked, stepping back to let him inside.

Simon rolled his eyes.

No, they're for the other person whose chest I just shoved them into.

"Yeah, yeah," Jack said. He peeled off the lid and inhaled. His eyes got big. "Are these those cinnamon things with the weird name?" he asked, clearly enthused.

Simon nodded.

"Snickerdoodles."

The word came out choked but audible.

"Right, right. What the hell kind of name is that?"

What the hell kind of name is Bernard for a St. Bernard and Puddles for a dog afraid of puddles?

Jack's brow furrowed and for a moment Simon had the ridiculous notion that the other man could read his mind.

"German, maybe? Sounds kind of German." He shrugged and stuffed a cookie into his mouth.

His eyes got wide again.

"Mmmisooogood," he garbled and Simon smiled. Cinnamon and sugar gilded Jack's lips like they'd been caught in the sweetest flurry.

Jack grunted and held the container out to him.

Simon shook his head.

"Too early for me," he said. The words came out and in their wake a deep heat flushed through his throat and face. But Jack just smiled and shrugged, then shoved another cookie in his mouth.

Jack gathered the dogs and Pirate with a whistle.

"Did you make these?"

"My grandma."

Something flickered in Jack's eyes that Simon couldn't read.

"Wow. Real grandma cookies. Thanks."

He sounded utterly serious, as if cookies baked by a grandmother were categorically different than cookies baked by someone else, and he held the container reverently, tucked under his arm like a football.

A pillow with a head-sized indentation lay on the couch, a comforter half on the floor. Had Jack been sleeping here instead of in a bed?

Jack's eyes followed Simon's.

"Uh. I don't sleep well. Much."

Now that he said it, Simon could see that he looked weary, not sleepy.

"Why?"

Jack ran a hand through messy hair the color of copper.

"I haven't for a long time. Since I was a teenager. And usually when I can't sleep I draw. But…"

He shook his head.

Why did you stop sleeping as a teenager? What changed? What do you draw? Why can't you draw now? What do you do instead? How much sleep did you get last night? Does your leg hurt? How did you hurt your leg?

The familiar cacophony swelled in Simon's head and chest as he opened his mouth, and what came out was…nothing.

Jack's eyes on him were sharp and Simon looked at the floor. He blinked furiously and made for the door.

This part was always the hardest. The moment when he could see the person he would have been—the connections he would have made—if only he weren't like he goddamn was.

He still didn't entirely understand it, the war inside of him.

It had been raging as long as he could remember, and as in any war, all sides lost.

As a young child he'd been able to stay quiet, to watch the world from inside himself, and the only comment was to his parents at their luck that he was so well-behaved. He could press to his father's side and be lifted high above the fear. He could turn his face toward his mother's stomach and be gathered close in her arms, shielded and comforted.

But at a certain point—and Simon couldn't have identified it because it passed without him noticing—rescue and comfort were rescinded. There was no discussion, no negotiation. One day he simply realized that when he pressed close to his father he was given a clap on the back; when he turned toward his mother, he got a smile and a hair tousle.

Without warning, he had been set adrift on dangerous waters even as he still lived under his parents' roof. The praise for his good behavior was a thing of the past. Now the comments weren't complimentary, but questioning. Eventually, they stopped altogether because everyone knew.

Something was wrong with Simon Burke.

"Nothing's wrong physically," the doctor told his parents. "He's just a little shy, aren't you, Simon?"

That he would grow out of it was the general consensus, and Simon began to imagine the present as hard-packed soil and the future as the moment his reedy seedling would press through earth and grow toward the sun.

By high school he knew he was mired in the dirt permanently, buried alive, and instead of hoping to grow, he wished he'd stop.

His looks became less in sync with how he felt the taller and broader he got. Suddenly taller than most of the girls at school, taller than many of the boys, he wasn't small enough to hide anymore, and he began to hunch his shoulders and duck his chin to his chest.

It had the added benefit that he couldn't see the looks on people's faces when he didn't answer them. Teachers couldn't catch his eye in the hallway and give him the perplexed, disappointed look they reserved for students failing to perform to their potential.

Its downsides were the predictable ones. He walked into things. His neck ached constantly, as did the spot between his shoulder blades and the small of his back. Fists and elbows and shoulders could come out of nowhere and he didn't have time to evade them.

And no matter how low he kept his head, it didn't stop him hearing the things people said.

Freak. Weirdo. Retard. Then, as inevitable as the slide from fear into anger: *Faggot.*

It was said about him and to him before he ever considered where his desires lay. Especially because his main desire was simply to disappear.

But as high school progressed, Simon added one more layer of distance between himself and the students of Bear Creek High.

Being gay didn't bother Simon. It was being attracted to boys that was the problem. Because boys were awful. They seemed intent on making his life miserable in order to make their own more amusing, and the indignity of finding them beautiful or intriguing was humiliating.

Even if he could imagine a world in which a boy wasn't awful to him, there would still be himself to contend with. How could he do...anything if he couldn't even say hello?

Simon filed this curiosity and this desire away with all the others he'd quashed over the years. They stayed there, as quiet as he was, for a long, long time.

"I'm going to ask him a question," Simon told the pack. "I'll just ask one question and then he'll know that I want him to talk. Right?"

This sometimes worked for Simon. Some people were so eager to talk about themselves that one question was all that was required of him to unlock them permanently. Somehow he didn't think Jack was going to be one of those people, but he could hope.

His heart pounded harder and harder with each step back to Jack's cabin.

By the time he opened the door and began unclipping leashes he was wound so tight with intention that the second Jack came into the room he practically yelled, "How'd you break your leg!"

Jack's eyes widened at the bellow and Simon wished the floor would open up and swallow him. He sucked in a tight breath through nostrils narrowed with panic and squeezed his eyes shut tight so he couldn't see himself be seen.

Jack's voice, when it came, sounded normal. Too normal? Pityingly normal? Maybe not.

"Puddles got spooked and I took off after him. Rolled down this embankment or hill or whateverthehell you call it. Broke it on the way down. So stupid."

In, out; in, out. Simon made himself breathe evenly and quietly. Made himself as unremarkable as possible. He flexed his left hand, the one where the muscle twitches always began. Then, slowly, slowly, he opened his eyes.

"I hate it," Jack said. "Fucking hate being trapped here. Having to ask my brother to do shit for me."

Simon looked up at Jack for a moment. Jack was wearing that sweatshirt again. The one that looked like hugging him in it would be the most wonderful thing.

"Do you want some coffee?" Jack asked.

Simon shook his head. At least, he meant to shake his head. But the next thing Jack said was "Cool." So apparently he hadn't.

He followed Jack into the kitchen and sank into a chair, shoving his twitching hand under his thigh.

"Thanks for not offering to do it for me," Jack said, bitterness twisting his voice. "Swear if my brother offers one more pity hang or favor I'll lose it."

Jack puttered around, making the coffee slowly and in clear pain. Frankly, Simon hadn't offered to help because the last thing he could do was find more words, but seeing Jack's struggle—leaning one crutch or the other against countertops, almost losing his balance once or twice, and righting himself in the nick of time—Simon felt like he should've despite Jack's clear distaste for help. Must be nice, being accustomed to not needing it.

When Jack held two steaming mugs of coffee out to him, Simon took them and put them on the table, leaving Jack's hands free for his crutches. Jack thunked into the chair next to him and Simon held very, very still.

"So, uh. You don't talk much," Jack said.

There it was.

Simon's stomach knotted and he wanted to push his chair back and flee. Before he could, Jack went on.

"Do you not like to, or do you have stuff to say but you just don't...talk much?"

Simon bit his lip and held up two fingers.

Jack nodded assessingly. "Wanna text me? Is that better?"

Against all odds, something tiny fluttered to life in the black hole of Simon's stomach.

He slid his phone from his pocket cautiously in case it was a joke. But Jack took his own from his sweatshirt pocket and waited.

Simon's fingers itched with all the unspoken words. All the questions he'd wanted to ask earlier. But those had been in the moment. Now, with the ability to write anything, what his fingers tapped out was: Sorry. It's weird, I know.

Jack glanced at his phone and furrowed his brow.

"That you have a hard time talking? Well...yeah, I guess." He shrugged. "Why do you?"

Simon's face heated. In the question he couldn't help but hear the echo of years of words.

I'm not... Simon deleted. There's nothing wrong... Simon deleted.

He sent, I don't know. I get really nervous and I just can't make words come out.

Jack nodded. "Has it always been that way?"

Simon nodded miserably.

"Fuck. That really sucks."

Simon choked on an unexpected chuckle.

"Is it like that with everyone? What about your friends, or family?"

Simon rolled his eyes. Friends. Yeah, right.

I'm fine talking with my family, Simon wrote. But I don't see my parents much anymore. It's better that way. They just want me to be someone I'm not. My sister's cool and I can talk to her but she always wants to invite me to hang out with her friends or set me up. My grandma's my best friend.

He sent the message and instantly felt awkward. What twenty-six-year-old man's best friend was his grandmother? Then guilt swept through him at how hurt his grandmother would be to hear he felt that way.

"That's cool about your grandma. Nice she bakes you cookies and stuff." Jack sounded wistful.

Do you have a grandma?

He shook his head. "Well, I mean, I do, of course. But they're dead. Everyone's dead."

Simon reached for his phone but before he could respond to that rather bleak pronouncement, Jack said, "Why does your sister invite you to do stuff she knows you don't want to do?"

Simon snorted.

I know, right? Well...selfishness, I guess? She wants for me what she'd want for herself and she isn't quite willing to imagine that I might be different and want different things.

Jack said nothing, apparently waiting for more. Simon felt his pulse flutter, but not from anxiety; from pleasure.

She's my parents' ideal kid, Simon went on. Ambitious, outgoing, confident. Everything I'm not.

He added a grimacing emoji but accidentally hit the scream emoji instead and sent it before he noticed.

Jack smiled.

"You're not ambitious?" he asked.

Simon blinked at him, thinking about that, and for an unguarded moment, they were looking at each other—really looking at each other.

I guess my ambitions are just different. Less ambitious. Well, less...idk, career-y?

Jack nodded.

Mine are more like "Order a coffee without stammering" or "say 'thank you' at louder than a mumble when the pizza's delivered."

Simon couldn't quite look at Jack to see his response to that.

"That sounds so damn hard," Jack said, voice gruff.

Unexpected tears prickled in Simon's eyes to hear the empathy there. Not his abhorred pity; not scorn; not embarrassment. Just empathy.

It is.

From the corner of his eye, Simon saw Jack's phone light, knew he'd seen the message. But he still couldn't look up.

So why don't you draw when you can't sleep anymore? he added.

"Ugh," Jack grunted, and pushed back from the table with powerful arms, leaning his chair on its back legs. Simon looked up, startled, and Mayonnaise, who had crept in through the window cat door without Simon noticing, lifted her head at the disruption, but Jack was already levering his chair back down to earth. "Sorry," he muttered.

Simon sat very still, except for his left hand, which spasmed against his will. He shoved it back under his thigh.

"I illustrate children's books—well, I *did*." And that was all he said.

Simon hadn't given much thought to what Jack did, but if he had he'd have thought carpentry or lumberjacking—something physical and outdoorsy; something that would've honed the magnificent physique of the man sitting next to him.

But the image of Jack, powerful shoulders bent over paper, strong fingers wielding a pencil to bring a children's tale to life made something snaky happen in the pit of his stomach.

The questions came too fast for him to type them: *What's your art like? What kind of stories did you illustrate? How did you get into that work? Are they published? Are you famous? Can I read them? Have you always wanted to do that?* And, louder, bigger: *What happened???*

He fumbled his phone in frustration and familiar prickles of anger and humiliation crept up his spine. So many times he'd wanted to scream, "Why are you making me do so much work when it's so fucking hard for me and it would be effortless for you!?"

One-handed, he typed, Just tell me everything!!! and shoved his phone at Jack rather than sending the message.

He had his eyes fixed to the table, so he didn't see Jack's expression, but after a moment, Jack said, "Sure. Sorry."

It was kind, but the humiliation that came with relief was still humiliation.

"Do you want more coffee?" Jack asked.

Simon shook his head. More than a cup and he'd be buzzing.

"Okay. Um. I met my friend Davis in college. We were on the same freshman hall. I hated my roommate so I was always in the common room, and his room was right next to it. I didn't really want to be there. College, I mean. I thought— Anyway."

He gulped his coffee.

"I wanted to be an artist. Stupid, right?" He rolled his eyes at himself. "Eventually, he talked me into illustrating this story he was writing for a class. I don't know, I think I was drunk. But it was...good. I've never been any good at writing or coming up with ideas. Not that smart, I guess."

Simon glanced up in time to see hurt burning in Jack's eyes and wondered who'd convinced him of those things. Jack ran a hand through his messy hair and sighed.

Mayonnaise jumped soundlessly from the counter to the table and insinuated herself on Jack's lap. He stroked between her ears and let her make biscuits on his thighs. Then he pressed between her shoulder blades and she curled up contentedly.

"It just worked with Davis," Jack went on. "He had the ideas and I just made them happen. At first we wanted to do a whole comic book thing, but then his sister had a baby and he wrote this little story for the kid. I illustrated it and his sister went nuts over it. So Davis decided we should try and publish one for real. I didn't think anyone would want something I drew. Hell, what did I know about kids' books? Books at all, really. Or kids. But Davis... When Davis decides on something it always happens for him."

The sentiment was so like what Simon had assumed about Jack.

"After we graduated he moved to New York. It's where his sisters live and they encouraged him to come. Before I knew it, he'd made all these editor contacts—I don't know where. He was always good at meeting people and I didn't want anything to do with that part of it. But it was cool. It was...ah, fuck, it was magical. The book sold and we did another one right after. I couldn't believe I got to draw shit for a living. It was...perfect. But Davis—I dunno, it was like he was never satisfied. Anything good that happened he just wanted something better next time. He got an agent and wanted more money, he wanted to win all the awards, sell more books, I don't even know what all else."

Jack shook his head and gestured at the humble kitchen around them.

"I don't need much. Never have. This place was my parents'. I just winterized it. Davis still lives in New York and his sisters, all three of them are..." Jack gestured unreadably. "You know, what's the word. They like expensive stuff. Davis wants to be like that. Fancy. I dunno."

Materialistic, Simon offered inside his head.

Jack trailed off and looked right at Simon.

"Is this boring? Is this too much? You said tell you everything, but..." He shrugged.

A smile tugged at the corners of Simon's mouth and he shook his head and gestured for Jack to go on.

"'Kay. Anyway, it was fine with me if that's what he wanted. I had what I wanted, so. But, uh."

Jack's low voice went softer.

"I had this...idea. For a story. Kind of about me and my brother, but different. I dunno. It felt like something that I could write myself in addition to drawing. It wasn't gonna be instead of stuff with Davis. I just wanted to try. When I told him about it he didn't say much. He didn't seem upset or anything. Mostly I thought he wasn't very interested because it didn't involve him. He's kinda...he likes to be the center of attention. But then..."

Jack made to stand up in the move of a habitual pacer, but he'd clearly forgotten both his broken leg and the cat on his lap because he ended up grabbing Mayonnaise as she leapt onto the table and sprawling back onto the chair, wincing, the wood groaning beneath him.

"Fuuuuck."

Simon reached out a hand to steady him, palm skimming soft sweatshirt and hard muscle beneath.

He couldn't remember the last time he'd touched someone who wasn't Grandma Jean.

"Y'okay?" Simon got out.

"Yeah. God*damn* it."

He slammed a fist down on the table, face a mask of frustration, then put out a hand to soothe Mayonnaise when she bristled. She rubbed her cheeks against his fist and he let her nibble at his fingers and then flop down on her back, batting at his hand.

"Anyway. Two months or so after I told Davis about the project I get this email from him saying he sold it. I thought maybe he meant he sold it for me? He's in New York and I'm here, and I know he goes out for drinks with our editors sometimes. I thought it was weird but I was excited. It felt like a chance to really do something of my own."

Jack cracked his knuckles.

"But he didn't sell it *for* me. He pitched it as his own idea. The publisher loved it."

Simon sensed what was coming next and bit his lip, hoping he was wrong.

"Only, they thought it would have an older market than our kids' books and they wanted to pair Davis with an artist who does middle grade books. One who's a bigger deal than me. And that fucker agreed. Well—" Jack cut a look at Simon, suspicious and mocking. "He *said* his agent agreed and it was a done deal before he could get me on board, but I know that's bullshit."

Simon's heart ached. "Fuck," he breathed.

"Yeah, cheers," Jack said, toasting him with his empty coffee mug.

Simon raised his eyebrows to say, *What happened next?*

"I called him and he dodged me for days. Finally I got him on the phone and I put it to him straight. I said that I'd told him my idea and he'd stolen it. He acted like I was nuts. Said he thought I'd meant for us to work on it together. That he knew I couldn't've intended to do it myself since I wasn't a writer, so *of course* he'd thought I wanted to collaborate. And it was out of his control that the publisher had replaced me." Jack shook his head. "Fucker."

Simon asked, "What'd you do?" A flush of relief went through him when the words came out.

Jack's sigh seemed to deflate him. Mayonnaise chose that moment of weakness to strike, pouncing on his hand and sinking playful teeth into his wrist. He lifted her with one hand and cuddled her against his chest where she started purring immediately.

"Nothing."

"Huh?"

"What could I do? I told him to go fuck himself. That he was a greedy liar and he knew exactly what he'd done. I called our editor and explained what had happened but she wasn't the one who'd signed the book. She said that I could sue Davis, but what the fuck. Who *sues* someone? Whatever. Probably I couldn't have written it anyway."

"But—but it's your story! About you and your brother!" Simon said, outrage loosening his tongue.

"Yeah. Sucks. And now every time I go to draw it just reminds me of that. Of Davis. Thought he was my friend, man. Known the guy ten years. Guess trusting people is for suckers."

Jack looked so sad, so lost, that Simon desperately wanted to disagree. To say something that would comfort Jack. But what could he say? He had no experience trusting people. No experience at all.

Jack's broad shoulders were slumped, his full mouth

pulled into a scowl. He was cradling Mayonnaise to him like the cat was all he had to hold on to in the whole world, and Simon couldn't stand to see him like that.

Can I see your art? Simon typed, and showed Jack his phone.

Jack blinked at him. "You'd want to?"

Simon nodded and, in an act of bravery he couldn't quite account for, reached out a hand and stroked Mayonnaise's soft ears where they rested against Jack's stomach. His heart trip-hammered, Mayonnaise purred, and Jack said, "Okay."

Resentful at being displaced when Jack dragged himself to his feet, Mayonnaise scampered off, and Simon followed Jack through the living room where the pack sat and lay in various adorable configurations, and to a door that had always been resolutely closed when Simon had been in the house. He'd assumed it was Jack's bedroom, thought maybe the animals weren't allowed in there, but when they reached it, he looked to the right and saw a door open onto what was clearly the bedroom.

A huge, wooden four-poster bed was covered with a navy blue wool blanket on which Puddles cuddled with a cat Simon hadn't seen before.

"That's Louis," Jack said about the plump black and gray cat with wide green eyes and sweet, flicky tail. "He and Puddles are in love."

Before Simon could follow up on that, Jack opened the studio door. He turned, blocking the doorway, with the first hint of uncertainty Simon had seen from him.

"Just, um. It's not *real* art, you know? Just…whatever. Come in."

The room was small and smelled of wood and paper and something vaguely metallic that Simon assumed was ink. It was a bit musty, as if from disuse, but midday sunlight streamed in through the three large windows that made up the back wall, bathing the wood floor, with its collage of rugs and papers, in a cheery yellow glow.

There were sketches and torn-out bits pinned all over one wall and a huge whiteboard hung on the other, broken into squares like a storyboard. A bookshelf on the third wall showed the thin spines of comics and picture books and thicker, battered spines of art books.

Jack's drawing table was a huge slab of wood resting on two sawhorses in the spill of light. Simon walked to it slowly, giving Jack time to stop him. Sitting on the far edge of the table, a thin layer of dust gilding their covers, were three hardcover books, with stories by Davis Snyder and illustrations by Jack Matheson.

The first was called *There's a Moose Loose in Central Park* and the cover illustration was in gorgeously saturated greens and browns. The trees of what Simon could only assume was Central Park had movement to them like a breeze was ruffling their leaves. Peeking from between two trees was the familiar velvet of a large moose's antlers.

"Wow," Simon breathed.

He opened the book and was lost in Jack's illustrations. The story was cute—a moose that had traveled from Wyoming and made its way to Central Park made friends with a little girl who wandered away from her parents. When the horse-mounted police officers found them both, the girl was asleep on the moose's back and the horses made friends with the moose.

But the illustrations were glorious.

Jack had a hand with color that Simon could recognize instantly. He might be a graphic designer and not an artist, but he could see that much. And his work had a tenderness to it, from the cant of the little girl's head where she rested on the moose to the expression on the moose's face, as if it loved the child. Simon could see why the book had been successful. It was sweet and magical and amusing.

He flipped through the second book, *There's a Bear in Times Square,* and the third, *There's a Bison Stuck in Brooklyn.*

When he got to the end, and the bison was being safely led across the Brooklyn Bridge as the sun set, Statue of Liberty silhouetted in the background, Simon was nearly in tears.

"I can't believe you," he said.

"Um, in a good way?" Jack's voice was utterly sincere.

"Yes, in a good way, you idiot!" Simon heard himself say.

Jack's eyes went wide and Simon clapped a hand over his mouth.

"No, don't," Jack said. "Tell me."

"Tell you you're an idiot?" Simon mumbled.

Jack grinned. There was a tiny space between his two front teeth that Simon hadn't noticed before.

"Yeah."

The sound that bubbled out of Simon could only be described as a giggle.

"You're so t-talented."

"Yeah?"

Jack drew closer and ran a hand over the book Simon held, crutch caught under his arm. Simon had a moment of disconnect, imagining Jack's huge hands producing such detailed, tender illustrations. Then Jack gently traced the bison's hump with one thick finger and Simon realized there was no disconnect at all.

"It's like a combination of us. Wyoming and New York. Rural and urban. Davis said kids like animals, so." He shrugged. "Oh, look."

Jack touched Simon's shoulder lightly and pointed out the window. Two elk emerged from the tree line that must have been a hundred yards from the back of the cabin. One larger and one smaller, they bent their noble heads to munch on fresh grass.

Simon had lived in Wyoming his entire life, but every time he saw one of the beautiful creatures he shared the land with it felt like a blessing. A moment when two points in time—past and present—snapped together, coexisting in a harmony that made his heart race joyfully.

"These two come around a lot," Jack said softly, as if he didn't want to run the risk of disturbing them, even from inside.

"Wow" was all Simon could say.

They watched the elk nibble for a while, nosing around in what looked like it might once have been a large garden but was now overgrown, then wander back into the woods, heads held high.

Jack was standing close enough that Simon could feel his heat. He could also smell the intoxicating combination of coffee, fresh laundry, and some kind of earthy shampoo that made him want to lean into Jack and press his cheek to Jack's chest.

To prevent himself from doing that and probably getting shoved across the room, Simon looked at the other book on the drawing table.

It was a graphic novel called *Two Moons Over* by Corbin Wale, and the style was like nothing Simon had seen before. It looked almost scratchy, but the figures seemed to glow impossibly. The cover showed a large Victorian house that appeared to have had pieces added to it willy-nilly. In the garden were huge pumpkins, unnaturally large squash blossoms, and flowers that wound up every surface. Dogs—or were they wolves?—prowled the tree line protectively. And in the sky hung two crescent moons. Between them was a boy. Was he flying? Falling? Simon couldn't tell, but it also didn't matter because it was clear he belonged there. From the windows of the impossible house light glowed welcomingly. When he peered closer he could see two women's faces in a high window, their watchful eyes fixed on the boy.

Simon flipped the book open to the dedication page: *For the Aunts & for Alex.*

"It's my favorite," Jack said softly. "He's amazing. The stuff he does that's real but not real. It's... I love it."

Jack took the book out of Simon's hand as if he couldn't speak of it and not be holding it.

"It was kind of what made me think that maybe I could write and illustrate my own project. Mine and Charlie's story. I'm no writer; not really. But Corbin Wale... he doesn't really have many words. The drawings are the whole story. But it's not a kids' book. It's just… He doesn't need words, I guess."

Nothing had ever made Simon want to read a book more.

Jack set *Two Moons Over* down reverently.

"Too late now, I guess. Whatever."

Simon had so many questions, but it didn't seem like the moment to quiz Jack on the particulars.

"You could d-do it anyway," Simon said.

Jack's eyes narrowed and Simon's heart started to pound. He shook his head and waved his words away. Jack started to speak, but changed his mind. He rubbed at the stubble on his chin thoughtfully.

A flurry of barks and whines from the living room sent Jack lurching out of the room. Simon followed, closing the door to the studio behind him.

Bernard and Rat were fighting in front of the fireplace. Well, Simon wasn't quite sure you could call it fighting when a hundred-and-eighty-pound dog was sitting on top of an eight-pound dog and the eight-pound dog was barking aggressively while the hundred-and-eighty-pound dog whined, as if sad his friend didn't want to be sat upon.

"Bernard," Jack laughed. "Come here, ya lug." He gestured and Bernard sighed—if it was possible for a dog to sigh—and shifted off Rat. The second she was freed, Rat jumped up, skinny legs shaking, ready to do battle, and hurled herself at Bernard. Bernard yawned and threw a heavy paw over Rat, looking for a cuddle.

"Ridiculous," Jack muttered fondly. "Wanna sit?"

Simon sat on the couch next to Jack. Somehow sharing

a couch felt more intimate than sitting next to each other in the kitchen and Simon sat on his hand to keep it from twitching.

Jack opened his mouth to speak, but instead Rat let loose a volley of barks. This time, though, Bernard got to his feet too, looking toward the door.

The door opened and in stepped a man who looked enough like Jack that Simon assumed this must be his brother. The dogs circled the man a few times and then settled down again. Clearly he was a familiar presence here.

"Charlie," Jack said, resignedly.

Simon scrambled to his feet, heart pounding. Jack was quite a large man, but Charlie was huge.

Charlie's eyes widened.

"Oh, hi. Sorry, I should've called. I didn't mean to interrupt..."

Simon glued his eyes to Charlie's dirty boots.

"Charlie, this is Simon. Simon, my brother, Charlie. Simon's been helping me out with the animals."

"Right, sure," Charlie said. "Nice to meet you." He held out a large hand to Simon and Simon shook it. He thought maybe, since he'd just been talking to Jack, he'd try to say it back, but the words all came out garbled.

His neck got hot and he pulled his hand back, inching toward the door.

"Hey, you don't have to leave..." Simon heard Charlie say, but he was already out the door.

Chapter Six

Jack

A week later, Jack and Charlie sat, eating meatloaf, mashed potatoes, and peas. Charlie always cooked absurdly balanced meals.

"He's not weird," Jack was saying. "He's just shy."

Charlie raised an eyebrow.

"You scared him away with your hugeness," Jack grumbled.

"Mmhmm," Charlie said.

Jack bit at his lip. "He's...great. Sweet. I didn't expect him to be... I don't know. Cool."

Charlie snorted. "Cool? What are you, fifteen?"

"Shut up. He'll probably turn out to be an asshole just like everyone else."

Charlie's eyes grew serious.

"Not everyone will let you down, Jack."

Jack sighed. "Yeah, well *you* won't let me down even when I beg you to."

Charlie just kept coming over every day, helping without being asked. He cleaned the kitchen, did laundry, and brought groceries and sometimes meals. He asked Jack how his leg was and talked about people they knew who'd come into the hardware store. He gave the dogs baths that ended with him soaked to the skin. And, vexingly, he still left Jack's notebook and pens on his bedside table, a glaring reminder.

Still, every time he showed up, Jack was so glad to be distracted from mindless television or shamelessly spying on the house across the field. But within minutes of his arrival, Jack was snapping at him. He needed him—fuck, he knew he needed him—but he resented every moment of it.

Jack took a bite of meatloaf and it was so very familiar. His brother had made it the same way since he was seventeen. A week after their parents died, Charlie had cooked meatloaf, mashed potatoes, and peas for dinner, as if, with a well-balanced meal, he could somehow restore to their lives the balance that had been upset.

"Charlie? How did you know how to make meatloaf?" Jack asked, suddenly realizing he couldn't remember him ever cooking before their parents' death.

Charlie looked at him flatly. "I didn't *know* how to make it; I learned. Mom had those recipe cards of her mom's, remember? In the yellow plastic box."

"Kind of, but she never made meatloaf, did she?"

Charlie shook his head. "I didn't want to make some-thing she used to make. I didn't want it to taste like she was still there when she wasn't."

With a wave of vertigo that comes from realization, Jack thought of the meals Charlie had made in those first few months. They were plain and simple and balanced—noth-ing like their mother's slapdash combinations of whatever had been on sale at the market or in season in the garden. She'd been a joyful and absent-minded cook. Charlie ap-proached the task with military precision.

"Do you like cooking?"

It was something else he'd never thought of before. But he'd had a lot of time to think lately.

"I don't mind it," Charlie said slowly.

As always, Charlie seemed to be measuring his words. His revelations were as precise as his cooking.

After an awkward few minutes in which they both, as if by mutual agreement, shoved food in their mouths so words were impossible, Charlie said, "I saw Vanessa the other day. She said to tell you hello and that you're an ass-hole for never hanging out anymore."

Guilt and irritation jangled through him. Vanessa had been his friend since high school. The two of them and their friends Ed and Sarah used to meet up monthly for burgers and beers at a bar they'd frequented since before they were legal.

Other than those monthly meet-ups, Jack had never been very social—he was easily bored by small talk and preferred sitting around a fire or walking in the woods to dinner par-ties and birthday parties; casual fucks with few words exchanged to first dates—but since the incident with Davis, Jack had canceled more often than not. He hadn't been in any fit state to socialize and he certainly hadn't wanted to broadcast the humiliation of trusting someone who turned out to be a snake.

Though logically he knew the fault lay with Davis, he felt like a sucker, and learning he couldn't trust his own judgment where Davis was concerned left him doubting it in general.

"Yeah, I'll give her a call," Jack mumbled.

"You all have a fight or something?"

"No," Jack snapped. "We're not ten years old and we didn't have a fight." Charlie raised a calm eyebrow and Jack felt even worse. "I've just been..." He started to say *busy* but it was so patently untrue.

"Feeling sorry for yourself," Charlie finished.

Happy that Charlie had finally said something he could legitimately be pissed at instead of just being in a permanently shitty mood, Jack said, "Screw you."

Charlie's expression was impassive and he raised one massive shoulder in a shrug.

"It's not unwarranted. I just wish you'd get over it."

"Get over it? How about *your* best friend and collaborator who you've trusted and worked with for a decade totally betrays you and screws you over and steals something important to you and we'll see how quickly you get over it, hmm?"

"Bro, I'm not saying Davis doesn't deserve all your anger. He's an asshole and he did a terrible thing. But *you* don't deserve to *be* this angry. And you're not drawing. You're never not drawing. Not since you were a little kid. I just don't like to see you like this."

"Yeah, well, sorry you have to. I'll try to get over it so you aren't inconvenienced," Jack snapped, more hurt than he could explain.

"You know that's not what I meant," Charlie said stiffly. He took Jack's empty plate and his own into the kitchen and Jack was glad for the reprieve and furious he couldn't be the one beating a retreat.

Damn bones for breaking and gravity for functioning and greedy, egotistical bastards for being greedy, egotistical bastards.

"Sorry," Jack muttered.

He knew Charlie couldn't hear him.

A few days later, a storm blew in while Simon was out walking the pack. It started as a shower that sent Mayonnaise and Pickles scampering inside, but within twenty minutes was a gusting squall that darkened the sky and drove rain sideways against the windows.

Jack paced. Well. Jack swung himself back and forth in front of the living room window on his crutches until he had to stop because it was too tiring. It hadn't had the same effect, anyway.

After another ten minutes, he lowered himself to the floor gingerly and built up a fire, wanting the animals to be able to warm up when they got home.

Yeah, the animals. It's definitely them that you want to warm up.

After another ten, he brought armloads of towels from

the bathroom to the couch so he could dry the pack off when they got home.

After another ten, he was able to admit he was worried. Puddles hated the rain. Rat was so small, and…and… He huffed out a breath.

Simon. He was worried about Simon.

Simon felt like part of the pack.

As if conjured by the thought, Simon burst through the door, a sodden, dripping mess. Pirate, seeming unperturbed, made a beeline for the fire and began to clean herself, and Rat followed, shaking off her skinny legs as she went; Dandelion ran right to the kitchen in hopes of a snack.

If Jack had been in fighting form, he would've had the towels on Bernard faster, but as it was, just as he turned to grab them, the huge dog shook himself, and Jack watched as if in slow motion as Simon got sprayed with another round of rain.

"Oh Jesus," Jack said, as Simon slumped resignedly, but he couldn't help but chuckle at the picture it made. Bernard, satisfied he'd wrung himself out, flopped in front of the fire to toast, which left only Puddles and Simon, leaning against each other, soaked and miserable.

"Aw, buddy," Jack said. He was talking to Puddles, whom he approached with the towels he hadn't been quick enough with for Bernard, but he included Simon in his sentiment, if only to himself.

He rubbed Puddles as dry as he could and then the dog slunk off to the bedroom, no doubt to soak a dog-shaped damp spot into his blanket and sheets. Making a mental note to change them later—fine, to ask Charlie to change them—Jack turned to Simon.

"Simon," he said, and the man's eyes met his. "Come inside, man, let me get you some dry clothes."

Simon eyed his soaked boots, jeans, and sweater currently dripping onto the doormat. Jack wanted to tell him he'd already have to clean everything to get rid of the wet dog smell so a little more rain wasn't a big deal. But for some reason, instead, he picked up the remaining towel from the couch and swung over to stand in front of Simon.

"Here," he said, and he wrapped the towel around Simon's shoulders and drew him close enough to rub his arms through it.

He heard Simon's intake of breath and had the brief wild wonder if Simon's mouth would taste of rain if he kissed him.

Then Simon let the breath out and leaned ever so slightly into Jack.

"Get your boots off and you can take a hot shower, okay? I'll get you some clothes."

Simon blinked up at him.

"Okay?"

Simon nodded and gave a ghost of a smile.

Since the first time they'd really talked the week before, they'd lingered over pickups and drop-offs, sometimes talking; sometimes Jack talking and Simon texting. Jack still couldn't tell what made the difference in the times when Simon could speak and when he couldn't. He appreciated the gift of Simon's words when he managed them. But

Simon via text was smart and honest and a little bit snarky, and he liked that too.

Now, standing so close, he felt like he should be able to tell whether words were forthcoming or not, as if the fanfare that announced their appearance would stir the very air between them.

But, no. He still couldn't tell. What he could tell was that Simon was shaking with cold and his wool sweater was so sodden that it might as well have been dumping water down his back.

"C'mere, let me take this," Jack said, tugging at the sweater. Simon's eyelashes, spiked with rain, fluttered and he lifted his arms to help take the sweater off. It was plastered to his shirt beneath, so when the sweater came off so did it.

Jack couldn't help but notice that Simon was lovely beneath his clothes. Angular and smoothly put together, though he was shivering. Jack dropped the sweater to the floor with a *thlump* and slung the towel back around Simon's shoulders.

"Come on," he said softly, and led the way to the bathroom.

He left Simon to his shower and fetched sweats for him to wear from his bedroom, where he did, indeed, find a sheepish Puddles on the bed.

He stroked Puddles' damp nose and Puddles licked his hand. Worried Puddles might be chilly, Jack slung the blanket over him and gave him a rub.

"You like Simon?" he whispered. Puddles yipped. "Yeah. Yeah, me too."

He dropped the sweats outside the bathroom door for Simon and tried not to picture the way hot water would slide down his skin. The way his dark hair would cling to his skull and show off the angles of his face.

His fingers itched for a pencil and he could almost feel the first line he'd lay down.

That was the worst part. Davis' betrayal had been gutting, but it was something that had been done *to* him. Not drawing for the last eight months? Losing the joy that had carried him through the darkest times of his life? That was something he seemed to have done to himself.

In fact, in the first blush of rage that had followed Davis' news, Jack had been full of spiteful energy. He'd determined that he'd draw the most gorgeous book Davis had ever seen and it would be the ultimate revenge. When the wind went out of those sails a week later, it had felt like something deeper was ripped away.

Because betrayal for selfish reasons was grotesque, but it was base; comprehensible. His own heart's turn away from itself was a mystery he hadn't yet managed to solve.

Jack was absently poking at the fire when Simon emerged, flushed and damp, from the bathroom. His dark, wet hair clung to his cheekbones just the way it had in the picture Jack hadn't drawn. His blue eyes burned, the cut of his cheekbone a perfect slash, and Jack couldn't look away.

The sleeves of his sweatshirt hung past Simon's hands so when he wrapped his arms around himself it looked like a straightjacket. Simon was only a few inches shorter than him but he was spare where Jack was muscular.

All in all he presented a picture so tempting that for the first time since it had happened, Jack was grateful for a broken leg because it felt like all that was keeping him from drawing too close to his new friend and breathing in every molecule of him.

"Better?" he asked, voice rough.

Simon nodded and picked his way through the maze of sleeping animals to get to the fire.

The storm still raged darkly outside, making it look more like sunset than morning; the fire glowed and crackled. It was Jack's favorite sound in the whole world.

Suddenly, Simon turned to him and smiled—a quick, bright smile that cut through him.

It took his fucking breath away.

"Hot dogs," Simon said, clear as anything.

"Huh?" Jack felt like the fog from outside had descended on him the moment he saw that radiant smile. Then he saw that Bernard, Rat, and Dandelion lay before the fire in a row, snoozing with their legs stretched behind them. Hot dogs.

He laughed, loud and deep. He laughed because Simon had smiled. Because Simon had made a dopey joke. Because Simon was in his cabin, with his pack, damp and warm, skin to Jack's clothes, happy.

Simon let out a small laugh, low and light, and Jack found himself in the surprising position of having to revise his favorite sound.

"You can move them if you wanna sit there," Jack said, just to say something.

Simon shook his head and sat on the couch instead. He seemed the most relaxed Jack had seen him.

Jack sank down on the couch too, easing his casted leg to rest on the coffee table.

"You aren't missing work, are you?" Jack asked softly, hoping to preserve Simon's relaxation. "I just realized you never told me what you do."

Simon shook his head. Swallowed. Tucked his hands underneath him.

"It's fine. I work from home. G-graphic design."

"That's cool. You're an artist too."

Simon scoffed. "Not like you."

"Lemme see?"

He handed Simon his phone. Simon blinked at him for a moment, then let out a sigh and pulled up his website. He scrolled peremptorily through a few pages before Jack grabbed the phone from his hand to peruse in detail.

Simon's designs were deceptively simple and Jack made note of the URL so he could look at the site later on his computer and see more of the detail. What at first looked like a simple border was, on closer inspection, words marching around the page. A clean layout of squares revealed itself, when you got to the bottom, to form the initials of the company. To the casual observer they were minimal and modern, but each design had a wink.

"These are amazing."

Simon ducked his head but he was smiling.

"Have you always worked from home?"

Given Simon's trouble speaking with people it would make sense that he sought out something he could do solo.

Simon shook his head.

"I worked at a c-company before." He shuddered. "It was awful. Cubicles and p-people and no one would leave me alone."

"What'd they do?" Jack asked, preemptively furious on Simon's behalf.

Simon turned to him, eyes wide with horror. "Talked to me! Had b-birthday cakes and—and holiday parties."

Jack laughed at his nauseated expression. "Monsters."

Simon smiled and rolled his eyes.

The fire crackled cheerily along with the chorus of animal whuffles and burbles.

"If you don't have to be at work," Jack said slowly, "do you want to hang out? Watch a movie or something? Doesn't seem like the storm's letting up anytime soon…"

Simon nodded and joy zinged up Jack's spine. He grabbed the remote before Simon could change his mind and started flipping channels.

He flipped past sports and news and reality TV and soap operas, finding nothing. He'd learned the hard way the last few weeks that television wasn't organized for people with nothing to do during the day. Jack switched over to Netflix and Simon perked up.

"You pick, okay?"

He handed Simon the remote.

Simon bit his lip and extricated a hand from where he was sitting on them to take it.

He scrolled directly to *The Great British Bake Off* and raised a questioning eyebrow at Jack.

"I've never seen it."

"What!?"

"I don't bake."

"That's— That—that," Simon stammered, but this seemed out of passion rather than shyness. "That has *nothing* to do with anything."

Jack held up his hands in surrender and settled in to watch.

After a few minutes of Simon looking over at him expectantly he said, "It's very... British?"

"What does that mean?"

"People are nice to each other and no one's an asshole and they're pretending they don't wanna win?"

"Yeah," Simon sighed blissfully.

After a few more minutes, Jack found himself having strong feelings about bakers and baked goods alike.

"That seems bad," he said. "That seems like a terrible choice. There's not time for that! Is there? I don't know; I don't bake!"

At his yell, Dandelion jumped up, startled. When she saw nothing was amiss besides underbaked cakes she flopped back down and didn't look up again until Jack's next outburst.

"You're scaring the p-pack," Simon said, swatting Jack's leg for emphasis.

Unfortunately, it was his broken leg and Jack cringed. It hadn't hurt so much as promised to hurt, but Simon babbled out a stream of apologies, face a mask of horror, until Jack twisted at the waist and grabbed his shoulders.

"I'm fine. It's okay, really."

"Sorry," Simon said for the twentieth time, and this time it had no sound.

Jack ran his hands from Simon's shoulders down his arms and took his hands.

"Seriously. You didn't hurt me."

Simon tugged one of his hands away.

"I'm sorry," Jack said, and let go, realizing suddenly that holding hands wasn't necessarily something that everyone was comfortable with.

Simon shook his head and sat on his reclaimed hand.

"It t-t—" He snapped his mouth shut and rolled his eyes, as if exasperated with himself.

Jack grabbed his phone and held it out to Simon.

When Simon gave it back to him it said, My hand twitches. It's from my medication, and an ☺.

"What medication?"

For anxiety, Simon wrote. It's a side effect. Muscle twitches.

Simon pulled his knees up and pulled the blanket from the back of the couch over himself.

"Do they happen more when you're nervous? Uh, anxious?"

Simon shook his head. He reached for the phone, then seemed to change his mind.

"It j-just happens. Once it starts, it happens f-for a while. Hate it."

"Is it just your hand?"

He shook his head and pulled the blanket tighter around himself.

"My thighs somet-times. My…" He trailed off, scowling.

"Does massage help?" Jack asked.

Simon's eyes snapped to his. He shrugged. And Jack wanted to kill every single person in the world who hadn't offered to massage Simon's twitching muscles.

"Want to try?" Then, realizing what that sounded like, "Your hand, I mean."

He held out his own hand, palm up, in offering. Simon blinked. Then slowly he leaned closer, slid his hand out of the covers, and placed it in Jack's.

"Watch the show," Jack said.

For the next twenty minutes as they watched the bakers measure, mix, shape, and decorate, Jack massaged Simon's hand. At first, he could feel micromovements that Simon was trying to stifle. Slowly, as Simon relaxed again, the twitches would flex his thumb up and back.

"It's okay," Jack murmured softly, massaging up Simon's wrist.

Simon sighed and let his head drop onto the back of the couch. The episode ended and another began. Jack dug his thumbs into Simon's palm.

Simon tipped his head to look at Jack. His eyelids were heavy and there was a slight smile hovering at the corner of his mouth. Or maybe that was just what his face looked like when he wasn't clenching his jaw.

"Feel okay?"

Simon nodded, eyelashes fluttering.

"Want me to keep going?"

Simon nodded again.

This close, Jack could smell his shampoo in Simon's hair.

He was aware of every shift and breath. Jack wanted to pull him close, kiss his lips, twist his fingers in that unruly hair.

A rip of thunder split the air. Simon startled, jerking upright, and the animals whined.

"It's okay," Jack soothed, and though he'd been talking to the pack, Simon settled too.

Lightning flashed and a whine came from the bedroom. Puddles.

"Puddles is scared of lightning," Jack explained, regretfully pushing himself off the couch. A sweet smile touched Simon's lips and he nodded.

In the bedroom, Jack could just make out a lump at the foot of the bed. Puddles had rucked all the covers off and buried himself beneath them, not an inch of fur visible. On top of the pile sat Louis.

"Aw, buddy."

Jack perched on the edge of the bed and patted the pile, feeling the trembling dog beneath. Louis fixed him with an even look, on guard but not unwelcoming.

"It's good he has you to protect him," Jack told Louis. Louis slow-blinked at him magnanimously.

Simon appeared in the doorway brandishing his phone.

"I'm gonna check on my grandma," he said, but he walked toward the bed.

He raised a questioning eyebrow at the blanket mountain with Louis perched on top and Jack nodded.

"Hey, Puddles," Simon crooned. He got to his knees on the floor and lifted the very edge of the blanket to slide one hand underneath. "Being scared sucks so much. I'm sorry."

He put his chin on the bed and after a minute Jack saw

a trembling nose emerge from the blankets and inch toward Simon's. Puddles gave Simon's cheek a lick, then retreated back to safety.

Jack felt a funny emptiness in his stomach.

Louis, as if he could sense the danger had passed, put his
head on his paws and closed his eyes.

Instead of leaving the room, Simon dialed his phone with
the hand that wasn't under Puddles' blankets.

"I just wanted to check on you," he said. "I know. I
know you can." He rolled his eyes but his smile was fond.
"No one is debating that, Jean. Because!" He laughed. "Yes,
ma'am. Yeah. Just til the storm passes. Oh, okay." His eyes
flicked to Jack. "No you can*not*! Goodbye, I love you," he
said quickly and hung up the phone.

"What can she not?"

"She wanted, um. To talk to you. And make sure you
didn't let me leave until the st-storm ended."

Jack was charmed by that.

"I would've reassured her."

Simon was blushing and had looked away.

"What?"

He shook his head. "She's just… Never mind."

He turned even redder.

"She's just what?"

Simon buried his face in the bed like a little kid and
spoke into the mattress.

"Didn't catch that."

Simon put his arms over his head in a gesture that was
so adorable and ridiculous that Jack's heart ached.

Cursing his leg for the umpteenth time, Jack lifted himself off the bed and came around to where Simon was. Simon's comfort language was clearly touch and Jack wanted his body back so he could speak it fluently. Laboriously and slowly, he lowered himself to the bench at the foot of the bed to sit beside Simon and put a hand on his shoulder.

Making his voice light so Simon would have no doubt he was joking, he said, "Don't make me call your grandma back myself."

Simon groaned and peeled himself off the bed, but still wouldn't meet Jack's eyes. But he didn't look shy, just embarrassed.

"She wants to play m-matchmaker," Simon mumbled. His face and throat were flushed and lust tore through Jack. He wanted to be the one to bring that flush to Simon's skin. He wanted to do everything to Simon.

"Is that right." His voice was low and rough. He'd never gone from finding someone adorable to wanting to ravage them in five seconds flat and it was wreaking havoc inside him.

Simon's head jerked up at his voice, eyes wide and hot.

"And why does she think we'd be a good match?" Jack drawled.

Simon blinked. Blinked again. His pupils dilated.

"I... Um, I... I might've, um." He shook his head in frustration and squeezed his eyes shut. "I said you were handsome," he whispered, eyes closed.

Handsome. The word ricocheted around in Jack's brain before sliding sweetly down to rest in his chest. It was so unassuming, so...grandmotherly a word, but it was so very Simon.

Not *attractive*, not *hot*. *Handsome*.

"Thank you," Jack said. "I think you're handsome too."

At that, Simon's eyes flew open.

"Not just handsome," Jack went on. He reached out a hand slowly—so very slowly—and traced Simon's eyebrow, cheekbone, chin. "Gorgeous. Beautiful. Fucking stunning."

Jack hadn't thought it was possible for Simon to turn redder, but it was. His eyelashes fluttered wildly and he gulped.

"Wow," he said on a breath.

Then he hiccoughed. He clapped a hand over his mouth but hiccoughed again. He groaned. Jack had never seen someone look so mortified in his life. This eclipsed even Charlie's expression when their mom had found out he'd been reading the sex scenes in her romance novels.

Simon pulled his knees up and dropped his forehead to them. Jack couldn't tell if he was hiding or trying to cure the hiccoughs.

Jack put a hand on his shoulder and when Simon didn't shy away he began slowly rubbing Simon's back. He could feel the hiccoughs as well as hear them. Simon muttered something to himself that Jack couldn't make out. After a few minutes, Simon peeked at Jack.

"Doing okay?"

Simon glared and Jack laughed.

"Not my fault you're gorgeous and your body revolts at a compliment."

Simon smiled a little.

"I don't suppose..." Jack started. But he lost his train of thought as Simon sat upright. The redness had faded to just a blush on his cheeks, and his hair was mussed. He was so damn beautiful.

Simon raised an eyebrow and Jack cupped his cheek.

"Don't suppose you wanna kiss me?" Jack said, voice rough with desire.

Simon's eyes went wide and his eyebrows shot up. But he pressed his cheek into Jack's hand and Jack knew he wanted to. He waited. Simon's eyes dropped to his mouth, then slid back up again. He licked his lips. He blinked. Finally, he leaned in.

Jack had kissed a fair few people in his life. In fact, if you'd asked him, he would've said that he'd sampled near every kind of kiss in the books.

But nothing had prepared him for the gutting sweetness of Simon's lips slowly pressed to his; the brush of Simon's long eyelashes against his cheek.

Simon pulled back, blinking at Jack, mouth parted sweetly.

"Okay?" Jack said.

Simon nodded, eyes fixed on Jack's mouth.

Jack pulled him in, Simon's hands on his shoulders, Simon's face to his. And Jack kissed him. Jack kissed him with all the reassurance and desire he could possibly transmit.

He felt Simon's gasp, felt the shudder that ran through him when Jack touched his tongue with his own, and he made himself a promise that whenever the time was right, he would see Simon dissolve into gasps and shudders and screams.

Simon pressed closer to him and Jack brushed his fingers down Simon's throat. Simon made a shocked sound of pleasure that tore through Jack, sent his mind racing in a dozen directions at once as he imagined all the things they could do.

Jack slid his tongue against Simon's, slick and hot, tasting him. Simon gasped again and Jack groaned.

Then Simon hiccoughed.

Simon jerked away so quickly Jack almost fell forward off the bench. He clapped his hands over his mouth and his eyes were huge. He hiccoughed again.

"Hey," Jack said, reaching out a hand. "You okay?"

Simon rolled his eyes and Jack could recognize his look of mortification by now, even with his hands covering half his face. He scrambled to his feet, face turning red again.

"Simon, hey. It's no big deal. C'mere."

Simon groaned, and this time it was *not* in pleasure. He was about to bolt, Jack could tell. He struggled to his feet as Simon ran through the bedroom door.

"Simon, dammit, don't make me run after you when I can't run! Fucking fuck," he muttered at his leg. He grabbed his crutches and made his way to the living room as quickly as he could.

"Seriously, you promised your grandmother!"

But when he rounded the corner of the living room, Simon wasn't pulling on his coat and shoes to leave. He was standing in the corner, face pressed to the wood, arms wrapped around himself.

"You look like the goddamn Blair Witch."

Simon snorted, which could have been a laugh or an angry exhalation.

"Okay, okay, come on. Tell me what the big deal is,

please. You hiccoughed. It's not the end of the world. Hell, I burped in a girl's mouth once."

And, okay, he hadn't quite meant to admit that, but anything to underline how little this mattered.

Simon shook his head, clearly not reassured.

When Jack got to him, he slid a hand up his spine. Simon didn't move away, so he rested his palm on the back of Simon's neck. He could feel his flush.

"Hey. You just embarrassed or is something really wrong? Cuz you're scaring me a little. Been a while since someone's actually hidden in a corner just to get away from me. And that was during dodgeball."

Simon slumped.

"Just emb-barrassed," he choked out.

"Okay." Jack rubbed Simon's neck and into his hair.

Slowly, Simon relaxed. He muttered something Jack couldn't make out.

"What's that?"

"Can't believe I r-ruined it."

"You didn't ruin anything," Jack said. "Hell, kiss me again right now and pretend it never happened, if you want to."

"Can't," Simon said, peeking at Jack.

"Can't kiss me again?"

Simon shook his head. "Can't pret-t-tend."

Jack was running his fingers through Simon's hair, entranced by how soft it was.

"Yeah, how come?"

"C-cuz," Simon said.

"Oh. Well, that clears things up," Jack joked, giving Simon's neck a little squeeze.

Simon snorted and elbowed him.

Jack steered him around by the shoulder, wanting to see his face.

"What's up, darlin'?" he said. "Because why?"

"B-b-bec-cause. It was my f-f-f-first k-k-k-k—"

Simon made an exasperated face at himself and Jack felt like his heart stopped.

"Your first kiss?"

Simon nodded miserably.

Jack felt like his dick went from zero to *oh god* in the space of that one movement. He wasn't sure why that did it for him and he didn't, quite frankly, care to interrogate it. He just knew that the idea that he'd been sweet Simon Burke's first kiss set him on fire.

"Oh, fuck," he groaned, and dropped his head to Simon's shoulder. "That's just— I, wow."

Simon stiffened and Jack lifted his head to find Simon looking uncertain.

"No, sorry, I— Fuck, that's so... I'm honored."

He cupped Simon's face and watched the relief relax his jaw and brow.

"Can I be your second kiss too?" Jack said, brushing Simon's mouth with his thumb. "Please."

Simon blinked.

"I promise I won't burp," Jack said very seriously, and was rewarded with a tiny smile.

Simon nodded and Jack felt like he'd been given a great gift.

"Thank you," he breathed, and he kissed Simon. Gently

at first—slowly. Then he slanted his mouth over Simon's and deepened the kiss. The taste of Simon was delicious and the tentative way he touched his tongue to Jack's made him wild.

When Simon started to breathe heavily, Jack eased off, weaning himself of that gorgeous mouth with gentle kisses to his lips, cheekbones, temple.

They stood together, breathing hard, and Simon reached out a tentative hand to touch Jack's mouth.

Eyes burning and lips swollen, Simon said, "Wow."

Chapter Seven

Simon

Simon replayed the kiss in his mind a hundred times. Hell, make it a thousand. That night, after the storm had blown through and he'd made his way home, he lay in bed, shut his eyes tight, and went over every detail he could remember. It turned out he could remember enough to make his heart race, his dick go hard, and his breath come short just thinking about it.

He slid a hand down his belly and into his underwear and brought himself off in just five glorious strokes, shuddering and biting his lip. He couldn't help but wonder if maybe, 6.8 miles northwest, Jack might be doing the same.

He fell blissfully asleep, but woke up with a dragon of

anxiety curled in his stomach. What would it be like when he saw Jack this morning? What if Jack thought the whole thing was a mistake and everything they'd been building was ruined? Simon had *talked* to him! What if Jack pretended it had never happened? Simon couldn't bear to see him twice a day and pretend. Or what if Jack assumed they'd fuck now? That was normal for people who had sex, right?

By the time he got to Jack's he was nauseated and shaking apart. Jack opened the door with a warm smile, but it slid off his face the second he saw Simon's expression.

"What's wrong?"

He held a hand out and Simon followed him in.

"I didn't know if— What are— We don't—"

Too much, too many possibilities all intersecting, contradicting, overloaded. Choking.

"Hey, hey, c'mere," Jack said, leaning his crutches against the wall and opening his arms.

Simon stood face-to-face with something he'd wanted since the moment Jack first opened the front door. The chance to be held close to that big, warm body, in its soft, worn sweatshirt. Something he'd wanted far longer than just since then, if he were honest.

Someone who regretted kissing him and wanted to pretend it never happened wouldn't open his arms, right?

He stepped forward, heart racing, and let Jack's arms enfold him.

Jack squeezed him tight, then stroked his back.

"What's up, darlin'?" he asked softly after a few minutes. It was only when Simon pulled back that he found the pack sitting in a circle around them, watching them.

It felt right, somehow.

He tried to put his thoughts in order but they started to get tangled up again, and the tangle stuck in his throat.

"You wanna text?" Jack offered when he cleared his throat for the fifth time.

Gratitude for the unexpected kindness of this man flooded him and nearly leaked from his eyes.

He nodded and pulled out his phone.

Sorry. I got so nervous and I didn't know if it would be weird today bc of the whole kissing thing and then I freaked out like what if you regretted it or maybe I'm a terrible kisser or what if you thought that kissing meant I would just have sex right away and I don't think I'm ready and then I thought you might be mad at me.

He couldn't quite make himself send the message, held his phone until Jack gently took it from his hand. After a minute, Jack cupped his cheek.

"It's not weird for me. I definitely do not regret the whole kissing thing." He winked. "You're, *fuuuck*, the opposite of a terrible kisser. I thought maybe I scared you away with how much I, uh, liked it."

Simon flushed, thinking about touching himself to memories of their kiss, and shook his head.

"Well, that's good. I'd never assume that kissing me meant you wanted to have sex with me, even if you'd kissed a million people before, and anyone who'd be mad at you for not being ready is a piece of shit. And I'll knock their block off."

It was a ridiculous thing to say and from Jack it sounded like the most natural thing in the world.

"Okay," Simon said. He dropped his forehead forward to rest against Jack's shoulder. "Good."

"Good," Jack echoed.

Bernard howled, echoing it in his own way too.

The next week was perhaps the strangest in Simon's life.

He wasn't used to waking up excited about where he was going or who he was seeing. He wasn't used to getting out of his car and not feeling a sick sense of dread creep through him. He wasn't used to falling asleep with memories from the day that he *wanted* to ruminate on. And he absolutely, certainly, one hundred percent was not used to being gathered to a man's chest, his lips and cheeks and brows kissed; to the taste of someone else's lips tingling on his own as he walked the dogs, made coffee, did his work.

It was visionary, transcendent, addictive.

It gave him the unfamiliar sense of having a place in the world. Of being tethered, rather than floating, ghostlike, through a land that belonged to others.

He didn't suppose that a week of kissing was supposed to be able to change the world, but his world was sweetly, irrevocably altered.

Of course his grandmother had noticed. Simon worried she might tease him, but that was a worry from another time.

"What's Jack's favorite cookie?" she'd asked, taking out the flour.

Simon didn't know.

"Well, ask him, silly!"

Simon had stared at his phone. It had never occurred to him that he could contact Jack when they weren't together.

Hi. It's Simon. What's your favorite cookie?

Hmm, Simon who? came the reply. But it was followed immediately with a winky face and Simon realized that although it was the first time he'd texted Jack from afar, of course he'd texted him a hundred times while they were in the same room.

He tried to stop smiling, embarrassed that Grandma Jean could read his absurd happiness on his face.

He sent back: Wow, you just gave me a panic attack. But he also sent a wink of his own.

Jack wrote, I know you're a tough cookie. Mmm speaking of cookies, I like oatmeal.

For a moment, Simon didn't even notice the second part of the text. No one had ever called him tough before. Told him to toughen up? Yes. To tough it out? Definitely. The thing was that he *knew* he was tough. He'd never told anyone, but sometimes at the end of the day, when he closed the door on the world and pulled a blanket over his head, he thought: *You are so fucking tough. You just did hard shit all day. You are so brave for doing that.*

He felt a flush of pride and gratitude that Jack had seen that in him.

Then: OATMEAL??? That's your FAVORITE cookie??? Whose favorite sweet confection is made of GRUEL?!!!

Daaaaamn, Simon, I love oatmeal in all forms!

WOW. Well, okay, I'll tell my grandma, but she might not let me hang out with you anymore...

You tell your grandma that I'll fight her for you.

You'd fight an old lady? Cold-blooded, Matheson.

I'm gonna tell your grandma you called her an old lady, Burke. Now make me some damn cookies.

And then, as if it were as simple as pressing a button, Jack sent a heart. A red, clear-as-day heart that sat there staring at Simon and making him wonder what would happen if he sent one back.

With a trembling finger, he sent the emoji back.

Voop as it sent, and Simon blinked.

Because he hadn't sent a heart. He'd sent the green-faced vomiting emoji that was next to it.

He dropped his phone.

"Dick pic, dear?" Grandma Jean said sympathetically. "The bits not quite what you'd hoped for?"

"Grandma, no! God."

He grabbed his phone and scrambled to type: OMG I meant to send the heart! My finger hit the wrong emoji and OMG.

Jack sent back a flurry of crying laughing emojis and

then a kissy face. With relief shaking through him and great care in the emoji-choosing arena, Simon sent back one perfect heart.

"Phew," he said, collapsing on a kitchen stool.

"Just a bad angle, then?" his grandmother drawled impishly.

"You're a true menace," he told her. "Oh, and oatmeal cookies."

She pursed her lips pensively and cocked her head.

"Hmmm," she said. "Interesting."

"Is it?"

"Very interesting."

They'd been kissing for what felt like hours. Simon's spine was liquid and his thighs burned from kneeling over Jack on the couch. Every swipe of his tongue against Jack's, every trail of Jack's fingertips down his throat, sent a pulse straight to his cock.

He buried his face in the crook of Jack's neck, the skin there hot and smelling deliciously of Jack. He pressed a kiss to the throbbing pulse in Jack's throat and felt Jack's breath hitch.

"Jack," he whispered.

Jack stroked up his back. "Yeah."

"I... I..."

Jack eased him back so they were looking at each other.

Simon was burning up. He wanted everything and didn't know how to ask for any of it.

"Feeling shy, darlin'?" Jack drawled. His eyelids were heavy and there was a flush across his high cheekbones.

Simon shook his head.

"Not...with this." He pressed his palm to Jack's chest. "Just..." He gestured to his mouth.

"Easier to touch than to talk?"

Yes. So much easier.

He nodded, relieved Jack understood.

"No problem. I can do the talking," Jack murmured. "Want me to tell you what you do to me? What I wanna do with you?"

Simon knew it was a choice but he just nodded. He wanted it all.

"Mmm, okay." He put his hand over Simon's where it rested on his chest. "You make my heart race. So fucking hot. And knowing that I'm the first one—the only one—to touch you. That you've kissed? It's..." He groaned. "I don't know. Fucking *gets* to me."

He stroked fingertips up the side of Simon's throat and Simon's eyelids fluttered. The gentle touches made him squirm in the best way.

"It's like you're so sensitive because this is all new and it..." He sucked in a breath through his nose. "It *really* turns me on to watch you."

Simon's breath came faster. Jack's fingers moved from his throat to his chest, and he brushed his thumbs over Simon's nipples, watching for his reaction.

First nothing, then Jack pinched and bolts of sensation shot through him, arching his back.

"Damn," Jack breathed. He did it again and again until Simon was writhing. "Wanna take this off?"

Simon stripped off his shirt. His face was on fire and the

flush was spreading down his chest, his nipples standing out, rosy and pert. Jack pinched them again and now that Simon could *see* it he felt it even more.

His thighs were trembling so hard he could barely hold himself up. Slowly, he lowered himself to Jack's lap.

Jack's broken groan ripped through him and for a moment he worried he'd jarred Jack's leg. But Jack cupped his shoulders, holding him there firmly, and when Simon's mind cleared he felt the hardness he was sitting on. He moved experimentally, pressing this way and that, and watched Jack's eyes roll back.

"Fuck, baby, stop for a second." Jack sucked in a breath. "You're— Shit, that's so sweet. You wanna feel it too?"

Simon nodded, heart pounding in his ears.

"C'mere."

Jack pulled himself more upright and settled Simon's full weight back on his lap. Simon tipped his hips forward and *Oh, fuck*, there it was.

Jack rearranged himself and then they were moving together, hard cocks straining against one another in their pants. It was so very, very much, but with each minute that passed it became more frustrating.

Simon whined and Jack kissed him hard.

"Simon," he said when they broke the kiss. "I wanna touch your dick. I wanna—*fuck*—I wanna feel you lose it. Wanna touch you till you come all over us."

A bolt of pure lust ripped through Simon and set him shaking. He fumbled with his fly. He pulled at Jack's sweatpants until Jack got the hint and eased them down his thighs along with Simon's jeans.

"Jesus, you're beautiful," Jack muttered, tracing the head of Simon's cock with his finger. Simon's hips bucked violently at that first touch and he gasped, bracing himself on Jack's shoulders.

"Oh, yeah, darlin'. I want to touch you fucking everywhere." He stroked Simon's cock slowly, gently, then a little bit harder, a little bit faster, making everything go liquid and hot.

"I want to touch every inch of you, inside and out. Wanna make you scream and beg and come until you can't come anymore."

"Ungh!" Simon babbled, feeling like his skin was too tight for the arousal roiling inside him. "Jack, p-please," he managed. He held on with one hand and with the other, he reached down slowly and wrapped his hand around the first erection other than his own that he'd ever touched.

Jack was big and uncut and Simon could feel his pulse through his veins. At the first squeeze, Jack's hips bucked up and Simon fell backward, which sent Jack into a flurry of cursing.

"S-sorry. I'm too big."

"Goddamn my leg," Jack hissed finally. "I want to do fucking everything to you and this damn thing." Then, as if Simon's words had finally caught up with him, he furrowed his brow. "You're the perfect size. And if I hadn't fucked myself all up—" He broke off and blew out an angry breath.

Then he pulled his good leg up, foot resting on the couch, and held Simon's hips so Simon couldn't fall backward.

"C'mere," he said then, eyes hot. Simon let himself be

arranged so that his cock pressed to Jack's. His eyelashes fluttered at the sensation of that hot, velvet flesh against his own.

"So hot, darlin'. You just move however you want. I promise I'll fuckin love it."

Simon braced his hands on Jack's shoulders again and ground his hips down, undulating to the rhythm his body demanded. His pulse got stronger and stronger until he felt it in his ears and temples, in his cock and balls, in his asshole and in his gut. He was hard and leaking and so was Jack. That press of hot, slick, swollen flesh was all Simon could think about.

Jack's hips pulsed up too, tiny movements that spurred the heat between them even higher.

Heart pounding, cock pulsing, Simon kissed Jack desperately. Jack groaned when their mouths met, and his palms on Simon's back were strong and hungry. Tongue in Simon's mouth, Jack hauled him down so they were belly to belly, chest to chest.

"Oh, fuck," Jack said into the kiss when Simon's weight pressed their erections together again. He reached between their bellies and when his hand closed around their hard lengths, Simon nearly swallowed his tongue.

"Oh! Oh, oh," he heard himself say. He slung his arms around Jack's neck, suddenly afraid that the dark, pounding surf gathering deep within him would rip him away forever.

Jack's strong arm held him tight and Jack's other hand worked them, sloppy and straining and better than anything Simon had ever imagined.

He heard someone whimper and realized it was him but he couldn't care because suddenly the world aligned with a shocking snap. Jack's hand tightened just so and the drag of his palm against Simon's skin had him soaring, grinding, clutching, writhing. Then the sky cracked open and pleasure tore through him, shattering him apart.

In wrenching spasms he came into Jack's hand and over Jack's cock and as if from a distance he heard Jack shout and felt Jack's heat added to his own.

Simon shook and Jack kept stroking them lightly, which sent tingles and shivers skating along every nerve ending.

"Mmmmhh," Simon groaned finally, and slumped against Jack's chest, shaking.

Jack's heart pounded beneath his cheek and Jack started petting his hair and his back, his hand finally coming to rest on Simon's ass, and giving a little push, pressing them together again. Simon felt Jack's cock twitch and a ghost of pleasure ran through his own.

They lay like that for a minute or two. Jack's heart rate returned to normal, as did Simon's breathing. Then Jack slid a hand into his hair.

"You okay?" he asked softly.

Simon nodded. For once, his head was blissfully empty, every habitual inkling blasted away.

"Good."

They lay for another minute.

"We're gonna get stuck together," Jack warned.

But Simon was so comfortable. So comfortable and so very, very peaceful.

"The dogs are gonna try to lick our come," Jack warned.

At that, Simon sat up, horrified.

Jack half chuckled and half groaned, since Simon sitting up involved a redistribution of the mess between them.

"Okay, okay, don't do anything drastic," he muttered.

They eased apart slowly, Simon wiping at their come with his shirt.

Jack caught his hand and pressed a kiss to his palm.

"Hey." Simon looked at him. There was a softness to his expression—an uncertainty that Simon hadn't seen before. "Was it okay?"

Simon grinned and rolled his eyes. The notion that Jack might not know how mind-blowing it was for him was laughable.

But Jack's eyes had a rawness in them that made Simon remember how much it hurt when sincerity was treated as a joke.

Simon cupped Jack's face, kissed his cheek, and said very seriously and very firmly, "Yes."

When Simon got home, someone was breaking things.

At the first crash, he braced for a burglar. But this was Garnet Run so it was more likely to be a moose.

Then he heard the yell. It was indistinct and garbled with pain, but Simon knew. What he didn't know was whether to give his grandma privacy or go to her. It was something he was never sure of. When he felt at his worst, the idea of someone seeing him was mortifying.

Once, in tenth grade, after Mr. Warner had forced him to the front of biology class to demonstrate removal of the fetal pig's heart and his hand had shaken so hard as the man barked instructions at him that he'd nearly sliced the pig in half, he'd bolted from the room. A well-meaning class-mate had followed him, crashing through the bathroom door just in time to see him puke into the sink. At the sight of her Simon had shut himself in a stall, wishing he were dead. Finally she left, and she never followed him again.

It never helped to be witnessed in the depths.

But with Jack's scent on his skin and Jack's taste in his mouth, an unfamiliar image slid into his mind. What if, someday, Jack were the one to find him? The one to wit-ness his body and brain trying to tear each other apart? What if he didn't run? What if he didn't cringe? What if Jack just wrapped those strong arms around him and held him as he shook? That wouldn't feel the same, would it?

Simon nosed into his collar, hunting for one more whiff of Jack, when another crash came from the kitchen. He turned the corner and jumped back as the plate hit the ground inches from his toes.

"Grandma, it's me," he said, keeping his voice casual.

"Don't come in here unless you're wearing shoes," she said, voice choked. "There's...everything's broken."

Simon gulped.

Broken crockery littered the floor and a hole was caved into the wall next to the window, flowered wallpaper punched into the drywall.

His grandmother stood outside the entrance to the pan-try. For the first time since the funeral, Simon found him-self thinking how old she looked. How small.

She'd simply always been there for him. In the usual ways, when he was a child. Birthday presents and hugs and special outings and favorite meals. But it was later that mattered more. When his parents began to realize that their son wasn't going to be who they wanted him to be. Wasn't going to act the way they thought he should. When they lost patience with his fear and his pain and began to see them as inconveniences instead of needs. That's when his grandmother's open door and open arms, her empathy and her acceptance, her fierce protection, had meant everything to him.

At fifteen, when he'd left his job at the Dairy Queen after three days because they'd forced him to take orders when he'd thought he would only fill them—when his boss had barked at him to *Speak up, son,* and when Simon couldn't, let fly unsavory comparisons that Simon wouldn't repeat—when his father had thrown up his hands in exasperation and asked how the hell Simon thought he'd ever be an independent adult if he couldn't even keep a job at a fucking Dairy Queen—his grandmother had stood up for him. She'd told his father to back off and she'd told him that it wasn't being able to ask strangers what kind of ice cream they wanted that made you an adult.

At sixteen, when he'd failed three classes because the teachers wouldn't waive the participation and presentation grades and the school had sent home a letter warning that he might be held back a year, she'd been the one to pluck the letter from his mother's hand, announce that she'd take care of it, then march into the principal's office and give him a piece of her mind that had, Simon was sure, been what let him enter his senior year.

At seventeen, when he wanted to apply for college but

didn't have a single teacher who could write a recommendation letter on his behalf, his grandmother had been the one to suggest he ask Cindy and Bill, who ran the Humane Society where Simon had spent the weekends since he was fourteen, to write instead. He hadn't gotten in anywhere, but he still had the letters. They were the only endorsements of his character he couldn't deny.

She'd been there for him more times than he could count, always warm and fierce and unrufflable.

But now she looked small, uncertain, angry. She looked heartbroken.

Simon crossed to her, not sure what to say.

"I can't believe he left me," she choked out. "Bastard." Simon put his arms around her and gathered her close. "Can't believe that bastard died and left me all alone," she sobbed. Simon had never heard his grandmother say *bastard* before.

"Bastard," he cooed in solidarity about the kindest man he'd ever known.

His grandmother swatted him. "Don't talk about your grandfather like that," she admonished through her tears.

"Sorry," Simon laughed. His grandmother laughed. She cried and laughed and then Simon found himself crying and laughing.

"Good lord," she said, wiping her tears and taking a deep breath. "What now?"

Simon knew she wasn't talking about this very moment, but sometimes the next moment was all you could really deal with.

"Well," he offered, "we could break more stuff?"

His grandmother's eyebrows rose.

"We could," she said thoughtfully. "We could break more stuff."

Simon reached into the open cupboard and took out two plates. He handed one to his grandmother. Then he clinked the rim of his to the rim of hers in a defiant *cheers* and threw the plate at the wall.

It exploded, then the pieces hit the tile floor and shattered again. Simon grinned, giddy with glee.

"Wow," he said. "Good thing you replaced those linoleum floors you had when I was a kid. They wouldn't have yielded nearly such a satisfying result."

"True," his grandmother said. Then she threw her plate at the wall and let out a holler of joy as it exploded.

They looked at each other, wide-eyed and grinning like naughty children.

"Again?" his grandmother said.

"Again," Simon agreed.

Chapter Eight

Jack

It was so infuriatingly stupid, but Jack had the urge to call Davis. Not the real Davis, who'd shown he didn't care about Jack at all. The Old Davis. The...fictional Davis?

The Davis who'd been his best friend since freshman year of college; the Davis who'd listen wryly when Jack would grumble about wanting a relationship but hating people, shake his head and say, "You don't hate people, bro. You're just a romantic and no one's lived up to it yet." At which point Jack would invariably huff and puff and change the subject, then wonder about it for days afterward.

Did it make him a romantic that most people irritated him and when he imagined waking up with them every morning for the rest of his life he wanted to barf at the tedium and annoyance?

Did it make him a romantic that, on the few dates he'd capitulated to, questions like *What are you afraid of?* and *What's the best thing that's ever happened to you?* killed the mood when in his fantasies they created intimacy, depth?

And now: Simon.

Simon, who didn't irritate him, but fascinated him. Simon, the thought of waking up next to whom every morning filled him with a fizzy lightness like the air on a cold, clear birthday morning just after sunrise. Simon, whom he now desperately wanted to ask what was the best thing that had ever happened to him. Simon, who he didn't hate, not even one little bit.

So, despite every possible betrayal and disappointment, sitting in his cabin with his pack, Simon's kisses lingering on his lips and the image of Simon's face in ecstasy—trembling mouth open, eyes shut, throat taut—as he came by another's hand for the first time, Jack wanted to call the Davis of his past and say:

Maybe you were right. Maybe I am a romantic. Because I am feeling romantic as fuck right now about a man called Simon Burke.

Jack organized his sock drawer. Painstakingly easing it from the dresser so he could sit on the bed, he divided white from black; wool from cotton. He hung his shirts in color spectrum order in the closet.

He alphabetized his spice rack. He sharpened every pencil and perfectly aligned his books' spines with the edge of the bookshelf.

The smoke hadn't come from the house over the hill this morning, though Jack had watched for over an hour. Had the birds and squirrels seemed quieter too? It felt like it, but he couldn't be sure. He marked an X on the piece of paper where he'd been keeping track, then a large, irritated question mark.

He sat in his studio with the binoculars and stared out the window at the defunct garden instead. He'd never been one for gardening though he remembered a time when it thrived. When his mom spent hours on her knees with her hands in the dirt. As a child, he'd sit at the corner of a bed of zinnias and hold as still as he could, hand outstretched, palm full of birdseed, waiting for the chipmunks to get used to him enough that they would eat from his hand.

Suddenly, for the first time, it felt essential that he plant the garden. If he could've willed his leg to heal in that moment, he'd have planted the whole field. He wondered if there were still seeds in the green metal box by the back door, but when he rose to check, a jolt of pain shot from his leg to his spine and he sank back down. Instead, he pulled a sheet of paper toward him and tried to remember all the things his mom had planted. He imagined delicate pea tendrils snaking up stakes and the creep of mint over potato mounds.

He stared out the window for hours. Watched the sun climb high and drop low again. Watched squirrels and chipmunks dart and flash in chittering configurations. Watched birds soar. Watched larger creatures move in the woods and smaller ones run from them.

Finally, exhausted from doing even these small things,

he sank onto the couch and watched episode after episode of *Secaucus Psychic*. When he found himself starting to wonder if maybe spirits really did linger after death and send messages to the living he got an uncomfortable feeling in his stomach.

Do you believe in ghosts? he texted Charlie, even though Charlie was at work.

I don't know. Not really, Charlie responded. Why?

So you don't think mom and dad ever tried to send us messages from beyond the grave or anything?

There was a long pause before Charlie answered and Jack didn't know if he was thinking or working.

Finally, when his answer came, Jack didn't know what to make of it.

I hope not.

"Fucking mother goddamn uggh!"

Jack swung his crutch like a golf club at the dog toy that had nearly tripped him and collapsed (gently) on the couch in a massive sulk, which is where he still was twenty minutes later when Simon arrived, only now Puddles was sitting on his left foot.

"Come in!" Jack yelled.

Simon brought the smell of autumn inside with him, fresh and intoxicating and Jack wanted to punch something. Jack wanted to punch everything.

"Hey," Simon said. He was wearing grayish-brown cor-

duroys and a wool sweater the color of blackberries; a soft
gray scarf that looked hand-knit was wrapped around his
throat. His dark hair was windblown and he was smiling
a little.

He looked so gorgeous and soft that Jack wanted to bury
himself in him and never come up for air.

Jack held out his hand and Simon came to him without hesitation.

"Hi," Jack said and pulled Simon down on top of him.
He wrapped Simon in his arms and breathed in the scent
of outdoors and wool and Simon himself.

Simon said something Jack couldn't hear.

"Hmm?" he asked, but didn't let go and Simon didn't
repeat himself, just nuzzled into Jack's neck. He thought
he caught just the slightest hint of sugar from Simon's scarf
and bet Simon's grandmother had knitted it.

"What's wrong?" Simon said low into his ear after a
while.

Jack grumbled and let Simon slide out of his lap onto
the couch beside him.

"Can't stand being cooped up here anymore. It's driving me fucking batshit."

"You don't have to stay inside, do you?" Simon asked.

"Well, no, but I can't fucking *do* anything," Jack groused.
He decided that perhaps sharing his recent habit of standing
outside the back door and obsessively stalking a smokestack
might not be in this delicate relationship's best interest.

"What would you do if you d–didn't have a broken leg?"

Jack huffed out a breath. He realized he was sulking, realized it was likely terribly unattractive, but couldn't quite stop.

"Walk the dogs," he said.

Simon shrugged. "Let's go, then."

He got off the couch and held out a hand to Jack.

Outside, Jack sucked in huge breaths, hungry for air that he or the animals hadn't already breathed out. He felt better already. It was chilly out, but the sky was clear. Turning leaves, dirt, wood smoke, and ozone filled his nose. Perfect.

It was extremely slow and painful going down the path from his house. By the time they got to the road, Jack was sweating and breathing hard, and he'd had to lean against Simon four or five times when his balance betrayed him. He had to stay on pavement otherwise his crutches sunk into the dirt and leaves, which curtailed their route options slightly, but Jack didn't care. He was outside with his pack and that was all that mattered.

Pirate rubbed up against his cast then trotted ahead like always, Rat at her heels. Dandelion turned this way and that, enjoying the walk. Puddles stuck close to Simon, and Bernard kept sniffing at Jack like he knew something was different.

Jack hadn't fully realized how much he'd missed this until now. It had been a month and every cell of his body had yearned for it. Even the fact that they had to go so slowly that Pirate finally got fed up and started running in circles around them didn't dull the shine of being out in the glorious morning air.

But after another five minutes, his shoulders and arms were on fire and his armpits chafed painfully. After another ten minutes he could feel the calluses forming on his palms and he was breathing like he'd run ten miles. Simon was shooting him looks that were likely supposed to be subtle but weren't.

"Let's stop for a bit," Simon said gently. Jack was panting and wincing and dizzy, sweat streaming down his back. He was furious at his body and wanted to argue with Simon, but he couldn't, because he needed to stop, and because he was already in a vicious argument with himself.

How did just breaking my leg make me this weak? Jack's mind screamed. *My arms should be strong enough to compensate! Why am I tired when I've spent all day lying around???*

The dogs didn't mind stopping. They wove their leashes together chasing each other and nipping at falling leaves, bugs, the air. Pirate chased a pika through the trees, catching it once and letting it go, then jumped on Bernard's back, inducing him to play with her. He obliged, harrumphing down on the ground and rolling around with her, practically tugging Simon down with him.

Simon's laugh drove away the pain in Jack's arms and the ache in his back. It even eased his resentment a little bit. He leaned back against a tree and looked up at the way each tree's leaves didn't quite touch, blue sky visible in rivers between them. Crown shyness it was called. A red-tailed hawk careened overhead and Jack envied its freedom.

"I'll drop them off and come get you in the car," Simon said.

The tentative edge to his voice was all that kept Jack from snapping at him.

"I'm fine," he said tightly.

Simon frowned at him. He slid the leashes up to his

wrists and took Jack's hand, turning it palm up. Jack hissed when Simon pressed on the skin there and snatched his hand away. He opened his mouth and closed it again.

"Sorry," Jack said softly. "I'm just so damn sick of being weak."

Simon's eyes snapped to his, blazing.

"You're not *weak*. You broke your leg. You're human, you know, with bones, that-that-that break!"

"Fuck bones," Jack growled bitterly, scowling at his cast. "I hate bones."

Simon's laugh rang out.

"You're such a baby," he said, but he said it gently.

Jack's eyes widened.

"You are," Simon said. "You think it's weak to have a broken leg? What do you think of people who can't walk? D'you think they're weak?"

"What? No, of course not!"

"What do you think of p-people who need help to get around all the time? Are they weak?"

"No, I—"

"What do you think of m-me, then? Am I weak because I c-can't t-talk to p-people?"

"No! Simon, no. I— Fuck, I'm sorry. You're right. Bad choice of words."

"It's not a choice of words, though," he said, cheeks flushed. "It's how you think. B-being strong means being able to d-do everything easily and by yourself and anything else means b-being weak. Right?"

Jack frowned. That *was* how he'd always thought of

things for himself. But he didn't think that way about other people. Did he?

"I…no, I…"

"And if you think it about yourself but not about me then wh-what makes you so damn special?" Simon went on. "Why do you g-get to be different?"

Simon's eyes blazed and Jack could see the anger there. Somehow, it shocked him. Had Simon's shyness made Jack think he couldn't get angry?

Jack hung his head.

"I'm not special," he said. "I'm just…used to being able to do things for myself. By myself. I don't like being help-less. It's frustrating and…"

Frustrating isn't all, though, is it? a sneaky voice whispered. *The last time you felt helpless was when Mom and Dad died and there was nothing you could do about it. You couldn't change what happened to them and you couldn't even help Charlie. He did everything for you and you just let him.*

Simon didn't answer, but his silence spoke as loudly as his words. After a minute, he said, "There's more than one way to be strong, Jack."

It's Ed's birthday, did you forget??? Are you coming???

The text from Vanessa was waiting for Jack when he got out of the shower. Fuck. He had forgotten.

He groaned. He was utterly physically exhausted from the walk this morning and spiritually exhausted from his argument with Simon. He felt like he'd deeply disappointed Simon and it had left a sick feeling of shame in his stomach.

The idea of sitting in a bar with Vanessa, Ed, and Sarah sounded terrible. *Everything* sounded terrible.

I don't think I can, Van, he wrote. I can't drive and I'm really tired.

She wrote back instantly. Dude. Are you pissed at us? Cuz you've been more of a dick than usual lately.

He sighed. He wasn't sure what he was. He wasn't sure why an outing he would have looked forward to a year ago had lost all its appeal.

No way, he wrote. He didn't have the heart to let Van believe he was upset with her to get out of going. Just kind of stuck here. And, you know, broken.

I'll pick you up! Van offered, which he should have predicted. Seriously, Ed really misses you and it's his damn birthday. Don't be a fuckhead. I'll come by around 7.

At that Jack smiled slightly. "Don't be a fuckhead" had been the Vanessa Carlson catchphrase since high school, and woe betide those who didn't heed it.

OK, Jack wrote, already dreading it.

True to her word, Vanessa's headlights cut through the dark at seven on the dot. She greeted the dogs enthusiastically, hissed at the cats companionably, then said, "You look like shit."

"Always a pleasure, V."

"No, I mean you look…" She cocked her head and looked up at him consideringly. "Sad."

Jack gestured to his leg and his crutches and shrugged. "Sucks."

Her narrowed eyes said she knew he wasn't telling the

whole truth, but she let it go, gave Bernard one last kiss on his huge head, and they left.

"His bed frame was made of *antlers!*"

Sarah gestured wildly enough that a frothy plug of beer slugged out of her bottle and streamed down her hand. She licked it off.

"He opened the door and it was like fucking *Hannibal* in there. And I was like 'Hell no, dude, I am not screwing you on that throne of death.' Like, how is it comforting to bring someone back to your house and basically say, 'Hey, I kill things bigger than you on the regular with no problem. Wanna bone?'" She paused, outrage turning to giggles. "Ha ha, *bone*, get it?"

Jack snorted. He was pleasantly buzzed and enjoying hearing Sarah and Ed trade dating horror stories and wondering why he'd avoided his friends for so long. As always, Sarah won because it was clear that men were horrible. Vanessa's expression suggested that she was extremely glad she already had Rachel and didn't have to suffer any of this.

"What about you, J?" Sarah said. "Any recent dating disasters to share?"

Ed feigned a thoughtful look and stroked his chin. "I don't believe it's *called* dating when you screw people in your truck outside of bars, is it?"

Everyone laughed and Jack rolled his eyes.

"Nah, no disasters."

Jack wasn't sure why he didn't want to tell his friends about Simon. There was a time when he'd have been just as eager to share as Sarah. But now...since Davis...there was a part of him that just couldn't trust them. A part of him that was newly aware that once he told someone something he couldn't know what would be done with his confession. *Anything* could happen as a result of his words. It felt like chaos and risk and...helplessness.

And then there was the way that Simon was one million miles away from the dudes he'd fucked and never seen again and he wouldn't even know how to tell his friends what made up that distance. Simon's strong chin and downcast eyes. His trembling lip and the way he'd glared at Jack when he told him off in the woods. His bravery and his sweetness and how he grabbed Jack so tight when they kissed, as if he refused to allow a single inch to separate them.

There was the way that Simon was one million miles away from anyone he'd ever known and how for now, he thrilled at knowing Simon was just his.

Chapter Nine

Simon

When Simon got to Jack's for the evening walk, Jack was outside chopping wood while leaning on one crutch. Splinters flew and Jack's back and shoulder muscles flexed beneath his sweat-soaked T-shirt. His biceps bulged. Simon's mouth watered.

"Hey!" Jack called after letting the axe bite into the stump he was chopping on.

Simon swallowed. As he drew even with Jack the smell of fresh cut wood mixed with clean sweat. Simon wanted to press his nose to Jack's neck and breathe it all in.

He realized he was staring when a lazy, self-satisfied smile slid onto Jack's face.

"See something you like?" he drawled.

Simon's face heated and he said, "Maybe."

Jack raised an eyebrow.

"Well, *maybe* you wanna stick around a while after your walk..."

"Okay, yeah, sure, okay," Simon garbled, and he shot Jack a glare for flustering him. Jack just smiled.

It was dark when he got back with the pack. They settled themselves around the fire and Simon stood in the middle of the living room.

Since he and Jack had begun whatever this was, Simon felt like his body had come alive. It wasn't just the pleasure of when Jack stroked him off—although that was sublime. It was that he'd discovered a new language. A language that didn't depend on his ability to speak.

He felt like a whole new world had opened up to him. If he wanted to give comfort, he could put a hand on Jack's thigh. If he got scared or uncertain, he could press his forehead to Jack's shoulder and know that Jack's arms would come around him. When he wanted a kiss, he could lift his face and receive one.

It was so simple. In fact, it was the reason he'd always loved animals. A pat, a lick, a nuzzle spoke volumes. But the ability to communicate with another person this way felt like it had changed everything.

Now, when Jack came up behind him from the kitchen, Simon only had to let his weight tip backward slightly to rest against Jack's chest and Jack nuzzled his hair and wrapped his arms around Simon's stomach, crutches hanging off his wrists.

The scent of Jack's shampoo and soap enveloped him as surely as Jack's sweatshirt-covered arms and he relaxed into Jack's embrace.

"Walk okay?" Jack asked, nosing his ear.

Simon nodded and tipped his head to the side. Jack pressed a soft kiss behind his ear that made him shiver. Feeling brave, Simon pressed his hips backward and felt Jack's cock start to harden.

"Mmm. Wanna go make out?" Jack said lightly, but when Simon turned to look at him his eyes were hot.

They made their way to Jack's room, closing the door quickly behind them to avoid canine or feline company.

Jack pressed Simon to the door, tipped his chin back, and kissed him. Simon melted into him and kissed him back. The image of Jack from earlier, muscles straining with effort, came back to him, only this time he imagined Jack's hips pulsing, his neck cording with pleasure as—

Simon groaned and dropped his head to Jack's shoulder.

"Y'okay, darlin'?"

Simon nodded.

Earlier, Simon's medication had made his thigh muscles twitch. Sometimes the twitches moved from there to the muscles of his ass. He hadn't told Jack this, worried it would be a turn-off. Because what he wanted—what he really wanted…

"I—I…" Jack slid his hand inside Simon's shirt and ran a hand up his spine, half soothing, half arousing. "I want, um…"

"Yeah?" Jack's voice dropped an octave, as if he knew what Simon was going to say.

Simon's face burned. He grabbed Jack's ass and pulled their hips together.

"Oh, shit," Jack gasped as their erections ground together. He kissed Simon again. Then he grabbed him and started to lift him to the bed, remembered about his leg, and roared in frustration. "Dammit, I wanna throw you on that bed," he growled, sounding so brutish and so pouty at the same time that Simon laughed.

"I want you to fuck me," he said, and this time the words came out just fine.

Jack was on him so fast it was like his leg had miraculously healed.

"Yeah?"

"If you want?" Simon teased.

Jack's grin turned hungry and his pupils blew.

"I want very much," he said, voice so low that it rumbled through Simon's chest.

They kissed until they were straining together, hands everywhere, losing clothing as it got in the way. When they were both naked, Simon took in the man lying next to him. Jack was strong and vigorous, every muscle engaged. There were freckles on his shoulders that Simon hadn't seen before. His broad chest and thick thighs were dusted with hair a shade darker than the copper on his head. The hair between his legs was even darker, and his erection was as impressively vigorous as the rest of him.

He was so gorgeous that Simon couldn't believe he was allowed to touch him. In wonder, he ran one finger from

Jack's belly button down to his cock and watched the muscles in Jack's stomach and thighs bunch. He continued, tracing his finger along the silken skin of Jack's erection. Jack was breathing heavily, but made no move to stop him.

He circled the tip of Jack's cock, gathering the moisture there, and brought his finger to his mouth. The taste exploded on his tongue, musky and salty, and Jack groaned, then drew him down into a slow, hot kiss, tasting himself.

Lying side by side they had easy access to each other's bodies and as they kissed they got tangled up together, stroking, squeezing, thrusting. Every inch of Simon's skin pulsed with a hot awareness. He threw his leg over Jack's hip to press them closer together. Jack palmed his ass, squeezing, then stroking, then tracing between his cheeks. When Jack's fingers found his hole and rubbed the sensitive skin there, Simon shuddered.

Jack pressed a kiss to his cheekbone and pulled his leg higher, exposing him to questing fingers. Slowly, so slowly, Jack stirred his nerve endings to arousal, stroking, tapping, pressing just a little. All the while, he kissed Simon, tongue hot and claiming.

"Wanna taste you," Jack said, and Simon didn't understand because they'd practically been consuming one another's mouths for what felt like hours. "But I need you to come up here," Jack said when Simon didn't move. Jack rubbed at his hole and realization dawned. Simon dissolved into a blush of lust at the idea.

"Oh god," he muttered, and Jack arranged him so he was on his hands and knees, facing away.

Jack's rough hands were hot as he dragged Simon's

ass toward his face then spread him apart. Simon's face burned—arousal, embarrassment, each driving the other higher. When Jack licked him Simon's hips jerked at the slick curling heat. Then Jack began to feast on him.

"Oh my god!" Simon's thighs shook and his hips thrust into the air.

"Mmmm," Jack said, clearly enjoying the reaction.

Simon let his arms collapse and pressed his head to the mattress between Jack's legs. He couldn't concentrate on holding himself up and on the exquisite sensation of Jack's hot, slick tongue teasing into him. The change in position tipped his ass up and Jack groaned, grasping his hips and sliding the tip of his tongue into Simon's trembling hole.

Simon panted and babbled things he couldn't keep track of. He was dissolving slowly, tendrils of hot pleasure crawling through him with every stroke of Jack's tongue.

"Jack, Jack," he realized he was saying.

"You wanna come like this, baby?"

Simon didn't know. Simon didn't know anything. He didn't *want* to know anything. He wanted Jack to decide. He buried his face in Jack's leg.

"Okay, I got you."

Then Simon was consumed, taken apart. Mouth sucking, tongue thrusting inside him, fingers pinching his nipples, and finally, finally, a rough hand cupping his balls and then stroking the underside of his straining cock and he was gone, waves of pleasure rolling through him and exploding as he choked on his own cries.

He came so hard he saw black spots and when the deluge had passed, he found himself with his clenching ass resting on Jack's stomach and his face pressed tight to Jack's thigh. Jack was stroking his back.

"Ungh," Simon tried. He found himself pulled up and suddenly he was face-to-face with Jack again. Jack's eyes were dark with lust and his gaze consumed Simon.

"You are so outrageously hot," Jack said.

"Ungh?" Simon tried again.

"Yup."

Clearly his mouth wasn't functioning to make words at the moment, so Simon used it to kiss Jack as deeply as he could, to communicate to him how gorgeously he'd made him come, and how he would do anything Jack wanted to make him feel as good.

Jack groaned into his mouth and pulled him to straddle his lap, then his fingers went right back to Simon's ass. This time, they were slick. Jack slid one inside him and little tingles shot through Simon.

He panted, cock starting to go hard again.

"That okay?" Jack murmured, eyes fixed on Simon.

Simon nodded so fast he practically gave himself whiplash and Jack smiled.

"Fuck, I want to finger you until you lose it all over me."

Simon gasped. Jack had no qualms about saying exactly what he wanted and seemingly no self-consciousness either. It hit Simon with a dark wave of lust. This was right. This was what he wanted. He wanted Jack to talk forever.

"I want to look at your gorgeous fucking face and just slide inside you." He slid a second finger inside Simon and curled his fingers.

Something white-hot crackled through Simon and he jumped. Jack groaned helplessly.

"God, Simon."

Simon blinked and braced his hands on Jack's shoulders. Jack did it again, stroked inside him with unerring fingers that had Simon writhing. He pressed himself deeper onto Jack's fingers, desperate to see what it felt like to be filled by him.

"More?"

Simon nodded and Jack pressed another finger inside him. For a moment it was uncomfortable, then his muscles relaxed and it was gorgeous. Before he knew what he was doing, Simon found himself moving on Jack's fingers, rotating his hips and trying to feel him everywhere.

"You're— God, fuck." Jack looked at him in wonder, spouting pure filth about Simon's ass and Simon's cock and Simon fucking loved it. When Jack looked at him like that he felt a sense of power like nothing he'd ever experienced. "Yeah, fuck yourself on my fingers," Jack said.

Simon felt the pleasure gathering in his balls, and he clenched around Jack's fingers, chasing the perfect combination of friction, angle, fullness. Jack was looking at him like he was the most amazing thing he'd ever seen and Simon was drunk on all of it.

Jack curled his fingertips as Simon sank down and the orgasm ripped through him, deeper than any he'd ever felt. His cock exploded onto Jack's stomach and Jack stirred the fingers inside him, drawing out his pleasure.

Simon collapsed on Jack's chest. He felt lightheaded and drained and so good he thought he might cry. He pressed kisses to every bit of Jack he could reach and Jack slid his fingers out gently and tangled the other hand in his hair.

"You're gonna kill me," Jack said tenderly. "Hottest fucking thing I've ever seen, Jesus."

An unfamiliar sense of pride bloomed in Simon's chest. He kissed Jack's neck and Jack settled him more firmly against him.

"You done, baby?" Jack said, stroking his scalp.

Simon could feel Jack's erection, hot and hard and straining, so he was definitely not done. He shook his head and reached back to stroke Jack's cock. One touch and Jack's whole body convulsed. He groaned into Simon's hair.

"You don't have to—" Simon cut him off by putting Jack's cock at his entrance and pressing down. "God, fuck, Simon, wait, Christ!"

Jack shuddered and Simon reveled in his power.

Jack cupped his face.

"You want that? You want me inside you?"

Simon nodded. He wanted it so much. He didn't think he could possibly get hard again but it didn't matter. He wanted to feel Jack, wanted to make Jack feel good, wanted to look into Jack's face as Jack lost it inside him.

"I don't think... I don't think I can last very long," Jack said sheepishly. "Next time, I promise, I'll make it so good for you," Jack babbled earnestly. Simon rolled his eyes and shut him up with a kiss.

Jack pulled a condom out of his side table and slid it down his erection. He slicked his fingers again.

"Kneel up." He tapped Simon's hip. He slid lube-wet

fingers back inside Simon and even though he'd just come it made Simon shudder.

"Stop me if it's too much. Okay?"

Simon nodded. Jack held Simon's hip and parted him, resting the tip of his cock at Simon's hole.

"I wanna be inside you so bad," Jack murmured. "I felt you clench up so fucking tight around my fingers when you came." He pressed his hips up, just the slightest bit of pressure. "I can't wait to feel that on my dick." A little more pressure. "You're so fucking gorgeous when you come. Mouth and your fucking eyes and—"

Simon felt the moment when Jack slid inside him, but by the time his brain processed it, he was seated on Jack's erection, body straining to reshape itself.

"Oh! Oh!" he heard himself gasp. Jack's eyes were squeezed shut tight like he was using every bit of resolve to keep himself from pounding up into Simon.

"Breathe, darlin'."

Simon breathed. Jack ran a soothing hand up and down his spine. Then he crunched up and pressed a kiss to Simon's trembling lips.

"It's a lot this way. Should've done it different your first time." Jack stroked his face. "Sorry. Stupid leg."

Simon shook his head, breathing through his nose. He leaned forward to kiss Jack and with the change in angle a beautiful heat washed through him. He gasped and moved his hips. Jack bit his lip.

Simon lifted his hips experimentally and pressed back down and Jack's eyes rolled back in his head. Yeah, that was good. He did it again. Jack grabbed his hips, strong arms helping him move.

"Oh my fucking god," Jack said. "Yes, baby, fuck yourself on my dick, you're so goddamn gorgeous."

Simon felt amazing.

As his body adjusted, the sensation of being too full shifted. He felt perfect. He felt complete.

Jack was clearly trying not to be too rough but Simon wanted to see him come. He wanted to be the one to *make* this gorgeous man come. He rose and fell on Jack's cock, watching his face. Jack's mouth was open, his eyes unfocused.

"Simon, I'm gonna come," Jack groaned. Simon felt Jack's orgasm as it tightened every muscle. His cock swelled inside Simon and for just a moment, Jack lost control. He punched his hips up as he came and all Simon could think was that he couldn't wait until they could do it again.

Jack's groan tore through him and when Jack's muscular body went slack in the aftermath, and Jack pulled Simon down to his chest and clung to him, Simon felt like a god.

"Fuuuuuck," Jack groaned a few minutes later. "That was amazing. You're amazing. You okay?" He lifted Simon's face to look at him.

Simon smiled and nodded. They were sticky and they smelled of sweat and lust and come. Simon's cock and balls ached from stimulation and as Jack slid out of him he winced. Still, as Jack swiped at their mess with the sheet, then gathered Simon close, Simon couldn't stop smiling.

He pressed his face to the crook of Jack's neck and breathed.

"I'm amazing," he whispered, and he felt Jack nod in agreement.

Chapter Ten

Jack

Jack woke from a doze at the sound of a dull thud against the closed bedroom door. He had a moment of disorientation where he didn't know why the door was closed. Then the warm form beside him stirred a little and he remembered everything.

Simon. His beautiful Simon riding his mouth and fingers and cock like he was born for it, jerking and trembling as he came with his head thrown back and his mouth open. The broken sounds he made that stirred Jack's blood, and the feel of that virgin ass clenching around him in pleasure.

Jack clapped one hand over his mouth and the other over his cock so he didn't wake Simon by groaning or humping him. Jesus.

In the thin light of the autumn moon, Jack could just make out the man curled up beside him. Simon slept as deeply as a child, covers curled around his shoulders, knees drawn up, face nearly buried in the pillow.

Jack chanced a kiss to his shoulder and Simon murmured in his sleep.

He slid from the bed with as little disturbance as he could manage and felt for his underwear and his crutches.

When he eased open the bedroom door, Puddles' head slid to the floor from where it had been resting on the door and he looked up at Jack, aggrieved. Louis was curled up on top of Puddles, uncaring about the venue.

"Sorry, buddy."

Given how much Simon loved the dogs, he probably wouldn't mind Puddles curling up at the foot of the bed, but everything was so new, and Simon caught him off guard with his reactions sometimes.

Jack hoped there would be a time when he would know Simon's reactions as well as his own. When he could read the other man just by a raise of his eyebrow or a curl of his lip. If he could just avoid scaring Simon off...

Jack went to the bathroom, checked the fire, and scratched the ears he could reach as he went along. Bernard's huge head lifted off his paws and he yawned, then settled back down, Rat using his paw as a pillow. A cat's eyes glittered at him in the darkness just before the white fluff ball that was Mayonnaise leapt, grabbing ahold of his crutch with her paws and curling her body around it to scrabble at it with her back legs.

"I think you killed it, bud," he told her, and extricated his crutch from her furry clutches.

The animals were used to him not sleeping at night, but usually he turned the light on, or the television, so—other than Mayonnaise's sneak attack—they were following his lead in being quiet.

Somehow, Jack found himself in his studio, in front of his drawing table, where he and Simon had stood the week before. Out the window, the tops of the trees swayed in the breeze and Jack imagined the coming winter. He loved the snow. Loved the clean smell of the cold air and the sound of a fire crackling merrily. He loved drawing as the sun rose and he watched the frozen world come to life. He loved drawing as the sun set and the world outside became the dark velvet distance his cozy cabin glowed against, a submarine moving silently through black waters.

Had loved.

He had loved drawing.

A wave of despair closed over him.

What if it never comes back?

He swore softly, fingers digging into the wood of the table.

There was a sound behind him and he waited for a furry body to press against his leg. When one didn't come, he turned to find Simon in the doorway. He'd pulled on Jack's discarded sweatshirt but his long legs were bare.

"Shit, sorry, did I wake you?"

Simon shook his head. Jack couldn't see his face in the dark, just his silhouette, but his shoulders were rigid, like they were when he was feeling anxious.

"C'mere," Jack said, transferring both crutches to one arm and holding out a hand.

Simon moved toward him like a ghost, moonlight catching the bridge of his nose and his messy hair.

His hand was shaking slightly, but when Jack pulled him in for a kiss, he twined his arms around Jack's neck. Lifting his arms bared his ass, and Jack's hand went to it like it was magnetized.

"I woke up and you were gone," Simon said softly against Jack's mouth, pressing his bottom into Jack's hand.

"Sorry, darlin'."

He couldn't believe he'd missed what it looked like to see Simon wake up and realize he was in Jack's bed.

"Couldn't sleep?"

"Guess not. But you should go back to sleep if you can."

Simon's eyes were sleepy, his head drooping to Jack's chest. A deep sense of peace settled there along with it.

They stayed that way for a minute, maybe two. Then Simon said, "Do you have a sketchbook?"

Jack plucked it from the window ledge. Dust plumed into the air. Simon took it from him and grabbed a few pens from the cup on the table. He turned and looked over his shoulder, then gestured with his chin for Jack to follow.

When they got to the bedroom, the door was open. Puddles was lying directly in the middle of the bed on his side, all four legs straight out in front of him, and Louis was curled up between his legs. Simon smiled.

"Puddles," Jack commanded, and Puddles yawned, then rearranged himself at the foot of the bed. Louis blinked one eye sleepily, rolled over, and very slowly made his way to curl up on top of Puddles.

Simon climbed into bed and Jack joined him, though he knew he couldn't sleep. Simon handed him the sketchbook and the pens. Then he stripped off Jack's sweatshirt and slid beneath the covers.

"Draw me like one of your French girls, Jack," he said dramatically, batting his eyelashes.

Jack's cock twitched, but Simon dissolved into giggles, burying his face in the pillow.

Jack reached under the covers, found Simon's bare ass, and gave it a squeeze and then an affectionate slap.

"I'll draw you like one of my..." Jack muttered, but Simon turned to him and gave him an evaluating look.

"What are you scared of?" he asked gently.

"I'm not—" Jack began automatically, but Simon's expression was so open.

This was a man who knew what it was to be scared.

"It used to feel like breathing. Pick up a pen and draw. Now I... It makes me think of everything that's happened. With Davis."

He shook his head. In the weeks after it had sunk in— that Davis hadn't just done something selfish, he had done something that proved he couldn't possibly care about Jack, because no one would do such a thing to someone they cared about.

It had made him question everything. And questioning was the opposite of how it used to feel to draw.

"What if I can't do it anymore?"

Simon slid closer and rested his chin on Jack's shoulder.

"You can," he said softly. "But I know what you mean."
Jack waited for him to go on. This, too, he was learning. That even when Simon's words came easy—as they
were more and more often with him—sometimes he had
to work up to what he wanted to say.

"It's a mental block. Nothing to do with your ability.
But a mental block's still real."

He kissed Jack's cheek. He was so damn sweet.

"Like right now, I can talk to you fine. But when I
leave...the next time I see you, I'll still think about it the
whole way here. What if I can't? What if right now is magic
and I can never repeat it."

Jack wanted to tell him that right now *was* magic, but
he bit his lip. Instead, he stroked Simon's hair.

"So what do you do? When you worry about that?"
Simon pressed closer and Jack could feel his sigh.

"First I try logic. I go through all the times I've done it
before, like evidence I can do it again. It usually d-doesn't
work because there's also evidence to the contrary."

He twined his fingers through Jack's.

"Then I think about what the w-worst thing is that could
happen. Like, I probably won't puke the way I used to in s-
school," he said with a shudder. "And I won't d-die. I'll feel
shitty, and embarrassed, and I'll want to run." He squeezed
Jack's hand. "But. Even if it's bad, I know I can handle it."

Jack turned and tipped Simon's face to his for a kiss. He
wanted to tell Simon how sorry he was that things couldn't
be easier for him. How much he admired his bravery, his
utter fucking guts. But it felt insulting or patronizing, so
Jack just stroked his hair and kissed him harder.

"So," Simon said, with a final kiss to Jack's lips. "What's your worst-case scenario?"

Jack closed his eyes, imagining years stretching out before him where he had no escape. No vocation, no projects, no other world than the real one.

"Being just...this. Just a guy who doesn't have...passion?" Jack said.

He couldn't meet Simon's eyes.

"That's pretty bad," Simon said.

"I don't think I could handle it," he said, realizing that he didn't have Simon's confidence that no matter how bad things got he could handle them. *There's more than one way to be strong, Jack,* Simon had told him in the woods. No fucking kidding.

After a moment, Simon pulled at his shoulder to get an arm behind him and hugged him tight.

"Then don't let it happen," Simon said, and though his voice was gentle, Jack could hear the steel behind it. "Don't let that asshole take this away from you, Jack."

"Simon."

But Jack didn't have anything more to say. Not really. He let Simon hold him for a minute, enjoyed the feeling of his arms around him.

Please don't let him leave me too. He's so lovely—please don't let him turn out to be something else.

The thought swooped into his mind like an eagle and without thinking he pulled Simon on top of him and held him close.

Simon came willingly, rested his forehead against Jack's like he could tell it was what he needed. But after a minute, he pulled back, traced Jack's mouth with his finger, and said, "Draw me something."

Jack swallowed emotion down. He hadn't put pen to paper in eight months but Simon wanted it and so Jack would try.

"What do you want me to draw?"

Simon rolled off Jack's lap and plopped the sketchbook there, then tucked himself to Jack's side.

"Draw Puddles baking cookies."

Jack snorted. Then he remembered he'd drawn a book about a Bison who'd taken the subway and he shut up.

He picked up one of the pens Simon had brought. It wasn't what he usually sketched with, just a regular ballpoint, but it didn't matter because this was just for fun, just for Simon.

It's not real, so there's no pressure.

He closed his eyes and the scene fell into his head. Puddles on his hind legs, measuring ingredients at the counter; Puddles turning the mixer on too high and being engulfed in a cloud of flour that settled on him, turning his fur from yellow to white.

Jack chuckled at that and Puddles lolled onto his back in his sleep, paws twitching as if he knew.

Jack began to draw.

Days later he was still drawing.

He wasn't drawing animals or landscapes like he usually did. He was drawing Simon. They were blushingly private drawings in a sketchbook he shoved under the couch cushions any time he got up.

It had begun with his face, in an attempt to capture the way that sleeping Simon looked like another person. Something in the lack of tension around his eyes, in the softness of his mouth…sleeping Simon was unburdened. The only other time Jack had seen him look that way was when they were fucking.

Simon, head thrown back, eyes hot with lust, mouth open on a scream.

Every time he remembered it he got hard. In fact, he was beginning to feel a little strange about how hot Simon got him. He'd never thought the virgin thing would do it for him. In the past, he'd gone for uninhibited guys who were just looking for a quick good time. Guys who made eyes at him in a bar or looked him up and down at the gas station. Guys who knew what they wanted and were ready for him to give it to them.

But Simon's surprised, wide-eyed sensuality got to him more than the most enthusiastic, knowing encounters he'd ever had.

Which was how Jack found himself transitioning from sketching Simon's beautiful sleeping face to drawing Simon facedown on his bed, legs akimbo, round ass raised and begging, hole glistening. The desire to be spread open and fucked hard eloquent in every tensed muscle and in his hand twisted in the sheets.

He didn't even mean to draw it. It'd been the middle of the night, he'd woken as usual, and, as if the previous eight months had just been a horrible dream, stoked the fire, flopped onto the couch, and lost himself in the lines of his pencil.

When he got up to use the bathroom hours later and focused on the page before him, it seemed almost to have been drawn by a stranger. His style, yes, his shading and his line work. But Jack didn't draw people—and he'd *certainly* never drawn people like...that.

That had been three days ago and to show for his recovered artistic impulse he had a sketchbook of fantasies that rivaled the *Kama Sutra*, a body that seemed to be on sex overdrive, and a renewed sense of hope that maybe his career and his artistic passion hadn't been snuffed out after all.

It was this last that he was thinking about when Simon arrived for the morning walk and Jack shoved the sketchbook under the couch cushion.

The shy smile that Simon gave him made Jack melt. He pushed to his feet, fumbled for his crutches, and let himself be carried toward Simon on the tide of the pack who instantly circled him, excited to go out.

"Hi," Simon said, then ducked his chin like he felt self-conscious about what he'd said, or how he'd said it. Jack couldn't always tell which it was.

"Hi," he said, in case it was the former.

Jack had found that if he kissed Simon first when he showed up in the mornings, Simon's shyness lingered, but if he put himself in a place where Simon kissed him, it dissipated faster. So he stepped close, enjoying the way Simon naturally tipped his face up.

He brushed his knuckles along Simon's cheek and looked at his mouth. Simon's lips parted and he slowly moved to press a soft kiss to Jack's mouth. Jack cupped the back of his neck and Simon kissed him again, deeper this time.

When Simon wrapped his arms around Jack, Jack pulled him close. Then they were hugging, mouths awkwardly pressed together and crutches smooshed to Simon's back, and Simon huffed out a laugh.

"Hi," he said again, and now he sounded more relaxed.

Satisfaction bloomed in Jack's chest the way it had when he'd realized the reason Puddles kept stopping in the middle of the road was the lightning shaped sticks. Jack had gently removed the obstacle and Puddles had looked at him with such gratitude, as if all the time he had simply been waiting for someone to pay attention.

Chapter Eleven

Simon

It wasn't often that Simon absolutely had to meet with clients in person, but when it happened, the day before the meeting was always spent attempting to distract himself so he wouldn't extend the period of torment longer than necessary.

Yesterday, he'd distracted himself by kissing Jack until he felt the bigger man shaking beneath him, every muscle tensed, mouth hot and hungry. Then he'd distracted himself by shoving his hand down Jack's pants and bringing him off with hard strokes to his magnificent cock, swallowing the sounds of Jack's groans in his mouth like he could grow stronger by consuming them.

Now he was sitting in his car outside an aggressively

busy Starbucks trying to ignore the sensation of his lungs shriveling to the size of raisins. He sang to himself to help regulate his breathing. The phrasing of most songs wouldn't let you hyperventilate and still keep to rhythm. But the second he stopped singing and got out of the car, it was there. The weight on his chest, the tongue that felt swollen enough to choke him. The shuddery stutter of blood not getting where it needed to be.

You are so fucking tough. You're gonna be fine. You've done this before and you survived, and you can do it again.

Then, sneaking in for the first time, a tiny, flickering joy: *After this, you can go see Jack. Jack would let you hide and it would be okay.*

But although he tried to hold on to the joy of *You can,* Simon didn't want to run to Jack. Didn't want to make this Jack's burden or make Jack too necessary to his survival. Because what if? What if it didn't last?

Still, Simon put his hand on the back of his neck where Jack's hand always seemed to land when they kissed. He squeezed gently the way Jack squeezed.

It didn't feel the same.

The meeting did not go well. Though Simon made it a practice to tell clients and potential clients that he preferred to communicate via email or text and that meeting with him in person was not indicative of the experience of working with him; and though the interactive designs Simon had prepared and walked this potential client through were, he thought, excellent, it didn't matter.

Mason Holeyfield, CEO of Holey Cow Steakhouse, was impatient with Simon's stuttering, interrupting him to ask the questions that Simon was trying to answer and attempting to finish his sentences. He liked the designs, Simon could tell, but in the end Simon could read the calculus Mason was doing on his face. It was an old arithmetic. Mason could find another good ole boy like himself— hearty, loud, direct, and confident—to do his website, so why would he bother making himself uncomfortable and awkward with Simon?

Simon slunk out of the bathroom where he'd fled the second the meeting was over and trudged to his car.

"Hey," a voice yelled behind him. He stared straight ahead and unlocked the car. *"Hey!"*

Simon glanced over his shoulder to find a young man loping toward him, holding out his scarf.

"You dropped this."

Simon reached out a shaking hand to claim the scarf. His attempt at *Thank you* came out a garbled mumble and the guy's expression turned sharp. Simon recognized him suddenly as the barista from inside.

"Okaaaay," the guy said. It was a universal comment on the ingratitude of customers casually offered up to the gods of the food service industry, Simon *knew* it was, but as he threw himself into the car and slammed the door behind him, tears flooded his eyes.

Those were the worst ones. When someone else felt disrespected or insulted by his failure and there was nothing he could do to allay it.

Simon was late getting to Jack's for the pack's evening walk. He'd gone home after the disastrous meeting and fallen into bed, exhausted and shaky, and only just woken up. He hadn't eaten all day, too anxious before his meeting and too nauseated afterward, and now his head throbbed with a hunger headache.

As he navigated the winding path to Jack's house, his heart beat harder and harder. His whole body ached to be held. To be pet. Comforted. But the shame he felt at the day's failure made it impossible to ask for what he wanted. He didn't even feel like he deserved it. He wasn't a child anymore.

But as it happened, Jack burst out the front door before Simon even dragged himself all the way out of the car.

"Guess what?" he said. He was grinning and his hair looked combed for once.

Simon attempted to arrange his face in an expression of enthusiastic curiosity.

"What?" he choked out.

His stomach roiled as the word rattled in his throat. He just had time to see the smile slide off Jack's handsome face before he retched.

Since he hadn't eaten, it was just a sick upchuck of water, coffee, and bile, and it burned in his throat and through his sinuses, leaving him coughing and sputtering on his knees in the dirt. His head spun.

He was dimly aware of a flurry of activity and then Jack was by his side, bent at the waist trying to peer at him without losing his balance.

"What's wrong? Are you sick? Are you okay? Simon?"

Jack's questions increased in volume as Simon couldn't answer. Finally, nausea past, he was able to look up. Jack's brow was furrowed, his eyes worried. Shame burned in Simon's cheeks and he closed his eyes. There was always the tiny, distant possibility that when he opened them again, Jack would be gone.

Jack wasn't gone. Instead, Jack was squatting on his good leg with his casted leg extended in front of him, trying to sit next to Simon. He looked so ridiculously like a lumberjack attempting a figure skating move that Simon almost laughed. Then Jack's heavy form landed beside him with an *Oof*, and Jack's hands were searching him as if he thought he mind find a bullet hole or a vial of poison.

Simon tried to say he was okay but nothing came out and he could tell he'd retch again if he kept trying. Sometimes the words he couldn't spit out hurled themselves down his throat instead, tickling and gagging until he couldn't swallow. When it got to that point it was hard to make it stop, so Simon set his jaw firmly and didn't try.

What now?

This was the part of the scene where—if he was unlucky enough to be in public—Simon usually waved off whoever could see him and scrambled away. But this wasn't just anyone; this was Jack. And for the first time in his life, Simon had another language, another way.

Taking a small trial breath, Simon eased forward on his knees and let himself stroke Jack's arm with two shaking fingers.

Jack's frantic movements stopped and he studied Simon's face. Simon forced himself to blink and swallow and breathe by distracting himself with Jack. He put his hand on Jack's shoulder and leaned closer. Just as he remembered that he'd recently puked and probably he should be staying as far away as possible, Jack pulled him into his arms.

Simon went. He let himself fall against Jack's strong chest, the position awkward but the relief undeniable. Jack's arms wrapped around him, one palm stroking up and down his back, and Simon felt tears of relief and shame wet Jack's sweatshirt as he buried his face in Jack's strong shoulder.

The sky darkened as they sat there, and still Simon couldn't make the words come. He couldn't conjure *I fucked everything up. I'm pathetic. I'm a failure. I tried. I'm tough. I survived it. Please just hold me. Let's go inside. I'm cold. There are ants crawling on me.*

He just burrowed closer and let Jack hold him.

It wasn't until much later—until Simon walked the pack, waving off Jack's concern, finally glaring at him to get him to back off; until Simon was home, lying in bed and pretending the pillow he was holding was Jack—that Simon remembered Jack had begun to tell him something when he'd first arrived.

And once he'd remembered it, he couldn't sleep until he knew. If he didn't ask, he'd lie here all night imagining a hundred different scenarios, all of them somehow ending with Jack hating him because he was self-absorbed and insensitive.

Hey, he texted Jack. What were you gonna tell me before?

Hey, darlin'. How're you doing? And a kiss emoji.

Simon closed his eyes in mortification. How? How could Jack stand him? How could Jack have seen him the way he'd been today and still want anything to do with him?

I'm ok. I'm so sorry.

Jack hadn't made him talk about it. Jack had just held him until they couldn't stand sitting on the hard ground anymore, then they'd pulled each other up and gone inside. Simon had washed his face, Jack had clipped on the dogs' leashes (after the glare) and off Simon had gone. When he dropped the pack back off, he'd kissed Jack and Jack had kissed him back, but Jack hadn't asked what had happened. He'd just asked, *Are you okay to drive?* When Simon had nodded, Jack had kissed his cheek, the gesture so sweet Simon had almost lost himself to tears again.

Nothing to be sorry for from where I'm standing, Jack wrote. But you can tell me if you want?

There was a pause, during which Simon was trying to decide how much detail he wanted to go into, and then another message came through.

Did someone hurt you?

Simon could almost hear the growl that would underlie that question if they were together. The one that promised retribution to anyone who hurt him and yet had nothing but gentleness for him.

No. Bad meeting with a potential client. He hated me and I freaked out in the bathroom and then just kinda lost it. It wasn't the most accurate or the most detailed gloss, but it was how it had felt.

Is that why you got sick?

Simon appreciated that Jack didn't try and police his language the way well-meaning therapists from his past had. He knew it wasn't productive to think of his actions and reactions in negative terms, but goddammit that was his business.

I get so nauseous. Nauseated? Which is it? And I hadn't eaten so I just felt all fucked up.

Did you eat when you got home?

A little.

Nauseated. I looked it up. Nauseous is causing nausea, nauseated is feeling it.

Simon snorted.
You're such a nerd, he wrote.

Excuse me, I think you mean Man of Learning.

Nerd of googling, Simon wrote, but he put a smiley face in case being called a nerd offended Jack's lumberjack-y soul the way having a broken leg did.

I'm glad you're feeling better, Jack wrote. Then, Will I see you in the morning?

Apparently he'd looked as bad as he'd still felt when he left Jack's if that was in question.

Definitely.

Good. Then the ellipsis of Jack's typing went on for a long time, then faltered. Then, I can't wait to kiss you tomorrow. Night.

Simon's heart fluttered. Jack still wanted to kiss him. He hadn't turned Jack off forever.

But how long and how many more humiliating episodes before he did?

True to Jack's word, when Simon opened the door to Jack's the next morning, he found himself soundly and thoroughly kissed. He squirmed with the pleasure of it, and a noise came out of him that had felt like a purr in his mouth but sounded like a giggle.

Jack laughed and leaned in for another kiss, but Simon stopped him with a hand to his chest.

"You still didn't tell me."

"Huh?"

"What you were g-going to t-tell me yesterday."

"Oh, yeah. I drew! I woke up and I couldn't sleep and I drew trees for an hour and fell back asleep. Like I used to."

Jack grinned and Simon found himself irrationally touched at the thought of Jack drawing trees.

"That's great."

"Yeah. I know it was only trees and only one night, but…" Jack shrugged, looking a little self-conscious. "It seemed like a good sign."

Simon smiled. "See? Worst-case scenario defeated." He kissed Jack again and then turned to the business of leashes and bags.

"Okay, see you in a bit," Jack said as Simon left.

Simon plastered a smile on and waved. He breathed in the fresh morning air, tasting the promise of winter. It was his favorite time of the year.

They walked for a while, Pirate chasing squirrels, Rat ranging along as far as her leash would go, Dandelion grinning her simple, contented doggy smile, Puddles' head swinging back and forth to search for threats, and Bernard a source of warmth next to his hip. But he didn't feel as peaceful as he usually did when out with the pack.

He patted Bernard's head.

"I'm jealous of your dad," he whispered.

Bernard *ruffed* in sympathy.

Simon didn't like this side of himself. The side that saw others' struggles—and how simply they could sometimes overcome them—and raged. Wished he could trade places.

Yeah, he knew that things were rarely as clear-cut as they seemed from the outside. After all, he'd felt Jack's fear in the middle of the night. But now, here they were, days later, and Jack had emerged victorious.

He'd rushed outside to tell Simon about his triumph only to be faced with evidence of Simon's defeat.

Simon sighed and let himself feel it. For five minutes, he let himself give in to every single petty, unkind, ungenerous thought.

Then, when the five minutes were up, he made himself stop.

"Wanna stick around a bit?" Jack asked when he got back.

"Okay." Simon unclipped leashes and watched the dogs run to the kitchen and their food bowls. He walked to

Jack and put his hands on Jack's shoulders. "I'm really glad. About your drawing." He infused it with all the sincerity he had now that he'd burned off the envy, and Jack's smile was pure joy.

"Thanks. I'm really fucking relieved. Hope it lasts."

Simon dropped onto the couch and let out a deep breath. On the floor, Pickles batted at something near him and he reached down to pet her. His wrist scraped against the hard corner of a book and he pulled it out.

"Are these your trees?" he asked, flipping open the notebook.

They were utterly gorgeous ink sketches. But they weren't of trees. Simon admired the lines of muscle and sinew rendered in smooth, confident strokes.

"Oh, don't—" Jack said, looking over at him. But it was too late. The lines had coalesced into...him. The drawings were of him.

"Um," Jack said.

Simon knew he should close the sketchbook. It was intrusive to look. But he couldn't tear his eyes away. On the next page he lay, head lolling off the bed, mouth open and eyes squeezed shut in pleasure. A messy-haired head and broad shoulders that could only be Jack's were buried between his thighs.

His eyes flew to Jack. Embarrassment wasn't an expression he'd ever thought he'd see on Jack's face, but there it was.

"Simon, I..." But then he bit his lip. Simon turned another page.

Him, on his back, cock hard and straining against his

stomach, eyes looking straight out of the drawing, desperate.

Simon stared at his own face. He looked...beautiful. He looked free.

On the next page, sketches of his profile, his eyebrows.

"I'm, uh. Simon, fuck, I'm sorry. I didn't mean to— I mean, I *meant* to, but I... I was drawing and it... Fuck."

Simon turned another page. He lay prone on the bed, legs spread, ass raised, looking back over his shoulder with lust-hooded eyes.

A dark, liquid heat sluiced through him, guts to balls, and his breath caught. He looked up at Jack, who was watching him closely.

"I'm sorry," Jack murmured again. But when Simon held out a hand to him, he lowered himself to the couch immediately.

Simon slid between Jack's legs, back to his chest, careful not to touch his cast, and opened the sketchbook again.

Jack groaned.

"Tell me," Simon whispered. He felt Jack's cock harden against his ass.

"Um."

In the drawing, Simon was naked and spread out on the bed. His mouth was wet and open, his eyes closed, and his hands were tangled in the bedclothes. One powerful shoulder and arm were visible, hand wrapped around Simon's erection as Simon's hips strained upward toward the contact.

"Tell me."

When Jack spoke, his voice was low and rough in Simon's ear.

"I want you to close your eyes so all you can do is feel. Then I would touch you, taste you everywhere." Simon jumped when Jack ran a palm up his ribs. *"Everywhere."*

Simon took a shaky breath, cock hardening.

"Then what?"

"Then I would suck you until you were almost there. Until I could taste you leaking in my mouth."

Simon's breath came faster.

"Then I would slide inside you so slowly you'd beg me for more."

Simon pressed his ass against Jack's erection and listened to his breathing go ragged.

"I'd fuck you so good, darlin'. Until you were begging and screaming. But I wouldn't let you come right away."

Jack's hand slid from his ribs to his nipple and he plucked at it as he spoke.

"I'd slow down until you couldn't stand it. Until you were desperate."

Simon writhed against him as frissons of pain and pleasure skittered through his nerves.

"Until all you cared about was the feel of me inside you."

"Oh god," Simon heard himself gasp.

Jack released his nipple and slid his hand slowly down Simon's stomach toward Simon's aching cock. Then he rested his hand there and began to touch him so softly, so gently that Simon was left chasing his touch.

"Sometimes I'd thrust myself so deep you'd feel like I was a part of you. And I'd stay like that, feeling you clench around me."

Simon's breath was erratic, his chest and face hot.

Jack adjusted himself so he could rub himself in the crack of Simon's ass. It made his heart pound and he squirmed backward to increase the contact.

"Mmm." Jack released a rumbling moan and flicked open Simon's pants, sliding a hot hand inside. With the other hand he stroked the inside of Simon's thigh.

"Jack," he breathed.

"What, baby?"

"Jack." He shuddered.

Jack's lips touched his neck and he let his head fall to the side.

"I'd stroke you while I was deep inside."

At the first touch of Jack's fingers on his aching cock, Simon cried out.

"Oh, yeah," Jack rumbled. "I'd stroke your cock and feel you clamp that sweet ass down on my dick like you wanna eat me alive. Like you want me to stay in you forever."

Jack humped against him and worked him and Simon felt his awareness begin to slide.

"Then sometimes I'd stop," Jack rumbled in his ear.

And he stopped.

Stopped thrusting against him, stopped stroking him, stopped kissing his neck.

"No!" Simon cried out. "No, please!"

Jack groaned and dropped his forehead to Simon's hair.

"You fucking kill me, Simon."

Simon was panting and writhing, anything to regain that gorgeous contact.

"I'd stop and I'd wait until you couldn't take it anymore. Until you had to have me."

Simon whimpered and tried to pull Jack's hand back where he wanted it, but Jack was immovable.

"Until you couldn't bear for me not to be touching you." His voice was cruel and hot, like he too was suffering.

"Jack!" Simon tugged at Jack's rough hand, his dick throbbing with frustrated desire. "Jack, please!"

"Ohhh god, yes. Just like that."

Then that rough hand was back, stroking him so perfectly, that hot mouth back on his mouth, making him shiver. He groaned, feeling like he would spill any moment. He thrust into Jack's hand and back against his hard cock, losing himself.

"That's so beautiful, darlin'."

Then he stopped again.

"No, no, no! Please, no!"

Tears streamed down Simon's face as he chased the stolen orgasm. Pleasure had been flooding through him and now it had been wrenched away.

Jack locked his arm around Simon's waist and slowly thrust against him.

"Yeah, I'd bring you right to the edge, over and over. Watch the way your face gets so pink. Watch you thrash around, trying to get more of my cock."

Simon's hole clenched at Jack's words and the feel of that cock hot and hard against him.

"Jack," Simon begged. "Jack."

"God, the way you say my name."

Simon squeezed his eyes tight shut, unable to stand a single stimulus that wasn't Jack.

"Jack," he whispered. "I n-n-need you."

Jack's shudder shook him.

"Fuck! Fuck, I need you too," Jack groaned, and Simon felt him come, felt the heat and the pulsing heft of him. It sent a bolt of lust through him that made him lightheaded.

Jack gasped one more time and shuddered out a low moan. Then the hand that had been on Simon's thigh slid into his pants as well, and Simon spread his legs wider. One rough finger rubbed against his hole, sending shivers through him. He threw his head back and let Jack do as he wished with him, all energy concentrated on the hum of pressure that was building inside him.

"Mmm, finally," Jack drawled, "when you couldn't take it anymore, I'd wrap my hand around you—" He wrapped his hand around Simon's aching flesh. "And I'd stroke you, and stroke you, and fuck you, and fuck you, until you lost it."

His questing finger pressed inside Simon and the pulls on his cock were long and slick and his voice in Simon's ear was low and hot. He curled his finger inside Simon, and the sparks caught fire. Every sensation raging through him coalesced into an explosion that snapped his hips and gushed from him in screaming pulses.

Jack held him and worked him until he was just shuddering pleasure, until his body was twitching with every touch, but couldn't feel a drop more pleasure or he might die.

A minute or two later, Simon's eyes fluttered open. Jack was stroking his stomach and kissing his hair. He felt liquid with ease and relished the steady thump of Jack's heartbeat against his shoulder.

Still a little shaky, he looked at the sketchbook again. The drawing was slightly smeared where he must've clutched it.

"Is there more?" he asked, voice raw.

Jack buried his face in Simon's hair.

"Not yet."

Simon turned the page anyway. Branches laden with snow, acorns hanging in clusters, tattered leaves, pine boughs.

"I wasn't lying about the trees," Jack said, arms hugging him close.

Chapter Twelve

Jack

"Haven't seen you in here in a while."

Jack jumped in his seat at Charlie's voice.

"Sorry. Thought you heard me come in."

Jack shook his head.

He'd wandered into his studio under the guise of dusting. He hadn't let himself examine why he'd need his drawing table dust-free because...well, that's why it was a guise. He'd dusted the bookshelves, pulling out a volume here and there and flipping through. When his armpits began to ache from standing with his crutches too long, he'd settled gingerly at the table. He'd flipped through *Two Moons Over*, as he often had before he started drawing in the past, and his hand had reached for a piece of paper automatically.

"Is that us?"

Charlie peered over his shoulder at the scattered pages.

"Um, yeah."

Jack started to gather the pages so Charlie wouldn't look, but his brother was already studying them.

"That's the time you hid in the woodpile and got swarmed by fire ants," Charlie said, chuckling at the memory. "God, your face. You really thought you'd found the best hiding spot."

Jack smiled and grabbed another drawing and shoved it at Charlie.

"Yeah, well, you weren't such a paragon of sense yourself."

Charlie groaned at the drawing. He'd been twelve and Jack had been eight and they'd gone fishing in the stream south of the cabin. Charlie had tried to show off and make up a new way of casting. He'd flicked his rod back like he was fly-fishing, and through some combination of coordination, wind, and bad luck, Charlie's hook lodged in the back of his shoulder.

"I really thought I'd invented fly-fishing with a spinning rod," Charlie said, soberly.

"And *I* really thought you were gonna fall in the stream the way you jumped around like you'd been shot."

"It hurt!"

"It was a fishhook," Jack scoffed.

Charlie smiled, then looked at him assessingly.

"You seem…strangely happy."

"Asshole," Jack muttered. But he *felt* strangely happy. Not just happy in comparison to how awful he'd felt the last eight months. But a deep, rooted happiness that had a lot to do with Simon. Simon who could cook casseroles and knew how to tat lace. Who liked to be held down and spread open and tormented with pleasure until he couldn't talk for moaning, rather than for shyness. Simon, who kissed him like he worried that each kiss might be the last and smiled at him like he wanted this to never end.

"I am. Happy."

"It's that guy, right? The dog walker? The shy guy?"

"Simon."

"I want to meet him. Properly."

Jack snorted.

"Okay, Dad."

If he hadn't been looking at Charlie he would've missed the expression of pure hurt that flickered there for a moment before his brother shrugged, turned away, and walked out of the room.

Why did I do that? Why do I always do that?

Grabbing his crutches, he followed Charlie. He found him in the kitchen, removing groceries from the thin plastic Albertsons bags that Jack used to pick up dog poop on walks.

"Charlie. I… Sorry."

Charlie shrugged again, but his movements were stiff and jerky as he began to put things away.

"Dammit, I've told you a hundred times I can do that myself. I have a broken leg, I'm not helpless!"

Charlie spun around, cheeks flushed and mouth tight with anger.

"You've never been helpless in your goddamn life, Jack!

I know that. I'm putting away your fucking groceries, not trying to give you a sponge bath. Why won't you just let me *do* this for you?"

He was yelling now, looming over Jack.

"I don't get why you even want to! You care about where my popcorn goes all of a sudden?!"

Charlie slammed a meaty fist into the cabinet and the wood cracked. Mayonnaise, who'd been slinking in through the cat door, bolted.

"I fucking care that for the last year you've been a zombie! I care that you've been miserable and hurt and depressed and you wouldn't even talk to me! You've shut out every single person who cares about you, including me."

Charlie's clenched fist dripped blood on the floor.

"Charlie…"

"I've *always* been there for you. Always. And you…" Charlie's voice went rough, his shoulders slumped.

Jack's chest was hollow and his throat dry. He'd seen Charlie cry twice since childhood. Once when they'd buried their parents and once in the middle of the night, when Charlie didn't know he was watching. He'd gotten up to use the bathroom, seen the light on in their parents' room, and crept down the hallway to see Charlie sitting at their mother's dressing table staring into space, tears streaming down his cheeks.

"You have. I know that." Guilt at his ingratitude swallowed him.

"I don't have anyone else." Charlie's voice was so low, so choked, that Jack thought he must have misheard him.

"What?"

Charlie made a frustrated sound in the back of his throat.

"You've always had friends. People like you, even though you're such a moody bastard. I…" Charlie shrugged, but it wasn't a casual gesture, it was an awkward clench of his huge shoulders. "People don't like me," he said, turning to the sink to wash off his bloody hand.

"What? That's stupid. Of course they do."

Charlie had been on the football team, he'd dated cheerleaders, he was the head counselor at camp. He was strong and handsome and confident; he always had been.

Charlie shook his head.

"No."

"What about everyone at the store? They worship you."

Charlie snorted. "They're my employees. And they worship my ability to cite aisle and bin on every size of nail, not my sparkling personality."

"What about the whole football team?"

"The football team…in high school? Bro, I'm thirty-five. I haven't talked to those guys in almost twenty years."

"But not because they didn't like you. Because—"

Jack had been about to say, *Because you didn't keep up with them.* Then he realized when the chance to keep up would've come. In the year after their parents' death. The year Charlie was keeping their house together, and paying the bills from insurance money, and cooking and…taking care of him.

"It doesn't matter," Charlie said. "Never mind." He made a move to put away a jar of peanut butter then snatched his hand back like he'd been burned.

"You can put them away. It's fine."

"You sure know how to make a guy feel loved," Charlie said wryly.

But he put the peanut butter in the cabinet.

"Charlie."

His brother's movements weren't awkward anymore. They were the fluid, coordinated ballet of someone who was used to working with his body. The movements of someone who used the world outside of him to escape the one within.

"Charlie. I do love you. You know that. Right?"

Charlie paused for too long.

"Sure. Me too."

Charlie stacked cans of beans in the cabinet, turning each one label out.

"You can meet him. Simon. We'll come to dinner? Okay?"

"Yeah?"

"Yeah. I want you to meet him. *Properly*," Jack added, with a wink.

Charlie ducked his chin and nodded.

"Okay. Thanks."

And though he'd said it to drive the hurt from his brother's face, Jack found that he really did want Simon to meet Charlie.

Simon, however, proved far less enthusiastic when Jack invited him.

First he froze. Then he nodded manically. Then he got very pale and very quiet.

"We don't have to," Jack said into the charged silence.

But given the way he'd clearly hurt Charlie, Jack knew he didn't sound sincere.

Simon shook his head just as manically as he'd nodded it before, clearly frustrated.

Jack handed him his phone in case he needed it to text, but Simon pushed it away with a huff. He closed his eyes and crossed his arms over his chest.

"I want to b-be able to," he said. "I just know I'll be so shy and I'll get all anxious and he'll ask me qu-questions and I won't be able to answer and th-then he'll wonder why his baby brother is dating this f-f-freak who c-can't even talk, and he'll hate me because I'm not g-goo-good enough for you."

Simon was glaring at his own hands as if they were the instrument of his betrayal. Jack took them in his own.

"He won't think that. And it's not true."

"You don't get it. You think because you like me he'll like me, but—but people don't like people who don't act the way they expect. It makes them uncomfortable. And being uncomfortable makes them m-mad or makes them want to g-get away."

Simon let out a miserable, shuddery breath and Jack felt an unfamiliar space open up inside him. A space that bloomed like a flower and belonged only to Simon. It hurt for him, it ached for him, it longed for him.

"Well, then, we'll just have to keep hanging out with him until you get comfortable and he can realize how great you are."

Hot hazel eyes snapped to his and Simon blinked uncertainly.

"You'd want that?"

"Hell yeah, I want that," Jack said, pulling him closer.

Simon rested his forehead on Jack's shoulder. He said something that Jack couldn't hear and Jack tipped his chin up.

"Hmm?"

"My grandma wants to meet you too."

Jack's grin was instant.

"You talking about me to your grandma?" he teased.

"No," Simon grumbled.

"I think you are." He kissed the spot behind Simon's ear that always made him shiver. "You totally have a thing for me."

"Shut up," Simon said mildly, and wrapped his arms around Jack's neck.

Which is how Jack came to be struggling out of a Lyft outside of Simon's house a few days later with two crutches, a bottle of wine, and a bouquet of flowers. Simon had offered to come pick him up, but Jack felt strongly that meeting the family meant arriving under his own steam and ringing the doorbell. Even if said steam *was* facilitated by a stranger he'd paid to stop at the grocery store so he could buy the wine and flowers.

Simon answered the door looking a little flushed.

"Hi. Wow, are those for my grandma? You really are trying to make a good first impression."

Jack kissed him hello.

"This is for your grandmother." He held up the wine. "These are for you."

Simon accepted the bouquet with wide, soft eyes.

"No one's ever gotten me flowers before."

"I'm honored to be the first," Jack said quietly and watched Simon swallow hard. Jack was honored to be Simon's first in every way he could.

"Let the poor man in, dear."

"Oops."

Simon shuffled aside, revealing a small woman with a white bob, glasses the same bright blue as her eyes, and an apron that said *THE ONLY THING I WANT YOU TO DO IS CHOP THE ONIONS.*

"I'm Jean," she said. "Welcome."

"Great to meet you, Miss Jean." He held out the wine to her. "I'm not sure if this goes with what you made, but if not I hope you'll enjoy it another time."

"Oh I didn't make dinner," she said. "Simon did. But you get full marks for textbook politeness. Did you google that?"

"Grandma!" Simon hissed.

Jack felt his cheeks heat. He actually *had* googled "meeting the parents" that morning, as well as "give wine to a host." He'd never met a boyfriend's family before. And since his own parents had died long before one would have met them, he'd felt at loose ends about the protocol. He hadn't wanted to embarrass Simon.

"Um. Well."

Jean burst out laughing, a warm, tinkling laugh that made Simon cough to hide a laugh too.

Jack smiled.

"Busted."

Simon had made lasagna and salad and they ate in a dining room wallpapered with roses. Not the delicate, tracery
roses of antique stores and flannel nightgowns, but bold,
lush roses with thorns that could draw blood. It put Jack
in mind of fairy tales and hidden castles.

Jean was lovely and funny and expressed such delight to
hear about his work in illustrating that she jollied him into
speaking about it in more detail than he usually would.

"Simon used to love a picture book about...what kind
of dogs were those, dear?"

"Shepherds," Simon said.

"Yes, shepherds. They lived in an old amusement park
and would roam through the overgrown tracks of roller-
coasters. It was quite beautiful."

"*Merry-Go-Hound,*" Jack offered. "That's a great book."

"Yeah, but I never got why it was called that when the
dogs were shepherds," Simon said.

"Psh, publishing," Jack said by way of explanation. "'If
it rhymes it climbs.' The charts, you know?"

"But...it *doesn't* rhyme," Simon said.

"It rhymes with merry-go-round—never mind."

"Teaching their kids the wrong dog breeds," Simon muttered seriously and Jack squeezed his knee under the table,
then left his hand on Simon's thigh. After a minute, Simon
rested his hand on top of Jack's and a smile played at the
corners of his mouth.

When Jack looked up, Jean was watching them with a
knowing look.

"Shall we have dessert?" she asked brightly, standing to

clear the table. Simon jumped up to help her, gesturing for Jack to stay seated. He glared at his leg.

"Soon, you bastard," he muttered to the cast. He had a doctor's appointment the next week to check in on his progress.

"Now, this I made," Jean said, setting a coffee cake drizzled with icing in the center of the table. She cut pieces for each of them and Jack noticed that she'd cut his significantly larger than either of theirs.

"That looks amazing," Jack said, mouth watering.

"I thought someone whose favorite cookie was oatmeal and liked snickerdoodles might enjoy something else with cinnamon and sugar."

"Wow. Yeah, I love cinnamon stuff. That's really smart. I see where Simon gets it from."

Simon groaned, Jean winked, and Jack took a bite of the cake, sighing in bliss as the tastes of brown sugar, butter, cinnamon, and walnuts burst on his tongue.

Chapter Thirteen

Simon

When Simon had arrived at Jack's an hour earlier, shaking out of his skin with anxiety over their dinner with Charlie, Jack had decided that the most logical course of action was to screw him to within an inch of his life as a distraction.

Now, Simon lay flushed and sated across Jack's bed, head on Jack's thigh, Jack's fingers combing through his hair.

"What if we had a signal?" Jack asked.

"Hmm?"

"If you can't talk. What if you gave me a signal and I could... I dunno. Give Charlie a signal to stop talking to you? Or whatever you want."

Reality broke over him like a wave, the blissful warmth and safety of the language of their bodies drowned.

Simon turned his head to rest his cheek on Jack's hip, feeling the jut of bone, strong beneath sensitive skin.

"The signal would be when he talks to me and I can't fucking answer," Simon said. "And he'll stop talking to me all right."

"Sorry," Jack said tightly, and Simon added guilt to his roiling mix of emotions.

Simon shook his head. It wasn't Jack. It wasn't Charlie. It was him. It had always been him. He tried to find the words to apologize but they wouldn't come. And somehow, after they'd been so intimate, to not be able to say something so simple to Jack hurt worse than it usually did. Why was the language of touch so much easier?

But since it was, he used it instead. He reached for Jack's hand and twined their fingers together. He kissed Jack's knuckles and kissed his stomach. He kissed his chest and his throat and then he placed a final kiss of apology on his lips.

"Simon, I..." Jack's voice was tentative. "We don't have to go. I want you to be comfortable."

I'm never comfortable, his internal voice snapped. But it wasn't true. He'd been perfectly, blissfully comfortable five minutes before. And not just because of the hot as fuck sex. Because in Jack's arms, in his own desires, he could lose himself.

Was there a way to do the same with Charlie? Not the sex, obviously, but a way to find a work-around. Another mode of communicating. Maybe not right away, but if this thing with Jack continued...maybe...?

Over the years, Simon had tried so many things. He'd tried glaring, tried smiling, tried a name tag that said *Don't talk to me*, which people had thought was a joke. He'd tried learning German in the hopes that another syntax might come out easier. It didn't, and even if it had, German speakers weren't thick on the ground in Garnet Run, Wyoming. He'd tried sign language, chat rooms, internet support groups, pen pals. He'd tried therapy, astrology, and alcohol.

But over the last few years he'd stopped trying. Stopped trying to change. And he'd started to try and enjoy his life the way it was instead. Starting his business. Planning to get a dog. He'd begun to try and accept himself. Begun to try and accept that he might have limitations but it didn't mean he couldn't also have joy.

Meeting Jack had felt like the rainbow at the end of the storm. A chuck under the chin from the universe saying he was moving in the right direction. And Simon refused to fuck it up. Refused to let this one thing about himself unravel this beautiful gift he'd been given.

No fucking way.

Simon shook his head and sat up.

"I want to go."

Jack looked for a moment like he might argue, then he nodded at whatever he saw in Simon's eyes.

"Okay. Let's go."

Charlie lived a ten-minute drive away and aside from Jack's directions, they were quiet. Simon did multiplication in his head in an attempt to keep out any *what-ifs*. He was struggling through 128 times 267—Simon wasn't actually terribly good at math—when Jack said they were there.

The house was clearly a work in progress. A central part looked mostly completed, but to each side raw wood framed in new structures.

"Wow, he's made a lot of progress," Jack said. "I haven't been here in a few months."

He caught Simon's hand before they got out of the car. "Simon. Look at me, please."

Simon looked into dark blue eyes that had become so familiar to him. Jack had a few days of copper stubble glinting over his jaw.

"No matter how things go with my brother, it won't change anything for me. You know that, right?"

Protests crowded one another out in Simon's head.

"I love my brother, but I—" He bit his lip. "Just, you can not talk to him and have five panic attacks and I'll still— I won't—"

Simon had never seen Jack at a loss for words before. He squeezed Jack's hand and watched his eyes go soft and unsure.

"I want you," he said simply. "All the time. I… I care about you so much. Please tell me you know that."

Simon only vaguely registered that Jack was squeezing his hand so tight it was slightly painful. All he could focus on was that soft, needing look in Jack's eyes. The look that said he truly wasn't sure his feelings were understood. And maybe reciprocated.

But Simon did know. Everything in the way Jack acted around him showed him that.

"I know," Simon said. "Me too."

A slow grin brightened Jack's face.

"Yeah?"

"Yeah."

Then Jack was kissing him, tender and hot.

"Good," Jack said fiercely, pressing their foreheads together. "That's good."

Jack was a large man, but Charlie was massive. He looked like the sized-up xerox of Jack—a bigger, rougher version. When he reached to shake Simon's hand, though, his grip was firm but gentle.

"Hi, Simon. I'm glad to meet the guy who finally dragged this grouchy ass out of his self-imposed exile."

"Hi," Simon said. But it came out thin. His ears were buzzing and his throat felt so dry he could hardly swallow. He was too nervous. He had known he would be but refused to capitulate and now here he was, standing in front of the brother of the guy he lo—

Just as his heart began to race, the largest cat Simon had ever seen ambled into the room. It was black with gray markings, fur-tufted ears, and a huge bushy tail. It rubbed its face against Charlie's leg and meowed, a sound like tearing metal.

"This is Jane," Charlie said as Simon bent down and offered his knuckles to the cat.

Jane. Apparently being bad at naming animals ran in the Matheson family.

Jane eyed Simon for a minute, then deigned to butt her head against his fist.

Simon wanted to sit on the floor with her, cuddle her tight to his chest, and bury his face in her luscious fur.

He didn't think that would go over too well with Charlie *or* with Jane, so he stroked between her ears and avoided looking up.

"Meatloaf?" Jack asked, sniffing.

"Spaghetti and meatballs," Charlie said.

"Yum."

"You'd eat anything," Charlie said lightly.

Simon thought of the horrid tuna casserole and grimaced.

"Hungry?"

The question lingered in the air long enough that Simon realized it must have been directed at him. He nodded and stood up, giving Jane a final pat to the top of her fluffy head.

On the table was a comically large bowl of spaghetti and meatballs. The things looked the size of Simon's fist and he would've bet they were the same recipe that Charlie used to make meatloaf. This was clearly a man accustomed to cooking hearty food for people who ate a lot. Was this how it was when Jack was young? The two brothers sitting down to devour a huge serving bowl of food like Lady and the Tramp?

"You're an animal person too?" Charlie asked. Simon nodded and smiled.

"When Jack was little he used to lure chipmunks inside with birdseed and try to keep them as pets."

Simon thought that was adorable, but Jack rolled his eyes.

"They liked me," he said.

"They liked your birdseed. And to burrow under the

carpet until the door opened again and then run out and leave you thinking they'd died somewhere in the house."

Jack muttered like he was still resentful about it.

"So what do you do, Simon?"

Simon's heart rate picked up. He went to step one: logic. *That is a completely normal getting-to-know-you question. There is nothing to be worried about. You know the answer to this question. You've answered it a hundred times before. No problem.*

"G-g-graphic d-design," Simon got out, then clamped his mouth shut.

"He's so good, bro. Hey, you should have him do a new website for the hardware store." Jack turned to him. "You'd laugh your ass off if you saw this website. It's from like 2003."

Simon nodded and tried to smile.

This is your job. You're good at this. Say something witty about old website design. Make a hardware pun. "I'll nail the design!" "I won't screw it up!" Hell, say anything at all.

Simon swallowed over and over, trying to clear the lump that had lodged in his throat. He reached for his water glass but it was already empty. If he could just *swallow* maybe he could say something.

The fear trickled in. First he wouldn't be able to swallow, then his lungs would close like two fists strangling him slowly from the inside. He'd breathe through his nose faster and faster and try to yawn, but the yawn would stutter out at his blocked throat and make him gasp. Once he gasped he'd start to choke. Once he choked he would panic.

He tried to stay calm. Fear of the panic made the panic happen faster. He pushed back his chair and tried to drag in a breath to apologize, but it was too much effort. His vision sparkled around the edges and he bolted from the room.

Vaguely he was aware of Jack calling his name, but all he could focus on was finding a bathroom and closing himself inside it. The first door he tried was a closet and the second was an empty room. The third opened into darkness and the temperature dropped.

Simon had the wherewithal for one absurd thought about a door to Narnia before he realized he'd stumbled into the unfinished part of Charlie's house.

The where didn't matter so long as it was away. Simon bent at the waist and breathed through his nose. Somehow this position always let him get a fuller breath if he caught the panic early enough. He didn't know why. A trick of the brain? The vagus nerve? Shift of his chest muscles? Whatever. He dragged in the sweet, cold air and concentrated on anything—*anything*—except his body's betrayal.

The air smelled of sawdust and freshly cut wood. Dust. Soil. He could hear the wind blowing through the trees outside, so that probably meant part of the structure was open. That would explain the cold too.

Still bent over he let his arms hang, fingertips trailing over the ground. It felt like cement. Concrete? What was the difference? He'd read it once but he couldn't remember. His breath came easier. He could taste the one bite of spaghetti he'd managed before humiliating himself. Sour tang of tomato, flat starch of pasta. Salt. Charlie wasn't a very good cook.

Tension in his legs made him bend his knees and slowly, slowly lower himself into a squat, then onto his hands and knees. He hung his head low, breathing to a five-count slowly, deliberately, not letting himself speed up no matter how much he wanted more air. Speeding up could became hyperventilating in the space of two breaths, and hyperventilating made him black out.

Was this how he'd die someday? Alone, in the dark, in the woods?

Something soft brushed against his cheek and Simon jolted. But a rusty-metal meow sounded in the darkness, and he reached out his hand.

"Hi, Jane," he whispered.

The cat twitched her tail against his face, then sat down on the floor next to him.

"Can I please hug you?"

He inched closer to her and tried to pull her into his lap but she skittered away with a yowl.

Typical.

"Hey, Simon?" He'd assumed if anyone came for him it would be Jack, but it was Charlie. "Are you okay?" He cleared his throat. "Tap on something if you're okay. Okay?"

Simon knocked on the floor and tried to breathe quieter. That made his breaths slower, which made him get too little air. And that made him feel like he was choking all over again.

To hell with trying to make a good impression. He sucked in loud breaths through his nose, tears dripping onto the cement floor—concrete floor—whateverthefuck.

He heard the shuffle of Charlie taking a few steps toward him, then sitting down.

"I'm expanding. This is gonna be a woodshop. Or maybe...no, a woodshop. I like to make stuff."

Furniture? Simon wondered. But something about the way Charlie was just talking told him he didn't require a response.

"Bowls and cups and stuff on the lathe. Spoons. I did a lamp the other day. Kind of."

That explained the sawdust smell.

"Jane rolls around in the sawdust and tracks it all over the house," he went on. His voice was low and gruff and yet he said this like he'd let Jane do whatever she wanted to the house.

Being bad at naming animals might run in the Matheson family, but clearly being a total sucker for them did as well.

At her name, Jane let out a little yip.

"You in here, Jane?"

A purr began to Simon's left.

"She's here," he croaked.

Jane tumbled onto her back, all four legs extended directly into Simon's face, and he wheezed a laugh.

"Thought she might be."

There was a long enough silence that Simon relaxed. When Charlie spoke again, his voice was softer.

"After my parents died I would wake up in the middle of the night terrified. Sit up in bed and feel like I was being crushed. They were dead. I had a little brother to take care of. Bills to pay, meals to cook, parent-teacher conferences to go to, a store to run or sell. I didn't know how anything worked."

Simon imagined being seventeen and waking up to stare

that in the face. When he was seventeen he vomited at speaking in front of his twenty-person history class.

"Don't know if it was anything like how you feel," Charlie went on. "But it was horrible. It was...worse than the way I felt when they died, honestly. So. I get it a little. You don't have to talk to me. We're good, okay? You're Jack's guy, I got your back."

Tears of gratitude replaced Simon's tears of panic.

Apparently being a huge goddamn sweetheart ran in the Matheson family too.

"Anyway, you can hang out in here, but if you wanna come inside, we're fine. You can just eat and hang out. Whatever you want."

Charlie stood up slowly.

"Did it ever go away?" Simon heard himself say.

"Yeah. Little by little it happened less often. Though sometimes, I still— Anyway. You come in when you're ready. Stay, Jane."

Simon was amused at the idea that Charlie thought a cat would obey an order, but as the door closed, Jane rolled closer to Simon and rested her paw on his leg.

This close, he could tell she was covered in sawdust.

"Your dad's pretty great, huh?" he said softly, stroking her back in a combination of petting and attempted sawdust removal. Jane's torn-metal meow turned into a yawn and then a deep purr as Simon combed more of the sawdust from her fur.

"They're both pretty damn great."

Warring feelings clashed in Simon's gut. Why hadn't

more people been kind the way the Mathesons were? And then: What if he'd simply never given people the chance?

The only reason he'd spoken more than three words to Jack was because it had felt worth seeing him over and over in order to walk the pack. It was happenstance that the person he'd matched with on PetShare was a kind, lovely, patient one, right? And now, the fact that Jack liked him explained why Charlie was being so kind.

And all of that had happened because Simon hadn't run away at the first twinge of discomfort, the first panic.

Horror began to eat away at his hard-won calm. If he'd just been able to stick it out, to open up, to make himself vulnerable to more people would more of them have turned out to be like Jack and Charlie? Had he done this to himself?

No! he screamed inside his head. *Stop it!*

He'd been down this path before. He had years of others' voices in his head telling him that if he just *tried* harder, just *socialized* more then it would all work out.

But it wasn't that simple. He'd attended school with people for years, seen them every day, and they'd tormented him. He'd spent months and months seeing his coworkers every day and never felt comfortable with them.

His anxiety was real, diagnosed, medicated. He couldn't *fix* it by just trying harder. It wasn't his fault.

It's not your fault.

"It's not my fault," he whispered to Jane. She purred.

Simon went to the bathroom and splashed water on his face. He was pale and redness from crying had left the blue of his eyes looking strangely violet. His hair was a mess. He sighed, tried to smooth it, gave Jane, who'd followed him into the bathroom, a final ruffle of the fur to dislodge the last of the sawdust, and took a deep breath.

In the dining room, Jack and Charlie sat like bookends, legs stretched out in front of them, hands resting on their stomachs. As he entered, they both smiled at him. Charlie warmly and Jack with concern in his eyes. He wished he could crawl onto Jack's lap and bury his face in his neck. Instead, he tried to smile back.

Jack caught his hand as he returned to his seat and kissed it.

"Charlie was telling me about the additions on the house," Jack said casually. "Just try not to lose consciousness directly into the spaghetti."

It was so clearly a tease on his behalf, a way to say he didn't have to participate, and Simon could tell he was about at the end of his capacity to be upright because it brought tears to his eyes.

He fixed his gaze on the cold plate of congealed spaghetti in front of him, knowing he'd throw up if he touched the meatballs, wondering if he could get away with just moving the food around on his plate. The last thing he wanted to do was insult Charlie's cooking, but he supposed it would probably be an equal insult to take a bite and immediately run to the bathroom to puke it up.

Charlie began talking about tongue-and-groove joints, the load-bearing capacities of different woods, and Jack's questions made it clear he knew what these things meant. Simon listened to every word, trying to move outside himself. Then he listened to every syllable, sense dissolving into sound. Then it was just two low voices, dancing, and Simon closed his eyes.

"Do you want to stay tonight?" Jack asked as they waved goodbye to Charlie and made their way to the car.

Do you want me to? Simon asked, but nothing came out. He raised his eyebrows in question.

"I'd love it," Jack said. "But I get if you just want to go home."

Simon shook his head. "No," he managed to get out, shocked to hear that his voice sounded normal.

They drove in silence, Simon forcing himself to concentrate on the road even though his head felt swimmy and his eyes burned.

At Jack's they were greeted with much yipping, barking, tail wagging, and licking. Simon put his arms around Bernard and pressed his face to the dog's huge head. Bernard wriggled with joy.

"Let's let them out for a few minutes," Jack murmured. "I'll just stand with them, okay? You want to take a shower?"

Simon nodded. The change of temperature sometimes did help him feel better.

Jack pressed a kiss to his temple and Simon closed his eyes.

You still have this. You didn't lose it. He still likes you.

Under the sluice of hot water, Simon let himself cry. It was the overflow that usually followed a period of panic—

not sadness but a kind of familiar hopeless exhaustion with a vein of self-pity and relief.

He dried off and pulled on a pair of Jack's flannel boxers and the sweatshirt Jack had been wearing earlier. It was worn soft and smelled like Jack. Simon put the hood up over his damp hair and flopped into bed. Louis' head popped up from the foot of the bed, so hidden in shadow that Simon hadn't seen him.

"Sorry," he murmured. Louis put his head back down.

Simon curled up in a ball and closed his eyes. He could hear Jack talking outside but couldn't make out what he was saying. He heard Rat's yipping bark and then the sound of the door opening. A stampede of furry feet followed, then Jack rambling around on his crutches, no doubt shutting off lights and stoking the fire. Every now and then he muttered or swore and Simon knew a crutch had caught on something or Jack had forgotten about his leg and hurt himself.

It sounded like home.

When Jack crawled into bed with him, smelling of toothpaste and displacing an irritated Louis, Simon realized he'd been half dozing.

"Hey," Jack said. "How are you doing?"

Jack's inquiry was sincere. He laid a soft hand on Simon's back.

"Kind of bad," Simon whispered.

He rolled over to face Jack in the comforting darkness. Jack took Simon's hands in his own.

"I'm so sorry, Jack."

He felt Jack stiffen.

"Darlin', no. No way. Don't you dare apologize. It's my

fault. You told me… I didn't… It's not that I didn't believe you. I just, I thought it would be okay."

"Same thing," Simon mumbled. Jack had thought it'd be okay because he couldn't imagine how it was possible to be as much of a basket case as Simon was.

Stop it stop it stop it.

Jack hesitated, then said, "Yeah. I guess you're right. My fault."

The air was thick with apology and Simon hated it. He hated that he'd let Jack down and he hated that he'd do it again if Jack spent any more time with him. And he was too tired at the moment to control his thoughts about it. He moved closer and threw his arm over Jack's stomach.

"It's not your fault. It's just…how I am."

"I like you how you are," Jack said fiercely. "But I hate— I fucking hate—how bad you feel."

Simon nodded and let Jack draw him into his arms.

"I'm used to it," he said. "And it still sucks."

The scent of outside clung to Jack's hair and Simon buried his face in his neck. Jack stroked up and down his back. How was it possible to go from feeling so bad to feeling so good?

"Charlie's nice," he murmured.

"Yeah. Too nice for his own good," Jack said affectionately.

"No such thing."

Jack squeezed him tighter.

He was exhausted, but his comfort was being eroded by the thoughts that had plagued him earlier.

"What…what did you think of me when we first met?" Simon asked.

"I thought you were the most beautiful guy I'd ever seen," Jack answered instantly.

"But what did you think about…*me*?"

"I thought I'd scared you or offended you because I was in such a bad mood. Here was this guy doing me a huge favor and I was all…grouchy and shit."

"What else?"

"I thought you were awkward," Jack said. His voice was so gentle, so fond. "I thought you were shy." He kissed Simon's hair. "I thought maybe if I didn't fuck it up I could get you to… I dunno, stick around a bit."

Simon was rummaging for something that didn't exist, he knew now. He'd wondered if everyone would turn out to be like Jack if he gave them the chance. But Jack *was* different. He hadn't thought Simon was a freak. He hadn't disliked him.

"That day I asked you to help me with the coffee filters? I just wanted an excuse to spend more time with you. But I hadn't thought ahead enough to have anything to ask you." Jack shook his head.

"I thought you were making fun of me."

"Yeah I kinda got that. I wasn't," he added unnecessarily.

"You never are."

"Simon, I… I don't know what you want me to say. I just liked you. I thought you were interesting. And yeah, part of that is probably that you were so different. That there was no quippy banter, no empty flirting. No boring small talk. Is that…bad?"

"No. No, never." He flopped onto his back. "Ignore me. I'm just having a thing."

"Tell me?"

Simon searched for the thread. Searched for the part of this that Jack might understand.

"I've had friends. I know it seems like I don't have any but… I've had friends I met online. I had friends when I was younger. But I never…"

There was no way to say this that didn't make him come off badly, so he just said it.

"I didn't care about them enough to—to put up with what I had to do to keep them. Making myself uncomfortable and t-taking risks. So we all just drifted. I would wish for friends—the kind of—of really close friends like on TV. The ones who feel like family—well, like family should feel."

Simon thought of Paul, his childhood best friend who'd tried hard to keep their friendship going as they moved into middle school. He'd asked Simon to walk home with him and his other friends; he'd invited Simon to every birthday party; he'd tried to get him to try out for the school play with him. But Simon didn't want to do any of those things—couldn't do any of those things without a cost greater than he could afford. So he'd let Paul go.

For years he'd blamed himself for being incapable, for losing the friendship. When he was older and first starting therapy, he'd blamed Paul for not realizing that all of his overtures were tuned to the wrong channel. Now he knew it wasn't either of their faults. Simon was himself and Paul was an oblivious kid.

Paul had gone to college in Colorado and Simon had never seen him again. But he still thought of him every year on his birthday: August 11. He still remembered his home phone number.

Simon gathered his thoughts.

"It's different with you," he told Jack. "B-because it's worth it to..." He was going to say *suffer* but that wasn't right. "Worth it to try and push myself if it means I get to...have you?"

He hadn't meant it to come out as a question.

"You do," Jack said, avid, pulling Simon on top of him. "You do have me, baby. I swear. It's different for me too. I've never..." He shivered. "I've never felt like this about anyone. I... Shit."

He wrapped his arms so tight around Simon that for a moment he thought Jack might press them together into one body.

Simon had been going to say that it felt worth it to try and push himself if it meant he got to have Jack, but that he worried he wouldn't be able to push himself far enough for it to work.

Simon kissed him instead. He kissed him with every ounce of energy he had left, and Jack kissed him right back.

Chapter Fourteen

Jack

Jack groaned in relief as the cast fell away, then recoiled as the smell hit.

"Jesus Christ, am I *rotting*?"

"Perfectly normal," the orthopedist said absently. "Oils and sweat and skin collect between your leg and the casting and form a layer of yeasty—"

"Okay, yep, got it," Jack interrupted. "Shower thoroughly. Noted. So when can I…do stuff?"

"What stuff are you referring to?"

Jack gritted his teeth to hold back his irritation. *No bedside manner-having asshat.*

He'd been waiting for the doctor for hours and was at the end of his tether even before the person who'd shown up had turned out to have all the compassion and humor of a nail protruding from a floorboard.

"Drive, walk, run, fuck my boyfriend hard in positions that require two legs, et cetera."

Welp, never mind about holding back the irritation.

The doctor cleared his throat. "Drive, as soon as the stiffness in your leg has eased. You can walk now. Short distances. Build up slowly. You'll want to build up strength for several weeks before you begin jogging, then jog at a light pace before running in six to eight weeks."

He sniffed and gathered his clipboard.

"The nurse will be in with a printout of exercises to strengthen the limb and your walking boot."

"And what about fucking my—"

"As long as you don't exert the limb to the point of pain you can…put weight on it."

"Thanks, Doc," Jack called after him. Then muttered, "Dick."

"Making friends and spreading joy wherever you go as usual?" Charlie said, walking into the room as the doctor was leaving.

"Doctors, am I right?"

"Not usually. Ready?"

"I just have to get stuff from the nurse."

He examined his bared right calf. It looked smaller, shrunken. But at the moment he couldn't care. All he felt was relief that he was back on his feet. That he could feel like himself again.

And he really hadn't been kidding about that whole screwing Simon up against a wall thing.

Or over the back of the couch.

Or over the side of the bed.

I have a surprise for you, Jack texted Simon.

What!?

Jack chuckled. Simon was so adorable.

If I told you it wouldn't be a surprise and all that. You'll see tonight.

Pout.

His shin ached and looked a bit swollen, and the skin that had been under the cast felt weirdly sensitive, but taking a shower without a plastic bag swaddling his cast and an ache in his hip from holding his leg up—not to mention the inevitable moment of almost losing his balance and falling on his ass—was heaven. He stood under the spray until the water began to run cold, then rubbed his leg gently with a towel as the nurse had recommended, her stern rejoinder about why he shouldn't scrub at the skin no matter how much he wanted to running through his head: *Because your skin will slough off and it'll hurt, tough guy, so just don't.*

He shuddered and rubbed even more gently.

The sensation of putting even a little bit of weight on his right leg after so long favoring it was strange, but Jack walked around the house slowly, gingerly, patting a dog here and tidying a pile of mail there.

The clutter annoyed him and he began to make plans to put everything in the cabin to rights. It had been too long since he'd cleaned, too long since he'd dusted. Too long since...everything.

At the bottom of a pile of mail and papers shoved in a corner was a large envelope. It had sat there for months, unopened, because Jack didn't need to open it to know what it was. Page proofs of his and Davis' book that would be out in a month. Their fourth together, completed before Davis' betrayal when Jack had imagined things would go on as they were forever: collaboration, publication, celebration.

But the wheels of publishing turned slowly enough to fossilize joy in bitterness, hope in fury.

Fury was perhaps too active a descriptor for the fugue state Jack had wandered around in for months before his fall.

Now, though, floor solid beneath both feet, Jack probed at the wound gingerly. It was still there, but it had diminished. It wasn't a raging storm any longer. It was a dull ache that felt more like foolishness and disappointment.

Jack slid a finger under the lip of the envelope and breathed in the particular scent of photo paper and ink.

A Lynx Slinks in the Bronx slid onto the table, a Post-it note from his editor on top: *Looks great! Can't wait until it's out in the world!*

Each line and color was familiar even all these months later. Jack had spent hours reading about the Canada lynx. He'd asked everyone he ran into if they'd seen one and listened to story after story from old men claiming they had. The accuracy of their sloping backs, hind legs longer than fore, had made his initial drawings look unrealistic until he'd figured out the angle he needed to draw them from to capture their size and grace.

Fuck, he missed it. All of it. In his horror at not being able to draw, he'd forgotten about the rest of it. The research, the chatting with people about what he was working on to get ideas. Seeing the world through the lens of his current project. Texting Davis ideas and getting his in return.

He flipped through the pages to find his favorite drawing. The one he'd spent days on to get the lynx's expression just right. It was beautiful, from the black tufts of fur on her ears to the little stub of her gray tail.

"I drew that," he whispered.

Then he took the pages and placed each one on the floor and sat on the couch. First Mayonnaise wandered over and plopped down on a page. That got Pickles' attention, who stretched out on another. When Pirate next walked through the room, she stopped, circled around, and came back to settle on a third page.

Rat saw that something was happening and started prancing around in circles trying to figure out what it was before placing herself directly on Pickles' legs, getting a tail in the face and a lazy hiss for her troubles. At the sound, Bernard came in from the kitchen where he'd been hopefully sitting next to the food dishes and, seeing the animal-studded living room floor, participated by flopping down in the middle, with no attention to the papers whatsoever. His wagging tail pushed one of the pages so close to the

fire that Jack tensed to get up and rescue it. Then he realized it didn't matter if it burned.

It didn't matter because the book already existed. As his
editor, Hailey, had said on her Post-it, soon it would be
out in the world. And the fact that Davis had turned out
to be a shit, that the way Jack had thought his life would
go had shifted in the space of an email, that chances were
he'd never see Davis again…none of that mattered either.
Not really.

Jack realized with a joyful twist of shock that he could
still have all of it. All the research and the conversation, the
talking about ideas. Of *course* he could. It was wanting to
do both the writing and the illustrations that had sparked
Davis' betrayal in the first place. Jack had already been on
the edge of trying it. He'd just gotten derailed.

And there were other people he could talk about ideas
with. He pictured telling Simon about the layout of a page
he was working on as they walked the pack in the evening. Simon would have great insight about layout from a
graphic design standpoint. He would ask thoughtful questions. He would never dismiss ideas out of hand. *Draw
Puddles making cookies.*

He imagined walking the pack with Simon *every* night,
talking about everything. They'd roam for miles, then
come home calm and tired and fall into bed to tire themselves out even more. They'd wake and walk the pack in
the cool morning air before each turning to their work for
the day. When Simon needed a break, he'd wander into
Jack's office and rest his chin on Jack's shoulder. When Jack

needed a break he'd chop wood for the fire and then lure Simon into a shower with him.

Fuck, it sounded like heaven.

He was startled out of his daydreams about Simon by Simon himself. The animals all perked up at the sound of the car pulling up and Jack sprang carefully to his feet.

When Simon opened the door and saw Jack standing there, he smiled instantly.

"Notice anything different?" Jack asked, raising an eyebrow. He was giddy with excitement and relief and something that felt like possibility. "Look, Ma, no cast."

"Wow—"

Simon hardly got the word out before Jack grabbed him in a hug and then spun him around, added weight on his leg be damned. He felt as unstoppable as a goddamn superhero.

Simon clung to his shoulders when Jack set him down, looking a little dizzy, then he grinned.

"Your leg's okay?"

"Yup. Good as new."

Well, it would be.

He towed Simon over to the couch and plopped down. The animals settled back down. Simon rested a hand lightly on his previously casted shin, the first time he'd ever felt Simon's touch there.

"You look so happy," Simon said.

"I am." Jack couldn't stop smiling. He flopped back on the couch. "It's been driving me fucking crazy not to be able to do all the things I usually do. Grocery shopping and going to get a pizza and going for runs. Picking things up off the damn floor. I haven't felt like *myself*, you know?

And now we can actually *do* things. We won't have to be trapped inside this damn house."

Simon patted his leg tentatively.

"And, man, I can't wait to walk the dogs and Pirate again. It's been so long. And you know what else I can't wait for?" Jack dropped his voice and pushed himself closer to Simon.

"Hm?"

"I can't wait to fuck you on every surface of the house."

"Eep" was what came out of Simon's mouth, which usually portended good things where sex was concerned. But now Simon's jaw was clenched, his skin pale. He was staring straight ahead blankly.

"What's wrong?" Jack asked. "You okay?"

Simon stood up, every movement stiff and controlled. He opened his mouth, then closed it, and Jack could practically see all the words warring to get out. But the trap of Simon's throat got them.

"Are you sick?" Jack stood too and reached out a hand, but for the first time, Simon didn't take it.

Simon shook his head but he'd gone pale.

Jack knew he didn't understand what Simon went through. He knew that even when he was pretty sure he was getting it he was *not* getting it. But he thought he did a fairly good job of giving Simon the space to feel however he felt and know Jack would still be there. But these moments—when Simon felt a thousand miles away, when Simon seemed in danger from his own mind and body, when Simon didn't reach out to him—left Jack unmoored.

"Do you want to text?" he asked.

Simon just blinked, like the words made no sense.

"Wanna write it down?"

Jack grabbed his sketchbook and pen and held them out to Simon. Simon didn't take them, but he also didn't leave.

"Do you just need some time?" Jack asked.

When Simon still didn't answer, Jack talked to himself instead.

He's not doing this on purpose. He's not ignoring you. This isn't about you.

But it was difficult not to feel foolish when you told your boyfriend you wanted to fuck him and he didn't answer, went pale, and zoned out so hardcore that he didn't even speak to you.

There's nothing to be upset about. It's not about you.

"Darlin', can I touch you?"

Simon nodded, hard, once, and Jack pulled him into his arms. Something was going on and he didn't know what it was, but this was still Simon. He adored Simon. Simon was the best thing on two legs.

Usually when Simon was upset, Jack could feel his heart pounding and his limbs shaking. But Simon was motionless in his arms, like he was a statue, shallow breaths the only indication that anything was going on.

Finally, he felt something damp on his neck and realized Simon was crying, silent and still.

"What's wrong?" Jack said as gently as he could manage. "Please."

"I c-c-c-can't do that," Simon said. And he sounded like his heart was breaking.

Chapter Fifteen

Simon

A war was raging inside Simon. On one side was his foolish, breaking heart. It reared and bucked and wept, wanting nothing but to be held in Jack's arms forever. On the other side was his seasoned, resigned brain. It packed its bags carefully and walked away the second Jack made it clear that now that his leg was healed he expected them to have a normal relationship—one where they went out and did things and hung out with people. Because it knew that Simon couldn't be what Jack wanted.

The battleground was Simon's stomach, which roiled, his palms, which sweat, and his throat, which had clamped up tighter than a furled peony fist.

Jack was holding him so gently, hands sweetly stroking his back and his hair. The battle left Simon bloody in
all the places no one could ever see, and his pain leaked
tracks down his cheeks. It wasn't the same as crying, but
it was close.

"What can't you do?" Jack asked. "Fuck on every surface of the house? I think you can, but we don't have to.
The bed's nice too."

Jack was being kind, trying to lighten the moment, and
it made Simon loathe himself with a deep, painful upper-
cut that he'd worked years to stop throwing.

"I can't j-just g-g-go out."

It was soft, but Jack heard. Jack steered him back to the
couch and he let himself be led because *god* how he wanted
Jack to magically have a solution. Wouldn't that be something? If all along the solution to his problem had been
held by a stranger.

But of course Jack didn't have a solution.

"I didn't mean like go to bars every night or anything,"
Jack backpedaled. "But we can go to the movies and out
to dinner and to ball games and…and…hiking?"

Simon imagined going to a football or basketball game.
Imagined the yells of thousands of strangers, the way they'd
stare at him when he didn't shout for the team, the gutting
exposure if the camera should land on him, projecting his
face for the whole stadium to see.

And even if it was just going out to dinner, sooner or
later Jack's friends would invite him to a dinner party or
a birthday celebration. Jack would want him to go. And
Simon would let him down the way he'd let him down at

Charlie's. Or he'd try and the whole event would become about Simon and how he was doing and was he coping all right and could he handle it, not about the event at all. And little by little he'd resent it and he'd stop saying yes. And Jack would resent that he stopped trying. And then... well, once there was resentment on both sides, how could they go on?

Simon was trying to find a way to say these things that didn't sound fatalistic, like he wasn't even willing to try, but Jack was looking at him so warmly. He was so beautiful. Warm. Strong.

Simon reached out a hand and pressed it to Jack's chest, trying to soak up his warmth.

"You don't understand," he said as gently as he could. "You want to d-do boyfriend things and I just c-can't."

"You don't know that."

Shame boiled into anger. It was so fucking unfair that this gorgeous, kind, perfect man couldn't grasp Simon's utter imperfection.

"I do!" Simon yelled. "You couldn't walk when you had a b-broken leg. No matter how hard you t-t-tried, you couldn't because it was fucking b-broken. Now it's healed but I'm n-not. I won't. I can't do these things! You won't w-w-want me outside this d-d-d-damn house!"

A look of almost cartoon puzzlement slid onto Jack's face.

"No, I... I do."

"Do you?" Simon demanded. "Do you want to take me to parties and-and-and restaurants? Do you want to know that I'll say no nine times out of t-ten? Or that halfway through I might lose my sh-shit like at Ch-Charlie's and have to leave?"

An engine of certainty was driving out the fear and heartbreak. This was all he had to do. Convince Jack this was doomed and neither of them would suffer any longer.

So he gave voice to his deepest fear as if it were an obvious truth.

"You've been bored out of your mind and I was here. You were interested in me because you had n-nothing else. But now you do again, so I know I won't s-s-seem as sh-shi-shiny."

"Wha… *That's* what you think?"

Simon set his jaw and stared. He nodded once. He watched the moment when the man he had fallen in love with winced as his words hit home. Then, with as much dignity as he could muster, Simon got his coat and left.

Chapter Sixteen

Jack

When Charlie drove up, Jack was sitting outside on a stump, walking boot in place, Pirate perched on his shoulder. She jumped down as Charlie approached and rubbed against Charlie's leg. Jack pouted.

"Traitor," he muttered.

"Can't believe you're not out doing everything the doc said you can do yet," Charlie said. He held up a paper bag. "Brought some sandwiches. I got one for Simon too. Not sure what he likes, so I got three different and figured he could choose first."

"He's not here."

"Oh. Okay. Well, you can just save it for him for later if you—"

Jack pushed himself up and stormed into the house before Charlie could finish his thought. He imagined Simon's tuna salad or turkey or ham sandwich waiting, neatly wrapped, in the refrigerator for a man who never came back. Jack's throat tightened.

Charlie closed the door behind him.

"What's up?"

His voice was infuriatingly gentle; inviting.

"Don't do that thing," Jack snapped. He wanted to rip the world to pieces, beginning with himself.

"What thing?"

"That *thing* you do where you sound like I can tell you anything and you know everything. Just…don't."

Jack closed his eyes.

"You *can* tell me anything," Charlie said, low and soft so Jack instantly felt like shit for being mad.

Jack banged around the kitchen, putting food in the animals' bowls and wiping up imaginary spills on the counter. The plastic of the walking boot made his right leg longer than his left so he had to stay up on his left toes a bit, making them ache. He wondered if he could get a shoe insert or something to even it out.

Charlie sat silently at the kitchen table and pet each animal as they ran to get their dinner. The bag of sandwiches lay untouched on the table until Mayonnaise jumped into Charlie's lap and, smelling something she liked, tried to crawl inside the bag. Charlie scooped the cat up with one hand and chucked the bag into the fridge.

Finally, when all the animals had eaten and there was nothing more Jack could pretend to clean up, he put the sponge down, took a deep breath, and said, "I think I fucked up."

They ate all three sandwiches (tuna, turkey, and ham; Jack had been right) and Jack told Charlie what had happened.

When he finished, Charlie frowned.

"What do I do? How do I convince him he's not some… some distraction?"

It hurt Jack to even say the word. Was that what Simon had been thinking when they kissed? When they touched each other? When they laughed together? That Jack was momentarily entertained. The sandwiches lurched in his stomach.

"I don't think that's the part to focus on," Charlie said slowly. "That's the thing he told himself *because* of the part you should focus on."

"And that is?!" Jack prompted when Charlie paused. He had a flash of Simon and himself sitting at this very table and Simon irritatedly instructing Jack to tell him every-thing.

"The part about how you want different things for the future. If you want a boyfriend who will go out and do things with you all the time and he doesn't want to go out and do those things, then it makes sense he'd tell himself that you would lose interest."

Anger sluiced through Jack, thick and hot.

"I would never *do* that; who the fuck do you think I am?"

"Bro, losing interest isn't something you do on purpose. It isn't something you *do* at all. Listen to what he was telling you: he cannot give you the things you told him you want. You *told* him you couldn't wait to not be stuck in the house. The house is where he feels safe. That's facts."

"I know that."

"Do you?"

Irritation flared Jack's nostrils and he felt fidgety and overheated.

"Stop," Charlie said. He put a heavy hand on Jack's arm.

"What?" Jack snapped.

"I'm not accusing you of anything. I'm asking. Would you want to be in a relationship with Simon if he could not go out to dinner with you or to a basketball game or to the market?"

"Well, yeah, of course," Jack said, barely containing his eye-roll.

"Yeah? Because Simon is worried that you won't. And— No, shut up, I'm not done. Simon is worried that you won't. Not because you're a bad boyfriend or a bad person. He's worried because he thinks you have an unrealistic understanding of what future you're choosing if you choose him. Do you get that?"

Jack opened his mouth to say that of course he did, then he remembered how still Simon had stood in his arms. He hadn't been vibrating with anxiety as he usually was in such moments. He'd been frozen. Resigned. He'd thought he'd already lost.

"Keep talking," Jack said, and slumped lower in his seat.

"You're such a romantic, bro. You think if you love him enough you can change the whole world. It's sweet, but it's not real. This is how Simon's brain works. You can't change that just by loving him to hell and back."

"I don't want to change him," Jack said, but he knew it was a lie before the words even hit the air. He *did* want things to be different for Simon. Easier. Less painful. "Well. Okay. I…"

"I know, bro. I've wanted to change shit for you a hundred times." Jack opened his mouth to ask when, but Charlie looked away. "Anyway, I think Simon sees how much you wish you could snap your fingers and make things better for him. But when you want that, what you're wishing is that he was a different person. One he's never gonna be. And that probably feels like shit."

Of course. Of course that's how Simon's ravenous brain metabolized Jack's careless words.

Jack thought about being able to reach out and take Simon's hand in his whenever he wanted. Being able to lean over and press a kiss to his cheek, his brow, his mouth. But the visions that he pictured were out in the world. Holding hands as they chose which flowers to plant or standing close as they reached the summit of a trailhead and gazed at the vista below.

"What was it like," Jack said slowly. "When we came to dinner. What was it like for you?"

He'd been so focused on Simon that he hadn't even noticed Charlie's reaction, other than being grateful his brother had been kind.

"It was hard," Charlie said. "Hard to see him so uncomfortable. I felt guilty, like it was my fault for trying to talk to him. But I would've felt rude if I'd just talked at him and not asked any questions. I wasn't sure what I could do to avoid hurting him, and that felt bad."

Jack's stomach lurched. This was what Simon had been trying to tell him and he hadn't understood. He hadn't understood even though he'd been with him the whole time. Simon was always choosing between hurting himself or feeling like he was hurting someone else. And if they were together, that someone else would often be Jack.

Puddles whimpered from the other room and Jack pushed himself to his feet, only wincing slightly at the weakness and ache in his leg. In the living room, Puddles had wedged himself against the couch and was glaring at the fire. A log had cracked at the bark line and left a jagged, burned out section that looked like a lightning bolt.

"It's okay, baby," Jack told him. He slid the poker into the fire and crushed the chunk to glowing coals. Puddles pressed against his leg and licked his hand.

Charlie sat on the couch while Jack stoked the fire and gave Puddles a rub.

"I hope you don't give up," Charlie said after minutes of silence.

"On Simon? I won't," Jack said, a bit hurt that Charlie'd drawn that conclusion from their conversation.

The mildness of Charlie's voice didn't mitigate the sting when he said, "Don't let Simon shut you down without a fight. Not if you want him in your life. Not if you're willing to work to make a life together. He's good for you. I hope you fight to be good for him."

Charlie plucked Pickles off his leg and set her down on the couch, then crossed to stand in front of Jack. The hand on Jack's shoulder was as familiar as his brother's intense gaze.

"Fighting sometimes means working your ass off to understand," he said. "Simon's been honest with you. Have you done the same?"

Jack blinked. Charlie wasn't usually so given to speechmaking and wisdom-dropping and something told Jack he should appreciate it while he had it.

"No," he said.

"Then that's where you start. Figure out what the truth is, then you can bring it to Simon and see where you are."

Jack looked down and nodded.

"Thanks."

He let his head tip forward just enough to feel Charlie's shoulder brush his hair. Charlie squeezed him almost painfully tight and ruffled his hair.

"I like him," he said.

"Yeah," Jack said. "Yeah, I like him too."

Chapter Seventeen

Simon

If you had told Simon Burke when he woke up this morning that he'd end the day with his heart broken, he wouldn't have been terribly surprised. After all, things with Jack had seemed too good to be true every single day they'd spent together—it was about time, right?

What *did* surprise Simon was his reaction. He could only remember having it once before, when his grandfather died.

He was utterly numb.

He was sitting in his car in the middle of a clearing in the woods somewhere a twenty-minute drive from Jack's house, and every part of him was numb except for a hot, tight pain in his throat.

His heart wasn't racing; it was slugging. His breath wasn't fast; it was deep. His hands weren't shaking or twitching; they were lead. In fact he'd pulled over because his entire body felt like it was moving at half-speed.

The only thing he could focus on was the voice in his head, explaining everything very, very clearly.

Jack would get back to his life. Going out with friends, spending time with his brother, and walking the animals himself. He might miss Simon at first, but then he'd be scrubbed from Jack's life as easily as deleting the PetShare app.

And when Jack's life went back to the way it had been, so would Simon's.

No more pack. No more touches. No more conversation. No more Jack.

Just Simon, alone, in his grandmother's basement.

Simon opened the car door and calmly, numbly, vomited into the rotting leaves.

Simon wasn't sure where he'd driven, but he'd sent his grandmother a text telling her not to expect him home that night before curling up in the backseat of his car and falling asleep. He awoke the next morning feeling even more frozen than he'd been the day before, like the cold had crept into his bones while he was unconscious.

He blasted the heat and drove some more. It was dusk when he got home. The porch light was on and his grandmother was cleaning the kitchen when he got inside.

He slumped onto a chair.

One of the best things about his grandmother was that she wouldn't force him to talk.

"Jack was here," she said.

"What? When? Why?"

Her raised eyebrow was only half scornful.

"He said you ran away."

Simon snorted, the phrase conjuring images of himself at eight, misunderstood, tying a jam sandwich into a bandana, and stomping off into the woods.

Then it struck him that he had done almost precisely that—sans sandwich—and he bit his tongue.

"What else did he say?" he asked grudgingly.

Grandma Jean gave the counter a final wipe and gathered an armful of baking supplies to return to the pantry. The cream of tartar next to the oven and the current lack of a plate of cookies on the counter told Simon they'd done more than talk.

"You baked him snickerdoodles!" he accused.

"I did," she confirmed.

Simon sulked in the chair, but couldn't quite bring himself to say, *He broke my heart and you betrayed me.*

"He seemed like he needed them."

"No one *needs* cookies," Simon grumbled.

"No, but sometimes people need someone to do something that shows kindness."

Simon slumped farther.

"What happened, dear?" his grandmother asked, sitting across from him.

"What did Jack say happened?"

He sounded sulky and childish even to himself.

"He seemed really disappointed you weren't here," she said very gently.

Simon shrugged again.

The numbness was back. Of course Jack was disappointed. Jack was kind and wouldn't want things to be uncomfortable between them. He knew that Simon loved the animals so he would probably tell him he could come walk them sometimes. But then winter would come and the snow and they wouldn't see each other much. By spring Jack would have forgotten all about him and the next time they ran into each other years from now, at the grocery store or the gas station, the last few months would fade to a hearty hail-fellow-well-met wave of Jack's strong arm and the nod that Simon would give because he didn't trust his hand not to shake.

"Did you hear me, dear?" his grandmother asked.

"What?"

"I said you should talk to Jack. Whatever he said that upset you, he clearly cares about you. He wouldn't want you feeling this way."

"I can't."

"Why not?"

"Because, he…" He shook his head. "It was fine when he needed a dog-walker. When he was stuck in the house. Bored and wanting a distraction. I was better than being by himself. But now… If things were normal for him we would never have met and I'd never have fallen—"

"Oh, sweetheart," she said, and mortification washed over him. How could he have thought this was real? How could he have thought that Jack would truly want him once he was healthy again.

"I don't want— I can't talk about it," he choked out.

"You don't have to talk, but you have to listen to me now. Are you listening?"

He nodded.

"Things can happen to us in the course of our regular routine that change our lives forever. We could be hit by a car crossing the street. Just because something's routine doesn't make it safe. Or right. Or best. Things can happen because we deviate from that routine too. It doesn't matter. What matters is being open and honest about where you are. And where you are is that you've met a wonderful man. You care about him. He clearly cares about you."

Simon blinked hard and avoided looking at her, but she tugged his hand.

"Don't make the mistake of letting fear convince you that you already know the end of the story. Don't cheat yourself out of something wonderful because you're too scared to take a risk."

"But I'm—"

"No," she interrupted. "You're not talking now. You're listening and then you're going to bed to think about what you heard."

"Yes, ma'am."

"Jack is very handsome."

His head jerked up. She had a dreamy look on her face. He nodded.

"He made the cookies. I just told him what to do."

Simon raised an eyebrow to say, *Okay, and?*

"He listened. He listened when I told him how to cream the butter and he listened when I told him that he might need to give you a little time to get your head around things."

Jack always listened. He listened to Simon's fears and feelings, his ideas and desires. Jack listened.

"Someone who listens—really listens? That's not someone to throw away, Simon. That's someone you fight to talk to because when they listen it's worth it. That's someone you have to listen to right back. Did you?"

Had Simon? Had he really listened to what Jack was saying, or had he stopped listening to Jack and begun listening to himself?

"Shit."

"Yes."

Simon dropped his forehead to the kitchen table.

"Go to sleep, dear. Think about things. But don't wait too long."

Chapter Eighteen

Jack

The first night after Simon left had felt long, but Jack had a mission then: to think honestly about what he needed. The second night after Simon left was the longest night of Jack's life. It didn't help that he'd eaten approximately a dozen snickerdoodles and couldn't tell if he was nauseated or hungry for something not made of cinnamon and sugar.

He'd gathered dead limbs from the clearing for kindling, chopped half a cord of wood by porch light, cleaned the kitchen and bathroom until they stank of vinegar, organized his office, and brushed the animals until their coats shone. Well, except for Rat's. Hers never shone, no matter what.

Every ten minutes he fought the urge to jump in his truck and go back to Simon's house. But Jean had told him to be patient; that Simon would come to him when he was ready. He believed her, but...he hadn't thought it would be this hard.

When morning came, Jack paused at every sound, hoping to hear Simon's car crunching up the drive. But it didn't come.

He threw on a coat and took the pack for a short and stumbling walk. The walk was short because he was obeying the doctor's orders to take it easy at first (not to mention it was slow going walking in the cumbersome boot), but the truth was it terrified him that Simon might come to find him when he wasn't there.

But Simon didn't come.

It was absurd: eight months of self-imposed exile in his cabin, followed by two months of wishing more than anything he could get out and not being able to. Now finally he was able to leave and he didn't dare.

He took the pack on another short walk that evening and finally passed out on the couch as the sun set, exhausted enough to sleep through the night.

He woke early, fed the animals, and took them for another short walk. He could tell he was overdoing it. His shin ached and his left calf was starting to complain about him walking half on tiptoes.

This was the thing he'd longed for every time Simon left the house, and now that he had it all he could think was that he wished Simon were with him.

He thought he understood what had happened. Simon

had convinced himself this would never work and when Simon convinced himself of things it was very hard to convince him otherwise. And Jack didn't know how he could. How could you tell someone that the things they had experienced time after time were not true in this instance? He couldn't.

But maybe he could show him.

When he got home he showered quickly, mind made up.

No more being patient, no more waiting for Simon to struggle through this alone. He might have had to wait for him to come to the house before, but now Jack was going to get him.

Jack dragged his clothes on over still-damp skin, shoved a beanie over his wet hair, and pulled on his boots.

"I'll be back," he announced to the pack. "And I'm bringing Simon with me. Hopefully. Fuck, okay, bye."

Pirate meowed in what Jack chose to take as encouragement and Jack whipped the front door open determinedly, beginning his quest as he intended to go on.

And almost ran smack into someone standing outside his door.

There, on his porch, stood Simon, hand raised to knock, just as he'd been the first moment Jack had seen him.

Only this time, he wasn't looking down with his shoulders hunched up to his ears. He was looking right at Jack, electric blue eyes burning, with shadows beneath them that spoke of his own sleeplessness.

Relief and desperation warred in his chest and he dragged Simon inside, suddenly worried he might bolt again.

"I was just coming to get you."

Simon dropped into a crouch to greet the animals who swamped him, scratching ears, kissing heads, and attempting to untangle his scarf from Pickles' grasp.

"Did your grandma tell you I came by?"

Simon nodded and stood. "You made snickerdoodles."

"Yeah. Though if I never see another cookie it'll be too soon. I kinda ate them all."

They stood facing each other, awkwardly staring. Jack reached out and put his hands on Simon's shoulders.

"Can we talk?"

Simon bit his lip and nodded. It was clear he knew Jack was actually asking if *he* could talk now.

Jack wanted to kiss him more than anything. Wanted to twine his fingers into Simon's soft, messy hair and cradle his skull, and kiss him so he didn't have to talk. But he simply squeezed Simon's shoulders.

"I didn't listen well the other day," Simon said softly. "I thought you were done with me—that we had to be done. Now that you can do everything by yourself again."

At Simon's tone Bernard let out a baleful howl and pressed himself against Simon in a sweet move that would have sent Simon pitching sideways if Jack's hands hadn't been on his shoulders. It felt so right to have Simon in his arms, leaning on him, and he pulled Simon against his chest.

"Not a chance, darlin'. Never be done with you."

Simon let out a *whuff* of breath that was half sob and half swallowed sound. The arms around Jack's waist were so tight it was nearly painful. He stroked a hand up and down Simon's back, relished Simon's breath against his neck.

"Let's go talk in the bedroom."

"Fewer paws and tails," Simon agreed absently and followed him.

Jack forced himself to swallow any bad *tail* jokes he might have been tempted to make and gently shooed Puddles and Louis out of the room.

"Can you—" Jack said at the same time as Simon said, "I was—"

"You go," Jack said. He sat on the bed.

Simon paced. When he spoke, it came out in a sluice.

"I got scared that if things were back to normal for you then what would you need me for? And then winter would come and by spring you'd have forgotten me mostly and maybe the animals would have t-too. And I would miss them so much. And you. Obviously. Of course you. And—and then once I got scared I wasn't listening to you, but I spent all day yesterday driving and thinking and it's not just that I was scared you wouldn't want me anymore but like if you did then what if I couldn't be a b-boyfriend—a good boyfriend—cuz I'm all me-like and then I just wanted to be walking with you and the pack and so. I'm here," he finished weakly.

Jack plucked out the key words and it was no surprise what they were. *Scared*, *scared*, and *scared*. Scared of losing Jack, scared that Jack wouldn't want him the way he was, scared to lose the animals. But also *want*. Simon was scared but he wanted him, this.

"I'm scared too," he admitted. That got Simon's attention. "I don't always know how to help you. How you want me to respond. I feel awful when I know you're having a hard time and I can't fix it."

"You can't fix it," Simon said flatly. "*It* is me."

Jack cursed his choice of words.

"I shouldn't have said it like that. I didn't mean fix you, I meant that I want to be able to make everything better for you. I would want that whether you were anxious or you had a headache. I don't like seeing you suffer."

"I can stay away when that's—"

"Christ, am I saying everything wrong or are you in a really negative mood right now?"

Simon glared and Jack remembered that he'd said nearly the same thing to Charlie when Charlie had said he hadn't liked seeing him suffer over the last eight months.

"Well, did you like seeing me suffer with my leg?" Jack tried.

Simon rolled his eyes.

"Please, that wasn't suffering, you were just a huge baby about it."

Jack was about to get annoyed at Simon for the first time when he saw the smile at the corner of Simon's mouth.

"I'm just being…careful, I guess," Simon said. "Sorry."

Jack could hardly fault him for it. He knew all about being careful.

"C'mere."

Simon stood between Jack's knees at the edge of the bed and Jack curled hands around his hips.

"I don't want to steal time with you," Jack said. "I don't want this to be some affair that plays out in my house but never sees sunlight. I want this to be real. That's what I was trying to say yesterday. That was all I was trying to say."

"Yeah, but when you say real, you mean…in p-public. With p-people. And—and—and I j-just…"

The quiver of Simon's lip made Jack want to wrap him up in his arms and never let him go, but he'd learned by now that Simon's stutter just happened and Simon got annoyed if Jack took it as an indication to treat him more gently.

"Yes," Jack said, stroking Simon's hair. "If I'm being completely honest. In public like we can go to the grocery store together or take a vacation, yeah. For me, yeah, that's what I imagine when I imagine being with you. And people? Well, they'd be there, yes, but I'm not under any illusions about how you feel around people. And it's not like I'm some social butterfly."

Simon nodded, brow furrowed.

"But I want to be with *you*, Simon. I don't want to be with an imaginary Simon who loves making small talk with strangers or singing karaoke in a crowded bar."

He watched the color drain out of Simon's face at the word *karaoke*.

"You could have anyone," Simon whispered.

Jack tugged him down onto the bed.

"What does that mean, darlin'?"

"You could have someone…" He shook his head. "I don't know."

Jack kissed him.

"I don't want anyone. I want you."

Simon let himself be kissed but he was zoning out. Jack

could practically see the thoughts zinging around in his head as if he were a translucent collection of energy transfers.

"Simon."

"Hm."

"Simon," he said louder.

"Huh?"

Simon blinked, eyes wide.

"Where are you?"

Simon blinked some more.

"What are you thinking right now?"

"I w-want a hug."

Relief struck Jack. He hadn't really expected an answer and he certainly hadn't expected that one.

He pulled Simon into his arms and pulled the covers over them. He held Simon tight and Simon clung to him.

There was so much he wanted to say, but this clearly wasn't the moment.

"'M so tired," Simon mumbled against his neck.

"Me too. Wanna sleep a bit?"

"Mm."

Simon fell asleep almost instantly. Jack breathed in the smell of his shampoo and the faint wool smell of his sweater. Simon's breath was warm and Jack was so happy to have him here, in his bed, in his arms. The rest could wait until tomorrow.

Chapter Nineteen

Simon

Simon woke slowly to the sound of Jack's quiet snores. From the light outside it looked like afternoon, which meant they'd slept for hours. Simon had rolled away from Jack in his sleep. He snuggled back into the larger man's arms.

He'd been out of it that morning, but now he could appreciate every smell and sensation, and nothing had ever felt better than being in Jack's arms.

He pressed a kiss to Jack's lips and Jack smiled in his sleep. Simon stroked his hair back and Jack pressed closer. He ran gentle knuckles along Jack's cheekbone and the several days of stubble gleaming on his jaw.

"Mmm." Jack woke, pulling Simon closer. "Love you," he rumbled into Simon's ear, then he kissed his ear and his temple.

Once, as a boy, Simon had been wading into the stream behind his grandparents' house, jeans cuffed to his knees. He'd seen a fish or a sparkle of sunlight that resembled a fish a few yards downstream and gone to investigate. One moment, he was standing on the slick but solid clay at the bottom of the stream. The next moment he took a step and the ground was gone. He plunged into the water as if water was all there had ever been.

Jack's sleep-tender words closed over Simon's head like the shocking embrace of that unexpected water.

In the next moment, Jack stilled. Simon could feel him wake fully and realize what he'd said, but he kept his eyes firmly fixed on Jack's throat.

"I… Simon, I…"

"You don't have to," Simon said quickly. "You were asleep. I know it doesn't count—"

"Would you hush?" Jack said.

He scooted down so they were face-to-face. His hazel eyes were soft, vulnerable. He cupped Simon's cheek in one warm hand.

"Simon, I love you. I've never…loved someone before. But I love the hell out of you."

"You…do?"

Jack's smile was slow and warm, and Simon thought it was for himself, which made it all the more beautiful.

"I really do. This is how it feels, huh? I've always wondered."

"But if you've never...how do you know?"

It wasn't at all what Simon had meant to say, but Jack just smiled and shrugged.

"Same way I know you love me back."

Something warm and light crept through Simon. Something easy and joyous and powerful.

"Pretty sure of yourself," he teased.

He felt as if every muscle in his body had suddenly gone loose and easy.

"Simon," Jack said, pouting. "Tell me. Tell me I'm right."

Simon's heart pounded the most beautiful rhythm. He shrugged and arranged his face into a casual, uninterested expression, then rolled onto his back, crossing his arms under his head.

"Simon!" Jack went up on an elbow and looked down at him. "I love you. Come on."

He playfully shoved at Jack's shoulder but Jack was immovable.

"See, you're used to me having a broken leg but now I'm back—ouch." He winced. "Uh, well, I will be anyway, and then you're in for it."

"Yeah? What am I in for exactly?"

The teasing fell away. Jack swung a knee over and suddenly Simon was looking up into his face as Jack straddled him.

Jack's eyes were intent on his, then they were kissing. Kissing like the world would end. Jack's mouth was hot and his hands were everywhere. They'd never been in this position before and it was instantly Simon's favorite thing.

Jack above and around him, the bed below him. There wasn't a molecule of him unoccupied.

Jack slid a questing hand under his sweater, running fingers along his ribs and around his belly button, then brushing his nipples. Simon slung arms around his neck and chased his mouth when Jack pulled back.

"Simon."

Simon groaned as Jack touched him, strong fingers stroking his cock through his pants.

"Simon, tell me."

If Simon could have formed the words, they would have been something like: *Jack, I'm so in love with you. I'm so in love with you that when I thought you didn't want me something inside me died. I want to stay here with you, forever, like this.*

Jack got his pants open and Simon tried to wiggle out of them but they got stuck around his thighs. Jack didn't seem to care, though. He dragged Simon's underwear down and his first rough stroke to Simon's cock made Simon gasp. He felt warm and relaxed and so turned on he never wanted it to end.

Jack wasn't letting him do anything but kiss him and hold on to him.

"Simon," Jack said hot in his ear, demanding and plaintive. "Simon, tell me you love me."

Simon gasped as Jack worked him, hard and fast and so damn sweet. He opened his mouth to moan and saw a flicker in Jack's eyes. Just the tiniest falter, as if he might not be as sure of Simon's feelings as he pretended.

Simon felt heat gathering in his balls and his guts and he clenched his stomach.

"I love you," Simon gasped. "I love you, Jack, please, I love you."

Jack's expression was so joyful Simon wanted to cry. Instead, Jack twisted his fist and pleasure blasted through Simon. He came hard and hot over Jack's hand.

Jack groaned and dropped his forehead to Simon's.

"Thank you," he said. "Thank you, thank god."

Simon stroked Jack's back the way Jack had done so many times to him and Jack kissed Simon's cheek.

"Love you," he murmured and Simon murmured it back.

"Want you," Jack said, pressing his hard cock against Simon's hip.

"I'm yours," Simon said, and he'd never meant anything more in his life.

Their clothes were gone in seconds and Jack fumbled lube and a condom from the nightstand. Simon still wasn't quite used to the sensation of fingers breaching him. It took a few moments for his body to adjust. But Jack seemed like he'd happily finger him forever, so Simon enjoyed it.

"You're so fucking hot like this," Jack said. "I love watching your ass take my fingers. Love the way you make that little sound every time I slide inside you."

Simon's breath caught as Jack touched him deeper inside.

"Yeah, that one."

Jack bent and took Simon's cock in his mouth, cleaning off his come and getting him half hard again in the process. Jack swallowed around him while he stroked over his prostate and Simon was writhing again.

"Yeah, baby, that's fucking gorgeous."

"Jack," Simon moaned. He could never find words when

he was in bed with Jack. It was as if his mouth was made only for kissing and sucking and all other communication was in the language of touch.

"I love you, Simon, fuck I love you."

Jack pushed inside him and they both groaned. Jack looked down at him, hazel eyes heavy-lidded with desire. They breathed each other's air and Simon smiled. He had never felt closer to anyone.

When Jack started to move, Simon squeezed his eyes shut and hung on, pulling his knees up so that Jack could fuck him deeper, harder. As Jack pulled him down at the shoulders and snapped his hips into him, Simon realized what he'd meant when he'd said he couldn't wait to fuck Simon after he got his cast off. The position was so intimate, Simon couldn't help but feel every breath and touch.

Just when Simon thought he couldn't take any more Jack shifted his hips up and each stroke drove Simon closer and closer to the edge. Jack closed a hand around his cock and Simon exploded, convulsing and babbling nonsense as the pleasure took him apart.

As his head swam, he heard Jack groan, and then he was crushed against Jack's chest as Jack lost it inside him.

"Fuuuck," Jack moaned, turning them to their sides as he collapsed so he didn't crush Simon and burying his face in Simon's neck.

Simon made a noise he hoped sounded like agreement but he was too fucked out to speak.

Later they dragged themselves out of bed and showered, but couldn't stop touching. Jack kept putting his lips to Simon's skin and mouthing something that Simon was pretty sure was *I love you*. It flushed him so full of joy that he mistook the feeling in his stomach for elation until it growled loudly enough to remind him there was a world outside of Jack.

But even as they ate, Simon couldn't stop reaching out to prove to himself with his own two hands that Jack was his for the touching.

When it was time for the animals' evening walk, they clipped on leashes together and walked out the door. This felt nothing like Jack's pained attempt to accompany them on his crutches. Jack's gait was uneven, but they strolled slowly together, not speaking, as if they had taken this walk a hundred times before.

And they had. Just not together.

Jack held Bernard's and Rat's leashes and Simon held Puddles' and Dandelion's. The dogs seemed delighted by this turn of events, happily sniffing and bumping at both their legs to start, then repeatedly weaving their leashes together, leaving Jack and Simon to navigate a nearly constant game of cat's cradle to untangle them.

Pirate pranced boldly in the lead, caring nothing for the chaos unfolding behind her.

"I wanted this," Jack said after they'd walked a while. "Once we started...you know, every time you'd leave with them I wished I was going with you."

It was so similar to what Simon had wished every time he'd been out here that it gave him chills.

"Me too."

They paused in a clearing and let the dogs off-leash to run around for a little while.

"I was thinking," Simon said. "You should write it anyway. The book about you and Charlie. If it matters to you, then you should do it and screw that g-guy."

Jack pressed his back against the trunk of a nearby tree and kissed him senseless.

"Thanks," Jack said. "I could. But I'm not sure I need to anymore."

"What changed?"

Jack cracked his knuckles and stared thoughtfully at the sky.

"It was the first thing I ever thought of doing by myself. The writing, the story, the drawing. That was a big deal to me. But... I don't know, it's not the only story I can tell. It was Davis' betrayal that hurt the most. The fact that he'd do that to me. But now that it's done, maybe I don't want to write about the past. Maybe I want to write something completely new."

Jack leaned in and kissed him gently on the lips.

"Completely new sounds good to me," Simon agreed.

Chapter Twenty

Jack

If you had asked Jack Matheson six months ago whether love could heal a hurting heart, he'd have scoffed. And sulked. And scoffed some more.

Now, three weeks after telling Simon Burke he loved him and learning he was loved in return, Jack found himself in the curious position of feeling like a new man.

Not because this new love had erased past scars. Those were still there. But because it provided him with a true north that pulled all other things into alignment.

Love was the morning mist in the Wyoming mountains—billions of water droplets containing whole worlds, suspended in air.

It had been three weeks since they'd said *I love you*, and now Jack was learning who boyfriend-Simon was. Learning his nature and behavior the way he'd done with each new animal that joined his pack; with each figure he taught himself to draw. If you could learn the truth of a creature then you could provide what it needed, represent it faithfully.

Simon was spending more and more time at Jack's cabin during the days, bringing his computer and working at the kitchen table. After a few hours he'd move to sit on the floor in the living room with his back against the couch so he could touch all the animals. They'd arrange themselves around him like a sundial and Jack would find him with his computer resting precariously on one knee to accommodate Dandelion sprawled over his feet, Bernard's head on his thigh, and Mayonnaise draped half on the couch and half on his shoulder.

Though the position was clearly awkward, Simon would look up and smile at him, playing with Bernard's soft ears with one hand and holding his computer up with the other.

One afternoon he was pulled from his desk by the unfamiliar sound of Simon ranting at his computer, beautiful face twisted into a scowl.

"What's wrong?"

He was met with a furious explanation that he didn't properly understand about why Bill fucking Einhorn was a fucking asshole who was making Simon's life miserable and ruining his design.

"I could kill him!" Simon concluded.

Since he couldn't offer anything in the way of content-based assistance, Jack said, "Wanna hit things with an axe?"

"Yes," Simon said without hesitation.

Which is how Jack came to know that when Simon got mad he got *mad*, and also that he looked incredibly hot with his face flushed from exertion, his muscles taut, and his hairline damp with sweat.

He learned that Simon liked to wake up with Jack's arms wrapped tight around him so that if his heart decided to start pounding or his breath decided to stutter, Simon would know that Jack had him.

The first time they'd gone grocery shopping together had made Jack's week. He didn't know why he'd fixated on that particular marker of togetherness, but walking through the brightly lit aisles with Simon had filled him with a deep satisfaction. He'd never done it with a date before. He could only ever remember going with his mother when she forgot and had to zip out at the last minute.

Simon had been grumpy about Jack's glee and Jack knew he'd really been scared the experience wouldn't live up to Jack's expectations of boyfriend-ness, though Jack had told him a hundred times that he didn't have expectations. When Simon had reached for his arm in the check-out line, Jack had pulled him close with an arm around his waist and felt Simon exhale and press closer and he'd been filled with utter smug contentment.

He'd begun going to dinner at Simon and Jean's on Tuesday and Friday nights, so he learned that when Simon and Jean had a few glasses of wine together they were funny

242 Better Than People

and giggly and got extremely passionate about embroidery. And knitting. And tatting lace.

In theory, Jean was teaching him to bake, but Jack preferred sitting on the stool in the kitchen and watching Simon and Jean's practiced ballet of baking together, listening to them finish each other's sentences. "Should we add more—?"

"Yes, because of the—"

"That's what I thought too."

Once Jack fell asleep in the armchair while Simon and Jean watched a Hedy Lamarr movie and woke to find a hand-knit blanket tucking him in and a note from Simon that said *If you wake up, come downstairs*, to which Jean had added the following proviso: *Or come upstairs ;)*. Jack laughed and left the note on the kitchen counter with a heart on it for Jean before he went downstairs and told Simon.

"What do you think she'd do if I actually did go upstairs?" he asked, nuzzling at Simon's ear.

"Probably hit you with the baseball bat she keeps under the bed."

"It's not our first date," Simon insisted again. "We've eaten meals and watched movies and gone on walks and—and you've devirginized the hell out of me."

"*Yeah*, I did," Jack growled into the phone. "Still. First date as far as I'm concerned. Want me to pick you up or do you want to pick me up?"

Simon's sigh wasn't audible but Jack could sense it.

The date had been Simon's idea.

He'd woken Jack up early a few days before, straddled

his hips, and told him, eyes burning, that he and Jack were
going on a date. Jack had put him off, stroking hands down
his sides and telling him in no uncertain terms that they
did not have to do it. That he'd meant it when he'd said
they didn't need to eat dinner out to be happy.

That was how Jack came to know that when Simon put
his mind to something he was immovable. And though Jack
was pretty sure Simon had only offered for his benefit, Jack
wasn't about to tell him he couldn't do it.

Now, Simon's nerves were coming out in arguing over
the details.

"Simon, you know we don't have—"

"Fine, pick me up I guess," he interrupted.

Jack grinned. His boyfriend was brave as hell.

"Great. I'll be there at seven."

"Don't forget my boutonniere."

Jack could tell from his tone that this was snark, but he
didn't know which particular kind.

"The hell's a boutonniere?"

"The flower thing that—never mind. I'm making fun
of you."

Jack considered letting it go. He knew Simon was joking and he knew he was joking because he was nervous.

"This matters to me," Jack said, making sure his voice
was gentle. "I know it's not your thing, but since you offered, I want to take you out. I want to... I don't know,
treat you."

This time he did hear Simon's sigh.

"Okay. Sorry. I know."

"How freaked are you?"

"Not freaked exactly. Just...spinning a little."

"Worst-case scenario it for me."

"Um." He gave a nervous laugh that made Jack wish he could reach out and wrap Simon in his arms. "I'm a bad, boring date and make everything awkward because I get shy and you finally realize that d-dating me is more t-trouble than it's worth?"

"Okay, got it," Jack said, because he'd also learned that telling Simon his fears weren't going to come true wasn't helpful. "Well, if I decide I'm done with you I promise I'll still drive you home, how's that?"

Simon huffed.

"Fine, I'll see you at seven. I'll be the one without a boutonniere."

Simon opened the door, looking harassed, and peeked over his shoulder before hissing, "She wants to take our picture."

Jack smiled. "Sure."

"Why are you both acting like this is the prom?" Simon mumbled.

"Well, maybe this isn't the best moment," Jack said, and held out the boutonniere he'd drawn on scraps of tracing paper and attached with a safety pin.

"Oh my god."

"And before you ask, yes, I googled it."

Simon's expression went soft and he looked closer at the flowers Jack had drawn: peonies and thistles. Lush and soft; strong and sharp. They reminded Jack of Simon.

"You're such a geek," Simon said, but he wound his

arms around Jack's neck and kissed him. "Thank you," he whispered.

"You're welcome. You don't have to actually wear it."

Jack figured he wouldn't want to attract any added attention.

Simon ducked his head.

"Well. Pin it on me, anyway."

Jack heard the unspoken sentence that followed: *I want to know how it feels.*

Simon was wearing a navy wool sweater, soft and worn, and Jack pinned the paper flowers over his heart, then leaned in and kissed his cheek. Simon's eyelashes fluttered.

Jean snapped a picture of them, winked conspiratorially at Jack, and ushered them out the door.

"Have him home by eleven," she called.

Jack saluted and Simon huffed as he got in the truck.

"Let me guess," Simon said, rather accusingly. "You went to prom with the prettiest girl in your class."

"Nope. I didn't go."

"Oh. How come?"

"Well, the boy I had a crush on wasn't gay, and there wasn't anyone else I'd've wanted to go with. Besides, dances...not really my thing. I went to Big Sal's Diner with Vanessa, Sarah, and Ed, and Sarah's boyfriend of the moment, I don't remember his name. We ate a lot of fries and pancakes and got coffee-drunk."

Jack remembered getting home at two in the morning, wired and giggly, to find Charlie sitting at the kitchen table, account books from the hardware store spread out, a calculator by his elbow, and his eyes red-rimmed.

"Who'd you have a crush on?"

Jack told him about Mason.

Mason had been a skinny, angry streak of energy who stalked through the hallways like he resented the very building itself. He'd moved to town at the end of their junior year and Jack hadn't known much about him except that his father was a mechanic and Mason had driven a car that seemed to be Frankensteined together out of bits and pieces from other cars. Jack wasn't even sure *why* he'd been so taken with him. They'd never interacted beyond a nod or a borrowed pencil, but something about him had been magnetic.

"What about you?" Jack asked. "Any high school crushes?"

They pulled into the parking lot and Simon stiffened.

Jack parked and turned to face Simon, taking in his slow breaths and taut shoulders.

"You don't have to talk to anyone but me if you don't want to, okay?" Simon nodded. "I'll even order for you if you want."

Simon glared.

"Okay, then. Wanna give me that?" He pointed to the boutonniere.

Simon let him unpin it, but when Jack went to put it on the dashboard, Simon took it and slid it into his pocket.

"You okay?"

Simon nodded.

"Don't...don't ask me anymore, all right? I'll get annoyed even if I know you're just being nice."

"Okay." Jack kissed his cheek. "Let's go, I'm starved."

Once they were seated, Jack said, "So about those high school crushes?"

Simon blushed and shook his head.

"I don't know if they were even crushes, just...boys I thought were...whatever," he said.

Jack thought that was pretty much the definition of a high school crush, but he nodded.

Simon blushed even harder.

"There was this guy. Tom. He, uh..."

Simon was saved by the arrival of their waiter, and stumbled through ordering a drink. He stared at the tablecloth when she ran through the specials. Jack ordered them an appetizer to share.

"Tom," he prompted.

"Nothing," Simon said, squirming. "Just. He looked kind of like you."

Jack couldn't have predicted the warmth that would stoke in his belly.

"I didn't really think of it until now," Simon said.

Jack took his hand under the table and squeezed it.

"I'm honored to fulfill your high school desires," he teased.

Simon grinned.

"He was a dick, though. So don't fulfill them too thoroughly."

"Did he fuck with you? I'll kick his ass."

Jack said it lightly but the truth was he sometimes fantasized about going back in time to when Simon was younger and being the friend Simon had needed and never had. He would have gladly protected him from the whole world if he'd only been there.

Yet here Simon sat, battered by the waves of the world, but so beautiful, so strong, so kind he took Jack's breath away.

They were smiling at each other when the waiter came to take their order. Simon pointed at what he wanted on the menu and smiled at her.

"So, I did something kinda weird," Jack said once they'd ordered. "You know that book I like?"

Simon shot him a look that said, *Of course I know it, you talk about it constantly.*

"Okay, so… I emailed him. Corbin Wale. I'm not sure what made me do it, but I wrote him…a fan letter I guess. Told him how much I loved *Two Moons Over* and asked him a couple questions about writing it. I've never contacted any artist like that. I dunno what I was thinking."

Simon's smile was soft.

"You emailed him because you're ready to write your own *Two Moons Over.*"

He said it so simply, and with such certainty, that Jack just stared at him.

He hadn't told anyone about what he'd been working on the last few weeks. He hadn't even quite acknowledged it to himself. He'd told himself the pages and pages of drawings were just playing around, just getting back into the habit of drawing. He hadn't even used his sketchbook, just done them on the back of scrap printer paper and then stuffed them in a drawer.

But he supposed the project was emerging whether he'd

admitted it to himself or not. That morning he'd woken before dawn and hadn't been able to fall back asleep, not—for the first time in a long time—because of insomnia, but because the ideas were coming so fast he had to stumble to his desk to get them down before waking life swept them away. He'd need to start keeping a sketchbook on the bedside table like he used to.

"I think maybe you're right," Jack said slowly, mind on the stack of papers in his drawer and how later he would spread them out and see—really see—what he had.

"You can tell me when you're ready," Simon said. His hot blue gaze was steady and Jack felt like he was glimpsing the steel that lived inside Simon but rarely showed.

"I will. I just need to…think about it a little more."

Simon reached for his hand when a shadow fell over the table.

"Jack!" Vanessa said. "Christ, it's been an age. I thought maybe you perished of a rare broken-leg complication that also impaired one's ability to operate a mobile telephone."

She said it as lightly as she said everything, but Jack knew she was hurt by his withdrawal over the last year. He owed her an explanation and an apology. But not right now.

"Hey, Van. Nope, I'm miraculously healed."

He stood to show her his un-casted leg, and gave her a hug.

"This is Simon. My boyfriend."

He reached out a hand to Simon, but it was awkward with the table in the way and Simon gave an abortive rise, then sat back down, cheeks flushing.

"This is Vanessa, one of my oldest friends. She's one of

the ones I was just telling you I skipped prom with," Jack said, hoping Van would take the bait.

She shot him a look that said she one hundred percent knew what he was doing and would capitulate for the sake of his poor, shy boyfriend but expected a full explanation stat.

"Psh, prom," Van said. "Prom's for losers. We ate pancakes. Pancakes are for winners." She winked at Simon. "Right, babe?" she asked Rachel, who'd come up beside her.

"That pancakes are for winners? Absolutely right. Hey, Jack. Good to see you drag yourself down from the castle to mingle with the commoners."

Jack introduced Rachel and Simon and saw the glance Rachel and Van exchanged. Yeah, he'd definitely be getting a phone call soon.

"So what do you do, Simon?" Van asked.

"He's a graphic designer," Jack said. "And he's amazing."

"That's really cool, *Simon*," Van said, glaring at Jack.

Jack gave Simon an apologetic look.

Simon glanced at Van and Jack could see he'd slid his hand into the pocket where he'd put the boutonniere. Jack pledged to make him any number of talismans if they helped him feel grounded. Loved.

"Jack's trying to p-protect me," Simon said, voice shaky but there. "I get all w-w-weird with new p-people."

Van and Rachel instantly softened.

"People are the worst," Rachel pledged. Simon smiled.

"Well, we should hang out, the four of us," Van said. "Then we won't be new people anymore."

She smiled warmly at Simon and Jack felt a rush of gratitude for her friendship. He hadn't been a good friend the last year, but he wanted to be better.

"I'd really like that," Jack told her.

Simon nodded and smiled, even though he was looking at the table.

"Okay, we're leaving. I'm so glad I got to meet you, Simon," Van said. "I'll talk to *you* later." She pointed at Jack and Rachel winked at him.

They swept out and Simon closed his eyes and breathed through his nose. Jack slid a hand to his knee and left it there.

"You o—" He cut himself off, remembering what Simon had said in the car. "Sorry."

"I'm okay." He took another deep breath. "No, really, I am." He opened his eyes and gave Jack a weak but genuine smile. "They seem really nice."

"They're great. I wouldn't call Rachel *nice* exactly, but she's awesome. She teaches third grade. Her students all live in fear and worship her."

"I should've asked what she did. I should've asked more questions."

Simon's *should have*s were usually the push he needed to slide down the ramp of bad feeling, so Jack kissed his cheek and said, "You can ask them questions when we all hang out. Rachel will tell you stories that will make you wonder how children ever make it to adulthood and why adults ever have children."

Simon smiled.

"Dogs are way better than children. So are cats. And, like, pikas."

"Softer too," Jack added.

The food was good, but Jack only had eyes for Simon. They both turned down dessert and walked outside hand in hand.

The moon was full and the stars shone overhead. Halfway to the truck, Jack felt a spot of cold on his cheek and looked up to see the first snowfall of the season drifting down.

"Snow," he said, and pulled Simon close.

They looked up, white snow falling from a blue-black sky, promising the peace and silence of winter.

"I love the snow," Simon murmured.

Jack turned him and lifted his chin. Simon's eyes were wide, his cheeks flushed with cold, and his lips red from the wine he drank with dinner. He was the most beautiful thing Jack had ever seen.

"I love you," Jack said, stroking Simon's cheek.

It was cheesy and geeky and Jack had never meant anything more in his life.

"I love you too," Simon said. "I never thought I'd... I didn't..." He shook his head. "Kiss me," he murmured.

And Jack pressed Simon to his chest so their hearts could pound in conversation, and kissed him as the snow collected in their hair.

Chapter Twenty-One

Simon

Simon had always had a thing about Christmas. It would be simplest to say he didn't like it. But the truth was that he'd always longed for a Christmas that would feel, well, Christmassy.

Instead, Christmas was spent at his parents' house and consisted of a marathon session of dodging his family's well-meaning suggestions about his life, meeting his sister's boyfriend of the moment, each of whom was treated like a part of the family, and wondering why he came year after year when he always left miserable, feeling like a disappointment, and lugging a stack of flashy clothes and gift certificates to social activities, all of which he donated, like clockwork, the week after Christmas.

So when he and Jack were lying in bed a few weeks before Christmas and Jack asked him what his favorite Christmas had been, Simon didn't have to think at all, because there was only one Christmas in memory that hadn't sucked.

"When I was nine I slept under the tree. My parents didn't want me to because they didn't want to leave the lights on all night, but all I wanted was to be able to look up and see it all lit up like stars in the dark."

Jack made a sound of satisfaction against his neck. Jack loved to look up at the stars.

"Maybe Kylie was sick or something and they were distracted, but they let me and it was magical. I took my duvet and pillows and made a little nest so my head was by the trunk and I could look up through the branches."

That night he'd dreamt that Santa was tiny—the size of an ornament—and that when he'd come down the chimney Simon had put him in his pocket and carried him around like a comforting friend.

It was also the year that Simon had realized other kids had grown out of their shyness while he was beginning to feel like his brain was wiped clean when someone spoke to him.

"What about you?" he asked Jack.

"I used to like it a lot. As a kid. After my parents died Charlie and I didn't really do much. It seemed too weird. Sad. Then I was off at school. When I moved back here we just never quite picked it up again. Usually we have dinner and watch shitty movies or something."

Simon said, "Hmm," and tightened his arms around Jack, but his mind was working double-time.

He got Charlie's number out of Jack's phone and sent the text with trembling fingers. Charlie wrote back right away to say that, yes, he wanted to come to the cabin for Christmas Eve. He also offered to help with whatever Simon might need.

What Simon needed first was the perfect gift. He started looking over Jack's shoulder when he was on the computer and peering at him while he went about his day, wondering what was lacking in his life that Simon could find for him and wrap in brightly colored paper.

After two days of this detective work, Jack pinned him against a wall and said, "What's wrong with you?"

"N-nothing?"

Jack peered at him.

"You're being weird."

Simon took this as a signal to stop looking for the perfect gift and turned his attention to planning the perfect celebration.

He could make dinner but all he could think of when he pictured a tree and lights and decorations was what if Jack didn't want Simon doing that in his home. So that put an end to the decorations.

"What should I do?" he asked his grandma over dinner. "I don't know what to get him, I can't surprise him with a whole house of decorations because it's *his* house, and I don't even know if he'd want to cut down a tree? No, he'd never kill a tree just for decoration. Ugh."

Jean smiled at him knowingly.

"Surprises are lovely, dear. But when you surprise someone you do all the work by yourself for the enjoyment of the one moment when they see what you did. When you plan something together, you get to enjoy the whole thing with them."

And hell if that wasn't the wisest and most sensible goddamn thing that Simon had ever heard.

He was all set to broach the topic with Jack the next day, when Jack said, casual as can be, as he fed the animals, "Do you wanna have Christmas with me?"

Simon glared.

It was so damn *easy* for Jack. After Simon's *days* of thinking and worrying and scheming, Jack had just tossed the question out like it was nothing.

"Whoa. Uh. So maybe...you don't want to?"

"Goddamn it," Simon grumbled. He shoved Jack's shoulders then hugged him tight. "Yes, please."

Jack rubbed soothing strokes up and down his spine.

"Also your brother is coming for Christmas Eve."

"He is?" Jack put distance between them so he could see Simon's face. "You...did you *contact* Charlie?"

He beamed and Simon nodded miserably.

"I was going to try and plan a whole thing, but I got..." He shook his head and buried his face in Jack's shoulder. "We could plan it together?"

"What's that, darlin'?"

"Maybe it's better if we plan together?"

Jack's smile and soft eyes made it all worth sacrificing the element of surprise. In fact, as he bundled up against the cold and followed Jack out into the snow, he wasn't sure why he'd ever thought a surprise was the way to go.

Jack was talking animatedly about Christmas trees when they got into his truck—local pines and root balls and ground thaw temperature and replant viability—and when they arrived at a tree farm twenty minutes away, Jack didn't even hesitate, just grabbed Simon's hand and pulled him into the fray.

Simon appreciated every accommodation Jack had made for him. Every questioning look to see if he needed to go home, every firm hug that soothed his nervous system, every massage that calmed his twitching muscles.

But this moment when Jack was so excited to do something with Simon that he didn't even think about making accommodations shifted something between them.

Jack *wanted* him. Wanted Simon with him, no matter what.

They made their way through a maze of trees with their trunks wrapped in burlap and perched in buckets.

"What's up with that?" Simon asked, pointing.

"That's to protect the root ball. I was just talking about this for like ten minutes."

"Sorry," Simon said, sheepish.

"I was saying that we can replant it when the ground thaws. I can't believe people cut down whole trees just to throw them away."

Simon squeezed his hand. He'd been right about that, anyway.

Jack continued on about deforestation and climate change as they walked. His copper hair gleamed where it stuck out of his maroon beanie and his shoulders looked impossibly broad in his heavy navy coat.

Simon couldn't believe that he was picking out a Christmas tree with this man. That he got to touch him, kiss him, wake up with him. His mind buzzed with dizzy joy but when Jack looked at him he couldn't remember one iota of what Jack had been saying. And he didn't really care.

He tugged Jack behind one of the larger trees in the corner of the lot and pulled him into a kiss.

"I like being shut up that way," Jack said.

Simon swallowed, then leaned to whisper in Jack's ear.

"I want to suck your cock."

Jack froze, then groaned and dragged Simon tight against him like he was about to fall.

"Fuuuuck, I can't believe you just said that. At a *Christmas tree farm*," he added, clearly scandalized.

Simon could hardly believe it himself but now that he had, all he could think about was dropping to his knees in a forest of pine trees and taking Jack in his mouth. The thought of Jack's big hands on his face and in his hair, of Jack in full winter gear with his cock out, of Jack coming down his throat while the cold air caressed him, made him shiver with want.

Jack cupped his cheek, eyes fixed on his mouth. He pressed his thumb to Simon's lips and Simon felt his mouth give just enough to let Jack inside.

"Fuck," Jack muttered.

Jack had a tree in the truck so fast Simon wasn't even sure he'd paid for it.

When they pulled up in front of the cabin, Jack hurried toward the door, but Simon stopped him.

"We don't have to—" Jack began, instantly gentle.

"I want to...out here."

Jack's pupils dilated and he nodded, then pulled Simon to the copse of trees at the side of the cabin.

Simon shoved Jack against a thick tree, dropped to his knees, and pressed his face against Jack's thighs. He was overwhelmed, which was different than anxious, and turned on. He wanted to touch Jack, pleasure him, not have to think.

He undid Jack's belt and pulled his pants down, sucking Jack's cock into his mouth before the cold air could chill him. Jack gasped and slid a hand into Simon's hair.

"You look so fucking hot like that. Swallowing my dick, hungry for it. Fuuuuuck," he groaned when Simon took him deeper.

Jack's powerful thighs were tight and Simon squeezed his ass, then pulled him forward, encouraging Jack to thrust in and out of his mouth.

"Fuck, baby, you feel amazing. You want me to keep talking?"

Simon moaned and nodded. Nothing got to him like hearing all the things Jack wanted to do to him.

Simon closed his eyes, focusing on the slick slide of Jack's cock over his lips and into his throat. He relished the sensation of *choosing* something to block his speech and breath.

"Shit, you look like a fuckin' angel, Simon. Like all you want in the whole world is to have your mouth on me. Maybe I should keep you between my legs all day when

I'm drawing, keep my dick in your mouth, just—oh god—have you kneel there and service me whenever I want."

Simon moaned and shoved a hand in his pants, so turned on it wouldn't take much.

"Don't make yourself come," Jack said sharply. "Just touch that hot dick and wait for me." Simon almost choked as lust rolled through him and he squeezed the base of his cock to keep from coming at Jack's command.

"So close, shit," Jack gasped.

Simon swallowed around him and Jack came, pulsing hotly down Simon's throat with each thrust.

Before Simon had gotten his breath, Jack dragged him off his knees and kissed him deeply, breathing hard. He slid a hand into Simon's jeans and fucked him with his tongue as he fondled him. When Jack fisted his cock and jerked hard, Simon's vision whited out and he came, gasping and swearing, into Jack's hand.

"Jesus Christ," Jack groaned and Simon whimpered and let himself fall against Jack.

When he could open his eyes, he let out a creaky laugh.

"Hmm?" Jack inquired.

Simon turned them slightly and pointed, too wrung out to speak.

Pickles, Mayonnaise, and Louis were lined up side by side in the kitchen window, staring at them, heads cocked.

The afternoon of Christmas Eve, Simon paced the basement and refreshed the UPS tracking link one million times. The perfect gift for Jack had come to him in the middle of the night and if it didn't get here on time he was going to flip his shit.

No, he told himself as his heart started to race. He lay down on his back on the rug and stretched. *You won't flip out. You'll just give Jack his present after Christmas. It's not that big a deal.*

He breathed in through his nose and out through his mouth for a few minutes, then practically screamed when the doorbell rang, startling him.

He bolted up the stairs and wrenched the door open to claim the package before he even thought about the awkwardness of having to see the delivery person.

He had the envelope in hand and was flush with relief that the heavy snows of the past week hadn't scuttled his plan when his grandmother came downstairs.

"Do you want your gift now or later?" she asked.

"Are you sure you wanna go to Mom and Dad's instead of coming to Jack's?"

Jack had been really disappointed when Grandma Jean had said she thought she should go to Simon's parents' house for Christmas and had asked for a raincheck for the next year.

"I think I can stand my own son for a few hours."

She winked at him and Simon smiled.

"I just mean…it's the first Christmas without Grandpa, and…"

Simon had his suspicions that she'd turned down Jack's invitation because she wanted a quick holiday visit and then the night to herself to remember him, so he hadn't pushed.

Jean patted Simon's cheek.

"I'll miss your grandfather wherever I am today. And every day," she said.

Simon swallowed and nodded.

"So. Presents?"

"Okay, now." Simon smiled.

He ran downstairs to grab hers and they met in the living room. This was their tradition.

They opened them at the same time and when Simon saw her face he knew he'd won before he even got the paper off.

The needlepoint pattern was of a photo of Simon and his grandparents when he was a toddler. He was wearing a red hooded sweatshirt and his grandparents each had hold of one of his hands, swinging him above the ground. Simon was grinning at the camera with glee, but his grandparents were smiling at each other.

"I made it on this site online where you can—"

Jean grabbed him and pulled him into a fierce hug. Her cheek was damp against his.

"It's wonderful."

She stroked his hair back and smiled through tears.

"Go on, then."

He pulled the rest of the paper off and found a needlepoint kit of a giant St. Bernard dog that looked very much like Bernard—wait, it *was* Bernard, and it had a decorative border made of bones.

"Is this—?"

"Great minds and all that," she said, smiling. "I got the picture from Jack."

"You're awesome," Simon said. "Thank you. Merry Christmas."

★ ★ ★

With all the snow the drive to Jack's cabin took twice as long as usual, but when he turned up the long drive, Simon saw lights glittering through the trees and heard happy barking from inside as he parked.

For a moment as Simon looked at Jack's front door he was back months before when he'd first taken the winding road and ended up here. That day, it had felt like it would take a force of energy greater than the sum of everything Simon had inside him to even open the car door. And once he had, his very hand had rebelled against knocking on the door.

Now, behind that door was everything Simon wanted. The man he loved, the animals he loved, the place that felt like home and safety and freedom. His future.

The door opened.

"Hey, darlin', need a hand?"

Jack was already tugging on a coat to come help him and Simon felt unexpected tears prickle in his eyes.

Jack hadn't shaved in a few days and it tickled Simon's face when Jack leaned in to kiss him.

"You okay?" Jack asked, catching his chin.

Simon nodded but he knew if he spoke he'd cry.

Jack stroked his cheek, then caught him up in a crushing hug. Simon felt like he could have lifted up his legs and gone slack and still Jack's arms would have held him.

Chapter Twenty-Two

Jack

Simon was leaky from the moment he arrived. A little teary-eyed, yeah, but Jack could *feel* the emotion pouring out of him. It happened sometimes. Like Simon felt so much it overflowed the bounds of his skin and poured out into the world. It always made Jack want to wrap him up in his arms or his bed and let Simon flow into him until he could absorb whatever excess Simon was emanating. Share in the aureole of pure feeling from a man who was used to trying to hold everything inside.

But today he couldn't just bundle Simon into the bedroom and hold him, so he made do with squeezing and kissing the stuffing out of him whenever he looked up from cooking.

Charlie arrived, smiling and hauling a bag of junk so big he looked like a very buff Santa.

"What's all this?"

"Merry Christmas, little brother," Charlie said, dropping the bag inside the door and patting Bernard, who'd come to investigate.

He held out his arms. Jack couldn't remember the last time they'd hugged but the feeling of his brother's arms around him was familiar and safe.

"Merry Christmas, Charlie."

Simon poked his head out of the kitchen, smiling shyly.

"Hi, Charlie. Merry C-Christmas."

Charlie smiled and tentatively held out an arm. Simon blinked, then gave Charlie a quick hug. Jack had never seen him touch anyone except Jean.

From the bag, Charlie pulled garland that Jack recognized from the shop, a fruitcake, and more dog and cat toys than any house should hold. He dropped them onto the living room floor and there was immediate chaos as the pack converged to nose and paw at the new arrivals and stake their claims.

One toy, a plush caterpillar with a crinkly nose that Jack felt sure was actually a baby toy, caused a tug of war between Rat and Dandelion that ripped it in half in ten seconds flat.

"Welp, that's my life," Jack said to Charlie. "Thanks anyway."

"No problem," Charlie said. Then from the bag he pulled a set of reindeer antlers on headbands and proceeded to try and stick them on various animals' heads.

"What's happening?" Simon murmured.

"Charlie's trying to recruit a team of reindeer dogs for his sleigh slash dogsled?"

Charlie stood from trying to put antlers on Puddles, who, it seemed, had another fear to add to his list—though whether it was a fear of headbands, of antlers, or of looking like an idiot was impossible to deduce with certainty.

"Just being festive," he grumbled.

Jack socked him on the shoulder, but Simon said, "It's nice."

Charlie smiled and Simon went to finish cooking.

"How's the store?"

"Pretty good," Charlie said. "I'm hiring another person for spring, I think."

He told Jack about the new line of paint he was carrying at the store and about the insulation he'd put in the addition to his house. Finally, he said, "You seem good, Jack."

"I am."

Charlie nodded.

"Good."

"You all right?"

Charlie looked up and for the first time Jack noticed grooves around his mouth and wrinkles at the corners of his eyes even when he wasn't smiling. He noticed a cut along his jaw from shaving and a Band-Aid on his thumb.

"Yeah, I'm just...you know. Tired, I guess."

"You work too hard, bro."

Charlie waved that away.

"Simon told me you've been drawing again?"

"Simon told you? He talked to you?"

Jack's heart swelled.

"Texted me, yeah. When he invited me here. I'm glad you're working again. Your drawings are... They're amazing."

Charlie had always been enthusiastic about Jack's love of art but Jack assumed he'd be just as supportive of whatever he chose to do. This sounded different, though. Particular.

"Do you wanna see?"

Charlie nodded and followed him into his studio.

Over the last few weeks, Jack's insistently casual sketches had ordered themselves into the roughest of stories in his mind.

At the center of it was a man—faceless and nameless— who walked the land. He spoke the language of the animals and the trees and the dirt beneath his feet but human language fell on him like violence. At his touch, plants flourished and wounds of the earth healed, but he was alone. Until a clearing in the trees opened and the man stepped through to a place that was made of a gentler material. In that place, he lay down and the animals came to him, arranged themselves around him, and he could rest.

"This is Simon?" Charlie said.

"What? Oh. Well, I don't know. Kind of."

Charlie closed the folder.

"I'm sorry he hurt you."

"Huh?" Jack said. "He didn't hurt me."

"Not Simon, Davis. It kills me that he fucked with you and I couldn't do anything to fix it. But it's over now, right? You're back. You're...better?"

Charlie's cracked voice was made of one part anger and

nine parts fear, and it inspired Jack to reach out and squeeze his shoulder.

"Yeah. I'm better. I'm great, actually."

The look of relief in Charlie's eyes was staggering.

After dinner they sat by the fire with the animals.

"I feel like we should be doing something Christmassy," Simon said. "But Christmassy things are s-stupid."

He was a little tipsy from the wine they'd had with dinner.

"We could watch a Christmas movie?" Charlie suggested, but no one was terribly excited about that.

"A walk?" Jack offered. The animals perked up at that.

"Okay," Simon said.

"Hey, look at that, Charlie, you'll get your reindeer dogs guiding your sleigh after all," Jack teased, pointing to Dandelion, whose antler headband was still firmly in place.

Charlie grumbled something unintelligible, but stepped into his boots.

With the pack leashed and the antlers affixed to varying degrees, they set off into the cold evening dark.

The snow fell lightly, dusting eyelashes and cheeks and making Pirate dance to catch it in the air. Puddles especially loved winter walks as the likelihood of encountering puddles or lightning shaped sticks was much diminished.

There was a magic in the air that felt like possibility. Jack caught Simon's free hand in his and Simon smiled up at him, soft and easy.

"We used to take walks with Mom and Dad on Christmas," Charlie said softly. He'd been quiet the whole walk. "Remember?"

"Only vaguely," Jack said.

"Oh. Well, we did."

Simon sent Jack a concerned look and patted Charlie on the arm.

Rachel's car was in the drive when they got home.

"Can you take them inside?" Jack asked. "That's your present."

"My…okay."

"I'm gonna take off," Charlie said. "Leave you guys to your night. Merry Christmas. I left you something in the kitchen."

He clapped Jack on the back, then bent and kissed Simon very softly on the cheek.

"Merry Christmas," he said again, then hurried to his truck.

"Merry Christmas," Simon said.

He shot Jack an inquiring look and Jack shrugged, then he ducked inside as the dogs began to whine.

"Hey," Rachel said, opening the door just wide enough to wiggle out of the car, then closing it quickly. "Special delivery."

"Thanks for doing this, Rach, especially on Christmas."

"Well, you know it's the Jewish friend's job to play Christmas angel and facilitate all of your surprise gifts."

"I hope it's a good surprise. She okay in there?"

"She's asleep and so far she hasn't peed in my car, so that's a good surprise for me, anyway. How's your guy?"

Jack smiled. "Good. Perfect."

Rachel looked awed, then vaguely disgusted. "Good for you. Okay, I gotta return to headquarters before Van finds her present."

She eased the door back open slowly and pulled a cardboard box from the passenger seat. Jack peeked inside and couldn't help going gooey eyed at the little ball of cuteness inside.

"Thank your friend for me," Jack said.

"She was just happy someone wanted the last one, but I'll pass it along."

Jack cradled the box to his chest as Rachel drove away.

"Hey, bud. You're gonna live here now. Hope you like it."

The puppy stirred and blinked open wide brown eyes at Jack, then yawned. Jack's heart turned to mush.

"Wanna know a secret?" Jack whispered. "I'm really hoping someone else is gonna live here with us too."

The puppy yipped, then collapsed in the bottom of the box with her legs in the air.

Jack decided to take that as a positive sign.

Inside, the animals had been fed and Simon was standing by the fire, holding a bowl.

"Look what Charlie gave you. Isn't it beautiful?"

It was a large, hand-turned wooden bowl, polished to a soft shine. Jack had seen smaller ones that Charlie had done, but he was getting very good.

He nodded in agreement and walked over to Simon. The dogs scented the air.

"Can I give you your present now? It's a bit time-sensitive."

The puppy picked that moment to poke its little head out of the top of the box.

"Oh my god."

Simon reached out a shaking hand and ghosted it over the puppy's tiny head. She sneezed. Simon's face lit with a look of pure joy.

"She's yours, if you want her," Jack said. "I know Jean's allergic, so she could stay here for..."

Jack trailed off because it was clear Simon wasn't listening to a word he was saying. He reached into the box and pulled out a small black puppy with a white belly, floppy ears and paws too big for her body.

"Oh my god," Simon said again.

He cradled the puppy to his chest and closed his eyes when she licked his chin and then yawned. Simon looked at Jack with love in his eyes and the puppy in his arms and Jack thought his heart might burst from his body.

"I thought since, you know, since Jean's allergic, she could stay here. And maybe... Um, maybe when you're ready, you could stay here too. Live here, I mean. With me."

Simon's eyes were electric blue, shimmering with tears.

"You want me to... You're asking if... I...what?"

He was cradling the puppy to him like a security blanket and Jack took them both in his arms.

"Move in with me, darlin'. Come live here with me. With us. We'll have Jean over for dinner all the time so she's not lonely. Whenever you're ready. It doesn't have to—"

Simon silenced him with a salty kiss and pressed their foreheads together. Jack closed his eyes in relief, then felt a tongue that he was fairly sure wasn't Simon's licking at his chin.

Simon laughed and cuddled the puppy closer.

"That a yes?"

"Are you sure?"

"Yup."

"Then...yeah. Yes. Hell yes."

Simon's smile was goofy and soft and he was bouncing—almost dancing—with the puppy.

"I'm moving in with Jack," Simon told her. "Did you know that? Yeah!"

Tears flooded Jack's eyes. He knew it was fast. Knew they still had things to figure out. But he also knew, in his guts, in his balls, in his bones, that it was right. That however many days he had on earth, he wanted to spend them with Simon as close by his side as he could get him.

"Are you crying?" Simon said, instantly attentive. "What's wrong?"

Jack shook his head.

"I'm so fucking in love with you." He wiped his cheeks. "So when do you think you might wanna—"

"Now. I live here now." He turned around the room, addressing the animals. "Pack! I live here now!"

Bernard howled, which made Dandelion bark. Rat jumped up to see what was happening, which stirred the cats. Puddles trotted in from the bedroom with Louis and sidled up to Simon.

Very slowly, Simon crouched down and held the puppy where Puddles could reach her. Puddles sniffed her small form, then licked her face. The puppy wriggled toward him to try and return the favor but Simon held her fast. He sat down with her in his lap and called the animals over, introducing her scent to them.

In his head, Jack ran through what they'd do over the next few days to make sure she was safe and welcomed as Simon worked his magic.

Pirate peered suspiciously at the puppy over Simon's shoulder for a few minutes before jumping into his lap and licking her from toes to nose. Rat ran in excited circles around Simon and the puppy. Dandelion approached the new addition with as much chill as he approached everything else. Pickles didn't care at all, and Mayonnaise sniffed her politely then went to the kitchen in search of food. Bernard nosed her curiously but when a friendly lick nearly sent her rolling across the room, Jack called him away.

Puddles lay down on the floor next to Simon as if he'd appointed himself the guardian of the new puppy and Jack realized that had been Simon's intention all along. Louis, the least welcoming to all but Puddles, in the face of his protection, sniffed the puppy, stared her down, then wandered into the kitchen after Mayonnaise.

Jack got out the puppy food he'd hidden under the kitchen sink and made a bowl for her. He put it in the opposite corner of the kitchen from the other animals' bowls and called Simon in.

The puppy attacked the food the second Simon set her down, all paws and ears and fumbling.

Simon pressed close to Jack and slid an arm around his waist.

"What are we gonna call her?"

"Your choice," Jack said. "She's yours."

"She's *ours*," Simon said diplomatically. Then, "Actually that's good, because given your naming habits you'd want to call her Jesus, or Santa."

Jack secretly thought Santa was a great name for a dog, but he just smiled at Simon.

"Or, god, you'd want to call her Box." Simon giggled, then frowned. "Wait. Is Box actually a really cute name? No, right? Why am I asking you."

Jack listened to Simon list every word that could be associated with the nature of the puppy's arrival, unbothered.

He didn't care about names. He'd started calling Bernard "The Saint Bernard" because that's what he was, but that was too long to say every time. Mayonnaise and Pickles had arrived within days of each other and in his mind he called them "The cat the weird color of mayonnaise and the cat that ate a pickle off my plate." He'd found Dandelion, injured, in a patch of dandelions. Rat looked like a rat. Et cetera.

"Box," Simon announced.

"Hmm?"

"Box. It's actually really cute, right?"

"Um, yes?"

"Is your name Box?" Simon cooed to the puppy. She yipped. Simon looked pleased with himself.

They spent the next hour playing with Box, getting her settled, and making sure the other animals didn't terrorize her. Jack had a crate that he'd used for each new dog upon arrival set up in his studio for her for the night. She really was an adorable puppy and she instantly declared her loyalty to Simon, jumping onto his lap and flopping over his knees. At one point she climbed into the bowl Charlie had given them and Jack snapped a picture and sent it to his brother with a note of thanks.

Sprawled on the couch, the puppy snoozing between them, they watched the fire and Jack gazed at the lit-up tree. When the ground thawed, he was going to plant it in the back of the house, a reminder of their first Christmas together.

"Jack? Can we go to bed now?"

They got Box settled and Jack encouraged Louis out of the bedroom, getting a glare for his trouble.

When the door closed and they were alone, Simon said, "Were you serious?"

"What?"

"About me moving in?"

Sometimes Jack felt what it must be like in Simon's head with a pang of sadness.

"Of course. Did you think I was just being polite for the sake of the animals?" he teased.

Simon dropped his forehead to Jack's chest, a move that meant he needed comfort. Jack wrapped him up tight and they swayed together.

"I can't wait to live here with you," he said softly into Simon's hair. "Wake up with you every morning. Fall asleep with you every night."

"Mmm," Simon said with his face hidden. "Juschecking."

They swayed a little longer, then got into bed, throwing clothes off from under the covers for warmth.

Usually when Simon was feeling a little unsure Jack loved nothing more than to touch him, tease him, bring him to the edge with hands and mouth and cock until he was begging, until he was taken out of himself and merged with Jack in every way possible. Then Jack would look into his eyes and give him that one touch that would shatter him, and hold him as he shook apart.

Tonight, though, all Jack wanted was to be here with Simon. To know they had infinite nights left to do with what they willed.

They came together slowly, kissing softly, hands roaming, just enjoying. They stroked each other as they kissed, hips grinding, until Simon clutched Jack's hip and rolled onto his stomach.

He was all graceful spine and luscious ass and miles of soft skin and Jack dropped kisses on his shoulders as he fingered him open. He knew he would never get over the shock of lust he felt as he slid inside his man. The way Simon's breath hitched and he shook his head against the mattress like he almost couldn't believe the way he felt.

It was dark and quiet and Jack moved languorously, eyes half closed, enjoying every sound and clench and sigh. He urged Simon up onto his knees and found his cock, hard and leaking against his stomach. He was so fucking beautiful. Jack kissed his neck as he thrust inside him, every movement as natural as breathing.

"I love the fuck out of you," he gasped as Simon started moaning and pushing back against him. Simon sobbed out his name and came over his hand, muscles clenching around him. The feel of Simon's tight ass was the end of Jack and he pressed Simon into the mattress and lost it inside him, every muscle clenching as the pleasure spun through him and he spilled.

Jack collapsed on top of Simon, groaning into his hair. They lay there, tangled together, until Simon jerked away.

"Shit."

"What's wrong?"

"I didn't give you your Christmas present."

Jack buried his face in Simon's neck.

"Gimme it tomorrow," he mumbled.

"No."

Simon wiggled out of bed and rummaged around in the closet. He slid back into bed and turned on the bedside lamp.

"Wake up," he said and kissed Jack's cheek, then pressed an envelope the size of a notebook into his hand.

Simon bit his lip and Jack turned his attention to the gift. It wasn't wrapped, just sealed with the envelope's clasp at the top. When he reached in, he found the edge of a piece of thick paper and slid it out.

The drawing was in pen and, even before he registered the familiarity of the animals, Jack recognized the style. Fluid lines that started and stopped in unpredictable places, the sense that everything was resisting gravity just the tiniest bit, light falling almost magically on the forms.

"Is this…?"

Simon was nearly vibrating with excitement on the bed.

"Corbin Wale drew it. For you."

Reverently, Jack flipped the drawing over, looking for a signature. In crabbed writing it said, *I got your email.*

More soon. Your animals are very truthful. So are your animals.
Here they are. Simon said you're the best thing to happen to him.
Corbin.

Simon leaned in to read it too and made an embarrassed
sound when he got to the end.

"I can't believe you did this," Jack said, fingers hovering over the words.

"I sent him scans of your books so he'd know what an
amazing artist you are. And pictures of the pack."

Jack imagined the email Simon might have sent, what
he would have asked for, what he said to get it done.

He flipped the drawing back over and examined it more
closely. The animals all looked amazingly like themselves
though the style wasn't realistic exactly. That is, he could
tell Bernard was Bernard because Corbin Wale had cap-
tured an essential Bernardishness in the drawing, even
though a stranger might not have been able to match them.
It was extraordinary. He'd even conveyed the fierce love
Louis had for Puddles with one line of his paw, though he
doubted Simon would have been quite that thorough in
his description.

"I can't believe it," Jack said again. He slid out of bed
and put the drawing on top of the tall dresser where none
of the animals could possibly get to it.

For a moment, he stood and took in the scene before
him. Simon, the love of his life, naked in his bed, hair tou-
sled and cheeks flushed, smiling at him softly. Their bed.
Naked in *their* bed.

A year ago, Jack had stood on the precipice of having his
trust crushed to smithereens. Now he felt so full up with

love and trust that the whole cabin seemed to pulse with it. He had ideas. Convictions. The pack. A future and someone to share it with. He had everything.

As if he could read his thoughts on his face, Simon reached out a hand to him.

Jack got back under the covers and switched off the light. Simon came back into his arms like they were magnetized at the heart.

"Our bed," Jack said, kissing him.

"Ours," Simon echoed. Then, "I live here now."

"We live here now."

They murmured to each other in the dark, pressed together tightly. In a few hours, Jack would get up and check on Box, make sure she was settling in all right. But for now, they just held each other in their bed, in their cabin, with their pack, as the snow fell on the roof and the trees and on all of Garnet Run, Wyoming.

★ ★ ★ ★ ★

Reviews are an invaluable tool when it comes to spreading the word about great reads. Please consider leaving an honest review for this or any of Carina Press's other titles that you've read on your favorite retailer or review site.

To purchase and read more books by Roan Parrish, please visit their website at www.roanparrish.com.

Acknowledgments

Many thanks to Jenny and Anni, whose thoughts on this book were invaluable.

Thank you to Wyoming, which made me fall in love with it, and the chipmunks, moose, dogs, fish, and other beasties that graced me with their presence.

Thanks to my agent, Courtney Miller-Callihan, who makes magic behind the scenes, and to my editor, Kerri Buckley, for shepherding this project so generously.

Thank you to my sister, as ever, for listening to me ramble as we amble.

To all the animals I've loved over the years, even the ones I tried to hug in Iceland that ran away from me. And my tenderest thanks of all to Dorian Gray, my little furry heart.

About the Author

Roan Parrish lives in Philadelphia, where she is gradually attempting to write love stories in every genre.

When not writing, she can usually be found cutting her friends' hair, meandering through whatever city she's in while listening to torch songs and melodic death metal, or cooking overly elaborate meals. She loves bonfires, winter beaches, minor chord harmonies, and self-tattooing. One time she may or may not have baked a six-layer chocolate cake and then thrown it out the window in a fit of pique.

Get exclusive free content and keep up with all Roan's new releases by signing up for her newsletter: bit.ly/2xHGvBjF.

Come join Parrish or Perish, her Facebook group, to hang out, chat about books, and get exclusive news, updates, excerpts of works in progress, freebies, and pictures of her cat: bit.ly/2hFOfBk.

You can order signed paperbacks through her website, roanparrish.com.

And you can find her online in all the usual places:
Twitter: Twitter.com/roanparrish
Facebook: Facebook.com/roanparrish
Instagram: Instagram.com/roanparrish
BookBub: BookBub.com/authors/roan-parrish
Pinterest: Pinterest.com/aroanparrish

*RITA® Award–winning author Elia Winters delivers a
sexy, playful frenemies-to-lovers road-trip romance in
Hairpin Curves, now available from Carina Adores!*

*Megan Harris had hopes of seeing the world, but at twenty-five
she's never even left Florida. Now a wedding invitation lures her
to Quebec…in February. When her ex-friend Scarlett offers to
be her plus-one (yeah, that's a whole story) and suggests they
turn the journey into an epic road trip, Megan reluctantly agrees
to the biggest adventure of her life…*

Read on for an excerpt of Hairpin Curves *by Elia Winters…*

Chapter One

Megan Harris checked the industrial-style clock on the wall, adjusted her glasses, and checked again. How was closing time still an hour away? She could count on two hands the number of tables she'd served since the diner had opened at six. After trying to avoid the clock since her midmorning break, she'd finally caved—and it was barely 1:00. Well, damn. She adjusted her headband, washed her hands, and left the back room to greet the probably-empty diner with a cheerfully insincere smile.

Instead of an empty diner, though, a familiar face looked up from one of the oversized menus, light brown curls pulled up in a pair of retro Princess Leia buns. Scarlett Andrews looked up and caught Megan's gaze, her expression turning cautious. Their entire history flashed through

Megan's mind all at once: childhood best friends, competitive but loving all through high school, their whole story coming to a swift end when Scarlett bailed on Megan right before college and left her scrambling to find another roommate at the last minute. They hadn't spoken since. Of course, Megan had seen her around, because in a town like Crystal River, you always saw people around. But they hadn't been face-to-face like this. And they certainly hadn't spoken.

Scarlett gave her a closed-mouth smile, no teeth showing, the smile that indicated she was not really happy. "I got a tip that I might find you here."

Megan leaned against the edge of the booth and folded her arms. "You want breakfast? Or lunch?"

Scarlett licked her lips and opened her mouth to talk, but then hesitated. It was so rare to see Scarlett look hesitant about anything; she had always been a bundle of confidence when Megan knew her well. Funny how a moment's conversation would take her right back to their high school friendship, back before everything fell apart, back when Scarlett was the person whose approval Megan craved most desperately. "I was hoping to talk to you, actually. You got a minute?"

Megan glanced over toward the open kitchen, where Winston was whistling while scraping the flat-top grill, his cloud of white hair tucked under a hair net.

"Come on. There's literally no one here." Scarlett gestured around. "Whose table are you gonna wait?"

Megan slid into the booth, her back to Winston. "Tell me if he starts looking grumpy."

Scarlett raised an eyebrow. "Winston never gets grumpy. Even I remember that."

"Yeah, well, it's changed a little since you worked here with me."

Scarlett glanced around. "Hasn't changed that much."

Before Megan could respond, Scarlett folded her hands on the table, all business, the menu still lying open in front of her. "Have you checked your email?"

Megan shook her head. "A couple of days ago maybe. It's all spam and mailing lists."

Scarlett's lip twisted. "You should really unsubscribe from those."

Really? They weren't even friends and she was going to give advice? "Thanks. I never thought of that." Megan flushed in annoyance. "Why should I check my email?"

"We got an email from Juliet last night."

"Juliet... Letourneaux?" Megan hadn't heard that name in years. The three of them were best friends as kids, back before Juliet moved away to Quebec halfway through high school. "She emailed both of us?"

"Yeah. She wanted to know if we could get online tonight for a video chat." Scarlett shrugged. "I don't know what she wants. The email was vague."

Megan tried to remember her last communications with Juliet, back in the final couple of years of high school, slowly trailing off over time. "Does she...does she know you and I don't really talk anymore?"

There it was, on the table where they both had to acknowledge it. Megan hated confronting stuff, but she hated ignoring it more.

"She must not. Otherwise she wouldn't write to both of us on one email." Scarlett looked like she wanted to say more, but didn't. She sat back instead.

"Okay." Megan had no idea why Scarlett was even asking her about this. "So that's it? You wanted to know if I knew what the email was about?"

"I didn't want you to miss the video call. It must be something important." Scarlett's lightly tanned skin turned pinker, a few freckles standing out on her cheeks with the blush.

Megan waited for something else, but Scarlett didn't say much. She just looked across the table at Megan in a way that made Megan feel weird and scrutinized and judged, and she didn't like it. Before Megan could slide out of the booth, though, Scarlett moved like she wanted to put a hand over Megan's. It was a weird, stilted gesture, that ended with Scarlett putting one hand over her other hand instead. "How have you been? Work treating you well?"

"Sure." Megan answered in a knee-jerk positive way, like she always did, but then found herself giving more info without planning to. "Another of the servers quit right after Christmas, so I've been taking his shifts, and Winston and Martha haven't made any moves to replace him. So it's been busy." She'd been meaning to ask them about that, but it never seemed like a good time. Scarlett might say that Winston was incapable of looking grumpy, but lately, Megan had been frequently seeing him poring over papers at his desk with a contemplative frown, or talking quietly to his wife Martha in the back room when Megan was busy waiting tables or covering the grill.

"Right." Scarlett nodded. "Sounds busy."

"I've been busy, but the diner hasn't. It's been dead." Megan looked out the glass front of the diner, out into the parking lot of this strip mall where the Starlite Diner had carved out a tiny niche between Winn-Dixie and the Top Coat Nail Salon. The parking lot was sparsely dotted with cars, and most were over by the Winn-Dixie.

"That's a shame. The Starlite used to be the place to be." Sympathy filled Scarlett's eyes, sympathy that made Megan itchy and uncomfortable. She was never settled under Scarlett's intense gaze. Megan didn't want to talk about this anymore, so she slid out of the booth. "Do you want food?"

Scarlett looked down at her open menu. "Yeah. Sure. thanks. Pancakes and sausage? And a large OJ?"

"Sure." Megan slid out of the booth. "Don't say I never did anything for you."

The words were intended like a joke, a throwback, but she regretted them as soon as they were out of her mouth. They didn't tease like that anymore. They didn't even talk anymore.

"Get me the food, and we'll talk." Scarlett gave her a ghost of a smile, and Megan left to deliver the order with the same sense of discomfort.

Winston took her order with an undecipherable noise of agreement and set about whipping up some pancakes while Megan drew an orange juice for Scarlett. She wiped down the counters for the millionth time today, wishing there was something else to do. Her time here at the diner was sucking her life dry. She hadn't gone to book group in months, hadn't played any of her favorite video games, hadn't done much of anything but work, sleep, and take care of the house. Christmas was a reprieve, a day off spent with family, but she'd been back into the grind almost immediately after. Adulthood was supposed to be about routines, sure, but this routine wasn't fun at all.

Was Scarlett any better off, though? Megan leaned on the counter and eyed her former friend, who was typing something on her phone. Scarlett hadn't volunteered what she was doing for work, but she was in the diner in the middle of the day on a Tuesday. Socially, Scarlett had the charm and grace Megan could only envy from afar. Scarlett was beautiful, funny, quick-witted, and adventurous. Maybe that was why she had a boyfriend or girlfriend every time Megan turned around in high school, but Megan herself had been a late bloomer. She'd only gotten into the dating scene once she was in college, and that had trailed off after graduating three years ago. There had been a handful of brief flings, but nothing lasting and nothing worth thinking about.

"Order up!" Winston's sing-song call jerked Megan out of her reverie, leaving her with weird guilty, unsettled feelings that rolled in her stomach like a confusing jumble. She slid the plate of pancakes and sausage in front of Scarlett, who put her phone away.

"Thanks." Scarlett flashed her a tight-lipped smile. Megan nodded once, curt and went into the back room to start washing dishes for pre-close.

Seeing Scarlett again, having Scarlett interact with her like things were normal between them — or at least somewhat normal — had her all aflutter in ways she didn't want to dig too deeply into. First off, she felt like her whole life was standing still sometimes, and having an old friend dip back into it after years of no communication made her feel even more like no time had passed. She was a goddamn adult. She was twenty-five years old. She wasn't the irritated eighteen-year-old who just had her best friend bail on their college roommate arrangement to flake off to some fancy private school and never talk to her again. She'd had seven years to get past it. After all these years, she'd thought she was over it. But here came Scarlett, smiling and talking about their childhood friendships and expecting everything to be normal. Megan felt itchy all over, a feeling that lingered with her as she loaded the dishwasher.

After Scarlett left, with no other customers coming in after her, Megan was free to start the closing process for real. She'd just finished locking up the safe when the sound of Winston clearing his throat got her attention.

He pulled the hairnet off his head, letting his white wispy hair free. Something in his expression gave Megan pause. He spoke with an uncharacteristic hesitation. "You, uh, got a few minutes?"

Well, this fucking blew. Scarlett put her hands on her hips and stared at the backed-up sink in her kitchen, bubbling disgusting brown water making no signs of retreating down the drain where it belonged. The landlord had told her the garbage disposal was working fine, even with the weird noises lately, and she'd believed him. What a dickbag.

"Jacen?" she hollered into the other room. "The sink's backed up."

"What the fuck do you want me to do about it?" Jacen's voice was muffled, like he had a pillow over his head. He probably did; Scarlett's insomniac roommate was prone to catching up from lost nights through naps.

"Fix it?" Scarlett stared back into the sink again. It wasn't moving.

"Did you use the plunger?" Jacen hollered, less muffled. Good; he'd probably taken the pillow off his face.

Scarlett wrinkled her nose at the plunger, now sitting in the other side of the dual sink, dripping brown gross sink-water. "Yes, I used the plunger. It didn't fix it."

Jacen sighed loudly enough for her to hear it from where she was standing. "I may have a penis, but I do not know how to fix a sink."

"What about Zayne?" Jacen's boyfriend had fixed their dishwasher once before.

"He's working, and I am not calling him to come over and unclog our sink. Look it up on YouTube."

Scarlett closed her eyes. Yeah, this was probably her responsibility, and unfair to pawn off on Jacen or his boyfriend. At least she'd had breakfast. Even if breakfast had involved seeing Megan again, Megan who she'd once been friends with, Megan who she had spent two hours this morning psyching herself up to go see. She probably could have just texted Megan about the whole Juliet thing, but Megan was notoriously bad about checking her phone back in high school, and Scarlett had no reason to assume anything had changed. From the sight of Megan still working at the Starlite Diner, still with the same unfortunately plain haircut as she had had back in high school, her theory that nothing had changed was more solid than she had expected.

A half hour later, Scarlett was set up on the kitchen floor with a disassembled pipe, a bucket of trash water, and a Youtube video she'd watched a dozen times that seemed to be missing a few key steps. Scarlett leaned back against the stove and took a break, surrounded by under-sink assembly parts. This was not how she'd wanted to spend her day. She still had actual work to do, another data-entry gig she was handling remotely. It wasn't hard, but it took time, and she'd hoped to be done by now. Maybe if she hadn't gone to the Starlite, she could have finished already. She still wasn't sure how to feel about that trip, or about seeing Megan. It had seemed like a good idea at the time, but Scarlett had often done a lot of dumbass things in the name of thinking they were a good idea at the time. Fixing a clogged garbage disposal made everything retroactively seem like bullshit.

The thing about seeing Megan again is how her judgment seemed to follow Scarlett home. Megan seemed to stand over Scarlett, arms folded across her chest, frowning slightly, casting aspersions on another one of Scarlett's choices like she always had back in high school. It wasn't mean, per se, but it always implied, I thought you were better than this. She'd run from that judgment once, and here it was again, settling into her apartment like another roommate.

Grumbling to herself, Scarlett watched the video again, zooming in on part of it, and leaned back under the sink again to start her work back up. She could do this.

"How's it coming?"

Jacen's voice drew Scarlett out from under the sink a while later, right when she was putting the last piece into place. She wiped her arm across her forehead. Ugh, she was going to need a whole additional shower after doing this. "I think I've got it." She pushed up to her feet, unsteady after so long on the floor. Her roommate was staring at her, frowning but also looking a little curious.

"You really fixed it? I was kidding about the YouTube thing."

"I fixed it. You look way too nice to have just rolled out of bed." Scarlett looked him up and down. Jacen had the whole "casual chic" look down, from his skinny jeans to his snug t-shirt, its deep cobalt blue bringing out the rich undertones in his dark brown skin. He had pulled his black dreadlocks back with a blue cloth headband to match, and had finished out the look with a leather jacket.

"Zayne's picking me up in an hour. We're going to the movies. I wanted to look nice." He struck a pose. "This is good, right?"

"Gorgeous. I look like I took a bath in our sink. But look." Scarlett flipped a switch and the garbage disposal roared to life, draining the brown water away in a whirlpool. "Très sexy, non?"

"Magnifique." Jacen chef-kissed his fingers. "What about you? Are you going out with—" He blanched, probably remembering she was single. "—anyone?" he finished, somewhat weakly.

"No dates for me." Scarlett started packing up her tools. Ever since she and Gwen had broken up a few weeks ago, she'd struggled to find the motivation to go anywhere. With a freelance job that she could do from home, this was a recipe for not leaving the house much.

"You want to come out with Zayne and me?" Jacen gestured vaguely toward the door. "I'm sure he wouldn't mind."

"No, I don't want to be your third wheel. That," she gestured to his outfit, "is clearly clothing for a date. I have work to do tonight, anyway."

Jacen frowned again. "You okay? This isn't like you, home on a Friday. I swear, you're here all the time, now."

"I live here, Jacen." She carried the tools she'd used back to the closet, then stripped out of her shirt on her way to take a shower.

"Well, let me know if you change your mind about going out," Jacen hollered down the hall. "I don't like to see you moping."

"I'm not moping!" She left her clothes on her bedroom floor and locked herself in the bathroom, in part just so she wouldn't have to continue that conversation. Sure, yeah, she'd been moping, but that wasn't Jacen's problem.

She took her hair down to rinse it, massaging her scalp with her fingertips. With the warm water running down her body, she could close her eyes and relax, if only the tension that had settled into her muscles these last few weeks would go away. It wasn't money; she never had enough of that, but always managed to get by. And she didn't want to think that it was Gwen. They hadn't been good for each other, despite making a healthy attempt at a relationship, and the breakup was the right move. Missing her was normal. But she wasn't actually missing Gwen as much as that physical closeness. Cuddling on the sofa to watch a movie. Spooning together in bed. Kissing, pressing against each other, hands and mouths bringing sweet, mindless pleasure. All that was gone, and her bed was empty.

Scarlett stood beneath the water until it began to run cold, then reluctantly got out and toweled off. Silence in the house meant Jacen had left. She put on fuzzy pajamas, even though it was the middle of the afternoon, and flopped down on the couch. Her phone stared at her, blank. No one was calling or texting. Gwen came to mind, and she grimaced. She had better find some way to shake off this funk. In the meantime, though, she had work to do. She pulled her laptop over with a sigh.

"Closing?" Megan had to repeat the word just to make sure she'd heard Winston right. "As in, no more Starlite Diner, forever?"

Winston rested his wrinkled hands on his desk and smiled sadly at Megan across the cluttered surface. His blue eyes turned down at the edges, the smile not reaching them. "We made it through Christmas, and that's as far as the missus and I were hoping to take things. I'm sure you've seen this day coming."

She hadn't, but she didn't want to tell him that. Obviously she hadn't expected the Starlite to stay open forever, but Winston and Martha hadn't given any hints of retiring. Well, other than the travel brochures that had been piling up on the desk...and the shortened business hours after the holiday…and the way Winston had started photographing the place and sighing wistfully after the New Year.

Oh.

Nodding, Winston leaned back in his chair. "We've had a good run, all of us, and you've been darn indispensable these past few years, but we got an offer from the Winn-Dixie that's too good to turn down."

"When?" Her voice cracked, and she tried again. "When are you closing?"

"End of the month."

The end of the month. That month. January. Megan's mind tipped on its axis, like her whole center of gravity had shifted, and she wrapped her hands around the arms of the chair. She'd been here for nearly ten years. Ten years. The Starlite had been her first job, a part-time dishwashing gig when she was still too young to get a job almost anywhere, slowly increasing in hours and responsibility as she got older. Scarlett quit to take a job at the grocery store, and Megan had continued at the Starlite. After college, without any immediate job prospects, the Starlite had taken her on full-time. She couldn't picture her life without these too-early mornings, brewing coffee before dawn and setting out paper placemats and silverware for the regulars.

Megan loosened her grip on the armrests, taking a breath and trying to regulate her tumult of emotions. "Have you thought about trying to find new owners? Instead of closing it?"

Winston chuckled. "Oh, we talked about it. Wondered if you might want to buy the place."

If she had the money, maybe she would. She leaned forward to say so, then froze, mouth slightly open. Did she really want to commit to buying this business and choosing this career for the rest of her life? This was only supposed to be a temporary job. The fact that a temporary job had grown to a nine-plus-year commitment was not because she loved it. She didn't want to give too much thought to the actual underlying reasons.

Winston barely paused, seemingly oblivious that she was about to speak and had stopped. "Martha told me, she said the worst thing we could do is try and saddle you with this place for the rest of your life. Restaurant's on its last legs, Megan. You've seen it. We've all seen it. No, the Winn-Dixie wants the space, and we're giving it to them. For a pretty penny, that is."

Megan's tumble of emotions settled into something like numbness, all feeling draining out of her and leaving an empty stillness behind. She'd been in this cluttered back room so many times, the sights were all familiar, but each object stood out like it was new again. The cork board covered with newspaper clippings from the restaurant's thirty-year history. Framed photos of the T-ball team the diner had sponsored for years, most of those kids grown up and gone off to college by now. Gray filing cabinets crammed into the corners, each drawer filled with decades of vendor invoices and god knows what, since Winston and Martha always resisted digitizing their systems. Stacks of papers on every available surface. There was a whole wall of employee photos from the years, everyone who had ever worked at the Starlite Diner, from busboys to line cooks.

Megan was there, right in the middle of the wall, from

back when she was first hired. Her sixteen-year-old face stared back at her. Not much had changed in nearly ten years. Sure, she'd upgraded her glasses, but she still had the same mousy brown hair, practically in the same shoulder-length cut, with the same hesitant, shy smile. Teenage Megan looked nervous about what was ahead of her. Her stomach twisted in discomfort. Was she still the same teenager inside, just in an older body?

And then, next to her, Scarlett's face smiled back. They'd been hired at the same time. Scarlett's hair was a wild light-brown cloud back then, and she had the same goofy smile as Megan. Back then, Scarlett had seemed so sophisticated, but this photo made her look like just another sixteen year old kid. All her memories were probably filtered through that same lens.

Megan's gaze drifted over the most recent row of faces in the photographs, the handful of other waitresses and cooks who traded shifts with her. Only a few, now, with the decline in business. "Does anyone else know yet?"

"We thought we'd tell you first." Winston shuffled some papers around, averting his gaze. "You've been with us the longest. I figured you deserved to know first, even if you probably saw the writing on the wall for a while now."

She must've looked stricken, because Winston frowned and shook his head. "Now, don't you worry. We're gonna take care of all of our employees, best we can." He patted his pockets, then got up from the squeaky office chair and began rummaging through the piles. "Let's see. Where is this. It's a big envelope. Ah, here it is," He pulled a manila envelope out from the file and reached inside, peering in as he sorted through the documents. "Here we go. We looked up what was standard, and we threw in a little extra because you've been such a big help, and because we got a good shake from the Winn-Dixie deal." He came around to her side of the desk and handed her a check.

Megan looked down at it, and then looked at it again, disbelieving. "Ten thousand dollars?"

"I know it's not everything, and it's not a salary, but it should at least keep you going for a while." He shifted awkwardly, pushing his glasses up the brim of his nose.

Megan's heart pressed against her ribs. "You didn't have to do this. I can apply for unemployment or something."

"It's the least we can do." He smiled sadly. "You've been part of the Starlite family since you were just a girl. We could barely keep the place open without you."

Megan got to her feet and gave Winston a hug, carefully, the kind of hug you'd give your grandfather if he'd just had surgery. She and Winston had never been on a hugging basis, but this was different. He patted her back awkwardly. "Thank you," she said.

"No leaving before the end of the month, though, all right?" He held her at arm's length and wagged a finger at her. "We're gonna have a lot of stuff to pack up, and a few dozen more breakfasts to cook. Your trip to Vegas will have to wait until February."

Megan laughed, even if she felt more sick than amused. "Sure. February."

Chapter Two

Ten thousand dollars. Megan stared at the check in her hand as she sat in her car in her driveway, not yet willing to move from that spot. What was she going to do with this kind of money? It would pay all her bills for months and months. She had good savings, what with never going anywhere and running up very few expenses. If she was frugal, she could probably make her savings plus this income last... eight, nine months?

But what was she supposed to do without the Starlite? She got tired by 8:00 p.m. She woke up every day at 4:00. Her rhythms were diner rhythms, patterns she'd forced her body into in order to keep this job that she—honestly— didn't really like that much.

Oh, wow, her world spun just thinking that. She said the

words out loud. "I didn't really like the job." Guilt, embarrassment, fear, all rushed through her system one after the other. She tried it louder. "I didn't really like that job!"

Her laughter bubbled up, hysterical, the kind of half-wild laughter that would get out of control if she didn't tamp it down. It wasn't happy laughter; it was the fraught, unstrung kind, the kind when a person had reached the end of their rope. She took a few deep breaths to steady herself and got out of the car.

Megan fumbled the key into the lock of her house, jiggling it a few times to get the tumblers to click. She should call the landlord about this one of these days. Still staring at the check, she nearly walked into the doorframe as she went inside. The warmth was a welcome change from outside, where Florida's damp winters made fifty degrees feel like half that. At least, that was what she imagined; she'd never been out of Florida before.

Megan stopped in her tracks, right between the living room and kitchen, a jolt running from her head to her feet. She'd never been out of Florida. And here she was, holding ten thousand dollars in her hand, convincing herself to squirrel it away in the bank and stay inside her little box.

Or.

She could do something crazy.

Teenage Megan came to mind, herself at sixteen in that photograph, looking scared and trying to blend in with the background. That Megan had wanted to get brave. She'd told herself she was going to do all these things someday, once she'd gotten out of high school, then once she'd gotten out of college, then any day now, always later, after she put a few things in order. There were always reasons to avoid what was frightening. Reasons to turn down invitations, to ignore job opportunities out of her comfort zone, to stay exactly as she was.

She could take this ten thousand dollars — or not all of it, even just a fraction of it — and go somewhere.

Not Vegas, as Winston had joked. Vegas wasn't her style. Honestly, what was her style? She hadn't lived enough of her life to even develop a style, but she had dreams. She had a whole list of places she wanted to go, a scrapbook full of "someday" visions for her future. With the check burning hot in her pocket, she pulled the scrapbook off the living room bookcase and sat down on the sofa.

"What's that?"

The voice from the kitchen made her jump and slam the scrapbook shut. "Jesus, Matt, I forgot you were home."

Her brother was already poking around in the fridge. "I'm always home."

"Tell me about it." Megan put the scrapbook back on the shelf. She'd look at it later, when Matt wasn't around to make snide comments. "Didn't you have work today?"

Matt chugged his water and leaned against the fridge. If he had work today, he'd wasted no time changing back into running pants and an old t-shirt. He didn't look like he'd shaved, either, and his hair was uncombed. "I took today off. I had a headache when I woke up."

Megan wrinkled her nose. Great, another day off for Matt. She approached him in the kitchen. "Speaking of which. You have your share of the rent money?"

"Didn't I Venmo you yet?" He looked at the calendar

hanging on the wall, then made a thoughtful noise. "Wasn't that due on the first?"

"Of course it was due on the first, and you told me you'd have it to me once you got paid, so I covered your half." Megan tried to keep her voice calm. If Matt got into a snit, he'd withhold rent for the month just to be spiteful.

"Oh, yeah." He nodded, sipping his water and rubbing his abs absentmindedly with his free hand. "Sure, I can get that to you. Remind me when I've got my phone." Before she could protest, he started out the door, grabbing his phone off the table as he did so. "See ya."

"You've got your phone now," she shouted after him.

"I mean remind me when I'm not busy." He was still on his way out.

"Where are you going?"

"I'm meeting Dan at the gym," he hollered, already leaving.

"I thought you had a headache."

If he answered, the words were lost as he shut the front door behind him.

Megan exhaled through her nose, a hot, angry puff of air. He knew just what to say to piss her off, and always had, ever since they were kids. If he weren't completely incapable of being a responsible adult, he could have his own rental instead of living with her, and she wouldn't have to babysit him all the time for things like paying the bills and cleaning up after himself.

He walked all over her, and she never stood up to him. Maybe that should stop. Maybe she could reinvent herself and go somewhere or do something. The farthest she'd ever lived from her hometown was an hour away during college, but otherwise, her life had occurred in and around the immediate vicinity of Crystal River, Florida. Not that she'd planned it that way. She had gotten a passport right after she turned eighteen, an indicator that she was going to head off into the world eventually.

Unfortunately, "eventually" was always easy to postpone.

Megan wiped up the edge of the counter where Matt had spilled some water. Even Matt had done his share of traveling, although he'd mooched off the generosity of friends and relatives to do so. But her? She'd been safe. She'd been predictable. She'd stayed home.

And now, she was laid off with ten thousand dollars burning a hole in her pocket and very little clue what to do next.

The email from Juliet said only cryptically that she had news for both of them, and asked to video chat around seven that night. Scarlett had already messaged back yes, probably assuming that Megan didn't have any other plans. The assumption would have rankled Megan if it wasn't so damn accurate. At 7:05, a message came through in a newly formed group chat.

Megan stared at the message for an inordinately long time. It just said, Hey! Are you two around?

At this point, it was getting weird not to just announce whatever news she had instead of demanding a video chat, but Juliet had always been a fan of grand gestures. It was part of what made her get along so well with Scarlett when they were kids. Juliet always had the best make-believe games, and Scarlett would be eager to build on their story, and Megan was just happy to be included.

It was also weird to be in a group chat with Scarlett. First, they had that conversation this morning, and then Megan was laid off, and now it was like she was in this twilight zone of worlds being overturned. Once upon a time, things were simpler between them. Scarlett had been the kind of best friend she would go to the moon for. Now? Now was a different story.

Scarlett responded to the chat first, the little circle with her cheerful face popping up on the screen. Sure! What's up? she typed. She was like some kind of poster for an antidepressant. Surely some of the intervening years should have taken some of that chipperness away.

Megan had to respond, then, because otherwise Juliet was going to think she was the only one in the chat. I'm here too! The exclamation point felt ridiculous. She wasn't an "exclamation point" kind of person, and she never had been. Would they think this looked as fake as she felt?

Hey girls! Oh my god. Let's video chat.

What could she say other than, Sure! With another damn exclamation point?

Within moments, all their faces were up on the screen. Nostalgia hit her like a wave of ocean water, the kind you don't see coming that knocks you flat on your ass. Juliet looked amazing, as good as ever, her blonde hair loose and perfect around her shoulders. She was older than when Megan had last seen her, obviously, but she still looked like a model.

Alongside Juliet was Scarlett, whose light brown curls

were still up in those two buns. Next to their faces, she looked like the friend who was going to tell them not to go to the party because the parents wouldn't be home. Straight brown hair, plain glasses, she was neither fashionable nor attempting to be, and the disparity had her pulling self-consciously at her glasses before either of them said anything. Of course, then she couldn't really see, so she had to put them on. Now she looked indecisive and nerdy. Perfect. Just the way she wanted this weird reunion to go.

"Girls! Oh my god, why haven't we done this before?" Juliet was looking down, staring at their faces rather than the camera, probably.

Because we're not friends anymore! Megan's inner voice said, chipper and too-perky, but Juliet didn't deserve that. Juliet hadn't pissed her off, after all. Juliet hadn't abandoned her at the most terrifying part of her life to go off to some other prestigious college like Scarlett had.

Huh. Maybe she was still a little bitter at Scarlett.

"What's new?" Scarlett sounded as cheerful as Juliet. Probably her life was amazing now; Megan didn't know.

"First tell me what you're doing! Megan, where are you living? What are you doing?" Juliet rested her chin on her hands.

"Uh. I'm renting a house," she said, trying to sound cheerful. She didn't need to mention that her brother lived with her. "And I'm, you know, I've been working at the Starlite. Trying to pay off that student loan debt. But uh… I'm making some big changes! Career change." She smiled.

"You are?" Scarlett raised an eyebrow, surprise or irritation in her expression. "You didn't mention that this morning."

"Yeah, well, it didn't come up then." Megan's face was so hot, she must look like a tomato. "It's all still up in the air right now. Very new."

Scarlett was still looking at her like she was trying to understand what was happening when Juliet piped in. "I'm so glad you two are still hanging out! I was worried that you might not be friends anymore and I'd be making everything super awkward by messaging." She smiled brightly, and Megan didn't have the heart to disavow her of her belief. "What about you, Scarlett?" Juliet asked. "What are you up to lately?"

"I'm freelancing, actually." Scarlett sat up a little straighter. "Telecommuting, mostly data analysis for private firms. It's a great setup, because I get to make my own hours, work from home, pretty much living the dream." She grinned with those perfectly white teeth that she hadn't even had to suffer through years of braces to get.

"I'm so glad." Juliet sighed. "The one downside of not being on social media is that I don't get to see what you're all up to. It is so good to see your faces."

"Thanks." Scarlett waved her hand in a "get on with it" gesture, and Megan was quite grateful for it. "Now we've got to know. Tell us why you're calling. What's your news?"

"I'm getting married!" Juliet fairly bounced out of her seat. "His name is Gabriel, and we've been keeping things kind of quiet because his family is very conservative and wouldn't approve of us living together, but we've decided to make it official. We're getting married on February nineteenth here in Quebec."

"Congratulations!" Megan and Scarlett said together, their words overlapping. Megan meant all her congratulations, too: Juliet was always so sweet. She deserved somebody really good. But…February 19th? Megan looked at the calendar and did some math. "But that's so soon. There's almost no time to plan a wedding."

"Tell me about it." Juliet gave a half-smile. "But his grandmother is not in good health, and we want everyone we love to be able to attend, so we decided to make it really fast. His father has wonderful business connections, and he pulled some strings, so we're at the Chateau Frontenac for the whole thing." She clasped her hands together. "I know we haven't seen each other since high school, but we were best friends growing up. It feels so important to me that the two of you attend. Is there any way you can make it?"

"Oh." Megan's heart fluttered. "I…don't know." Quebec? In February? "I've never been on a plane," she said, trying to stall her mind that was already spending the ten thousand dollar check she still had in her pants pocket.

Scarlett looked similarly uneasy. "I…don't know. It's a lot of money for tickets, and I want to say yes, but… I have to think about it, Jules."

Juliet's face fell. "Of course. I understand. I already mailed the invitations, but I didn't want you to get them without me talking to you first so you could know how much I wanted you to come. And Quebec will be so gorgeous then. It's Winter Carnival that week, and it's so different from Florida…" Juliet had those big, pleading eyes, like out of a cartoon.

"Maybe it's possible!" Megan found herself saying, with

another cursed exclamation point sneaking into her voice. "I mean, I don't know, but I don't want to say no right off the bat…"

"Well. Think about it, all right?" Juliet bit her lip. "If you made it, we could totally cover your hotel. But maybe you two could talk more? I'll hang up. Let me know! Please. I'd love to see you."

"Of course. Of course we'll talk." Scarlett was saying it like she wasn't going to hang up on Megan the minute she didn't have the social obligation to avoid her, the way she'd avoided all of Megan's attempts to reach out and then later made some attempts of her own that Megan had of course avoided, but who was keeping track of that?

"Okay! And let's not be strangers. I miss you both." Juliet gave them beaming smiles and then disconnected, leaving Scarlett as the only face on Megan's screen.

For a minute, they just stared at each other.

Scarlett rested her chin on her folded hands. "Career change?"

"Diner's closing, thanks. Telecommuting data analysis?"

Scarlett made a face. "More like data entry."

The silence stretched on some more, and maybe the mercy would be to just hang up and pretend they hadn't talked at all.

"What are we gonna do, Meg?" Scarlett asked.

"About what?"

"About Juliet." Scarlett made a face. "She really wants us to go."

Megan wrinkled her nose. "She also apparently thinks you and I are still best friends."

Scarlett laughed. "Who's gonna tell her?"

"We can't tell her," Megan insisted. "She wants us to go to Canada! I've never even been out of the state."

"Shit, I can't afford to fly to Canada." Scarlett shook her head. "We've gotta say no, right?"

"Right." Megan sighed. "I don't want to look at that sad face."

"Neither do I. I don't know about you, but I'm gonna take the coward's way out and just RSVP no when the invitation comes." Scarlett leaned back in her chair. "And change my name and go into hiding."

Megan looked at the screen. "I could…" She stopped, the possibility that had come half-formed to her mind suddenly dissolving. "No, it's dumb."

"What?" Scarlett asked.

"I was just thinking aloud. Never mind." Megan shook her head. "Have a good night. Good luck with whatever you're doing now."

"Yeah, thanks." Scarlett's sarcasm filled her words. She didn't even say goodbye before hanging up.

Megan stared at the screen, at her own face looking at her, and sighed again before closing the window. She had the whole evening to be sad and feel sorry for herself without worrying about what other people thought of her.

Especially Scarlett.

This was probably dumb. Most of the things Scarlett did were dumb. She wasn't even sure Megan still lived in the same house, but she'd gotten a Christmas card from this address a few years ago when Megan was maybe still trying to keep up appearances, and Megan wasn't the type of person to move. So she sat in the driver's seat of her car in front of a plain-looking beige house, which had a string of Christmas lights trimming the garage like the saddest scene in a depressing holiday movie, and stared at the light on in the bedroom. It was late. It was late, and she and Megan weren't even friends anymore, not after Megan had cut ties with her and Scarlett had decided to stop trying to apologize. Sitting in front of her house like a creeper wasn't a good look.

But.

If Megan had an ounce of adventure in her body, Scarlett could wrangle a trip to Canada out of it, and they'd both make Juliet happy. Which was probably the best thing to do in this situation.

So she got out of her shitty car and ran up the front steps to ring the doorbell.

Megan opened the door in her pajamas, her brown hair pulled back in a headband, wearing a matching pajama set because of course she wore matching pajamas, staring up at Scarlett with this expression of bewilderment that hit Scarlett like a punch in the gut.

She used to have a really, really big crush on Megan.

But now, they weren't there anymore, and Scarlett gave her a thumbs up, like that wasn't the most ridiculous way to greet someone. "Hey!" Scarlett said brightly. "Can we talk?"

"What. The hell." Megan looked past her. "Is this a prank?"

"It's not a prank. But it's cold! Let me in." Scarlet shifted from foot to foot.

Megan stepped aside, and Scarlett stepped into the house. It was the first time she'd ever been in here, and damn, the girl loved beige.

"Your house is nice," Scarlett said, because that is what you said when you were going into somebody's house for the first time. "Nice neutrals."

"I'm not allowed to paint it anything unless I paint over it when I move out." Megan made a face at her. Megan was always pulling these faces, scrunched up and irritated. "What are you doing here? It's late."

"I know it's late. I needed to talk to you."

"The internet is a perfectly reasonable option these days." Megan was wearing bunny slippers, like the kind that had actual bunnies on them, and something about that tweaked a weird little vulnerability in Scarlett's innards that she didn't want to question too deeply.

"Can I sit?" Scarlett went over and sat on the couch anyway without waiting for a response. She looked around the room again. Something seemed off. The art looked like the standard kind of art you'd find at Target, but hell, that wasn't weird. Scarlett got most of her wall hangings at big box stores. It was the stuff on the bookshelves. Megan had always loved romances, so those lined a whole shelf, but then she wasn't really a fan of video game tie-in novels, and there were three full shelves of...

"Metal Gear Solid?" Scarlett asked aloud, squinting to read the titles.

Megan flushed. "They're Matt's."

"Matt?" It took Scarlett a moment to remember. "Your brother?"

"He lives here with me." Megan folded her arms.

"Meg, you're not doing the South any favors here by living with your brother."

"Very funny. He lost his job a few years back and needed a place to stay, so I told him he could rent here with me."

"A few years back." Scarlett wasn't friends with Megan anymore, and she should probably keep her nose in her own business, but the curiosity was driving her into the questions she probably had no business asking. "And what's he doing now?"

"He picks up some hours here and there at a few different places." Megan's tone was evasive.

"Where's he tonight? Work?" The answer was probably no.

"He went to the gym with friends. And now he's probably gaming." Megan grimaced.

Of course it wouldn't surprise Scarlett at all if Megan's kid brother was a deadbeat who didn't pay the bills. He'd been a slacker in high school, but hell, lots of people were slackers in high school. Matt was the kind of slacker who liked to mooch off his parents until they stopped him, though. Maybe they'd finally stopped and he'd had to move in with Megan.

"What are you doing here, Scarlett?" Megan crossed her arms over her chest. Even standing while Scarlett was sitting, she looked slight. Megan had always been slim, unlike Scarlett's bold curves and wild hair, and her pale skin looked especially pale in the dim light. She didn't seem to ever get much color, even during the hot Florida summers when she and Scarlett used to spend all their time after school swimming and sunbathing outside. Now, the paleness made her look unwell.

"Are you okay?" Scarlett was asking before she thought about it.

Megan waved her hand. "I'm fine. I'm less fine if you don't answer me."

"Okay." Scarlett interlaced her hands, pressing her palms between her knees, and leaned forward on the couch. She'd been mulling this over ever since hanging up the call earlier that night. "Do you actually want to go to Juliet's wedding?"

A softness stole into Megan's eyes. "I can't." Her tone wasn't "I can't," though; her tone was "I wish I could."

"But is it that you don't want to, or don't think you can? Why don't you think you can?"

Megan sighed and spun in a circle. "Do we have to go through this now? It's almost midnight."

"Do you have to get up in the morning?" Scarlett asked.

"Yes," Megan shot back, and then paused. "Well, no." She bit her lower lip. "Wilson called and asked me not to come in tomorrow. They're cutting back on hours in the last few weeks the diner's open."

"Great. So you have time to talk."

Megan flopped into the recliner across from Scarlett. "You're impossible. You've always been impossible."

This was the closest they'd come to broaching their past. Scarlett wasn't sure if she wanted to. There were always questions involved, questions she wasn't ready to answer.

"Yes," Megan said when Scarlett didn't respond. "Yeah,

sure, I'd love to go. But it's ridiculous. It's a whole different country. I've never been on a plane."

That was the part that had settled in Scarlett's mind, the part she hadn't been able to let go of. "Are you scared to fly?"

"I don't know." Megan sighed. "What do you want me to say?"

"I didn't think it was a particularly difficult question. Lots of people are scared to fly." Megan might not admit that weakness to her, even if she knew it, though. Megan probably was scared to fly. A little voice in Scarlett's head reminded her that Megan was probably scared of almost anything.

"You said it was a lot of money." Megan's tone was accusatory. "Why are you asking me if I'm going to go if you can't afford to go?"

Time for the pitch. "I was thinking maybe we could drive," Scarlett said, and forced the last word out. "Together."

Megan stared at her.

Scarlett stared back.

"Together," Megan repeated. "In the same car." She drew back. "Wait, what car? Not your car, certainly. I saw that thing in the driveway and it's the same one you had in high school. I'm surprised it isn't currently on fire."

Scarlett couldn't even defend herself. "My car's a death trap. We'd take yours."

"So you want me to drive across the entire country with you in my car so you can save money on plane tickets?" Megan's eyebrows were so high up they were practically hitting her hairline. "You've got some nerve, Scarlett Andrews."

"Your car's a convertible," Scarlett tried.

Megan gave her a withering look. "It's February."

It really was a terrible plan, wasn't it? But Scarlett had already thought it up, and she was committed. "It doesn't have to be so bad. You and I used to be friends, once." She swallowed, the words suddenly hanging heavier between them than she wanted to. She forced herself to press on. "Juliet wants to see us both. She was the final member of our trio. We should try to go to her wedding."

Megan wrinkled up her nose. "Gross."

"What?" Scarlett snapped back.

Megan kept the wrinkled-prune expression for another moment. "It's gross that you're getting all emotional about this."

"Unbelievable." Scarlett flopped back on the couch and stretched her arms out over the back of it. "I didn't even want to ask you, you know that? I knew you were going to be an asshole about this, the way you've been a total asshole since we stopped talking."

"Right. Right. I'm the asshole. Obviously. And you're perfect." Megan was getting heated, color rising in her pale cheeks. "How am I supposed to do this road trip? I've never—" She cut herself off abruptly, mouth snapping shut.

"Never what?" Scarlett asked.

Megan shook her head. "Never mind."

"Never what?" Scarlett insisted. "Never been to a wedding? Never actually had a valid driver's license?"

"I've never been out of Florida." Megan folded her arms. "There, are you happy?"

"Fuck, really?" Scarlett gaped. "But this state is so bad!"

"This state is not bad. I happen to like it here. People come from all over the world to the beaches, and the cost of living is so low, and I have a Disney yearly pass…" Megan ticked off the pluses on her fingers.

Scarlett interrupted her. "It's hotter than Satan's taint, and you can't go thirty feet without hitting a nail salon or a Walmart, and alligators just fucking show up in the drainage ditches, and don't even get me started on sinkholes—"

"So move away, then!" Megan said, practically shouting. "Why do you even live here if you hate it so much?"

"Because it's cheap! And because I don't want to shovel snow! And because I grew up here and it's like a damn wart, you can't get rid of it. And…" Her voice fell. "And I like it." Scarlett hated that she actually liked the state, the sunny weather and the beaches and the quirky people.

Megan was nodding like she knew everything, and that was its own annoying bullshit. "I see."

"Ah, yeah, 'I see.' Don't act like you're my therapist." Scarlett waved her hand. "At least I've left the state."

"Don't hold it over me. I never had the opportunity." Megan looked off to one side, something sad coming over her face that made Scarlett feel like kind of an ass for picking on her.

Other obstacles were crashing into place in Scarlett's mind already. "Well, we couldn't drive, then. You probably don't even have a passport, and it would cost a fortune to get one expedited."

"I have a passport." Megan interlaced her fingers in her lap.

"What? Why?" Scarlett couldn't imagine why she'd want one.

Megan clammed up again, pulling her legs in to her chest on the chair. "I don't know why you care."

"I'm curious. For old times' sake."

"I got one back when I first graduated college. I thought— it's dumb." Megan's voice was muffled against her knees. Scarlett wanted to push her, but they didn't have that rapport anymore. She could try and pressure her, but that wasn't going to do them any good. But then Megan continued talking. "I thought I was going to travel, and I didn't." She picked her head up and rested her chin on her knees. "Is that good enough?"

She might drive Scarlett mad, and Scarlett might have some unresolved issues with her that she did not want to resolve now, but the curiosity was stronger than the resentment at this point. "Don't you want to use that passport? It seems perfect. We'll drive up to Quebec for the wedding. Go a few days early to see the city, go to that winter carnival thing, and then come home. Unless you don't want to leave the state."

"I want to leave the state," Megan said defensively. "You think I like never having done anything with my life?"

Scarlett didn't need to tell Megan that she wasn't the only one who hadn't done anything with her life. They would probably have to have that conversation eventually. If they became friends again. "What do you think?" Scarlett asked.

Megan's face went through a number of expressions. "How are we supposed to pay for it?"

"I've got a little money saved up," Scarlett lied.

"But not enough for plane tickets?" Megan asked.

"Okay, so I don't really have any money." Scarlett pulled her legs up onto the couch. "I don't know how we're going to pay for it."

Megan grimaced. She seemed to be considering something for a long time. "Okay. Look. I got a big check from Winston and Martha as thanks for closing the Starlite. I was...thinking of going somewhere with it anyway. I can pay for the hotels and food if you can pay for the gas."

Scarlett did not need to do the math to know she was getting the way better deal out of that over Megan, and her conscience wouldn't let her stay quiet about it. "Why would you even have me go if you're going to pay for almost everything?"

"Because I can't do all that driving myself," Megan said, like it was obvious. "And I've never done a road trip before. I don't know how to do it."

"You pretty much just drive north," Scarlett said, but then changed her mind. "Never mind. It's okay. I'm just letting you know you're really getting ripped off."

"I think that even if you were paying for half of everything, I'd still be getting ripped off," Megan said, matter-of-factly, "because of the fact that we're going to be stuck in a car together for a week or something."

Scarlett rubbed her chin. "If we drive straight through in shifts, we might be able to do it in less."

Megan raised her eyebrows. "Are you kidding? This is my one road trip, I'm going to make a whole trip out of it. I'm the one paying. We're going to all the places on my list."

"Wait a minute, wait a minute." Scarlett held up a hand. "This suddenly became a carjacking."

"It's not a carjacking when it's my car." Megan gave her a smug smile.

"Ugh. This is the worst." Scarlett rolled her eyes. Megan had her, and she knew it. "Do you at least have good places on the list? I'm not driving out to the fucking Grand Canyon on our trip to Quebec. You're allowed to go two hours off of I-95 in any direction, but no more. I want to get this over with as fast as possible."

Megan looked defeated, like all the fight went out of her. "I don't even know where I want to go, all right? I was just talking. I don't care."

That was clearly a blatant lie, but Scarlett didn't want to examine it or probe into it right now, and Megan was looking all sad, which hit some soft place inside Scarlett that should definitely have calloused over by now. She'd pressed her luck enough for one night. "Are you okay if I come by sometime to plan? And maybe message you in the meantime?"

Megan hesitated, then nodded. "Sure. Whatever. Now can you get out and let me sleep?"

Scarlett got up off the couch. "I'd hate to be a bother."

"Yeah, right." Megan ushered her out and closed the door in her face, leaving Scarlett standing in the cold wondering what in the world she was going to do now that Megan had said yes.

Megan stared at the closed door with her heart hammering in her ribs. For all her ability to seem unaffected by emotionally intense conversations, that evening with Scarlett had rattled her. If she hadn't been so exhausted and ready to drop off to sleep, she might have been able to process it better, but right now she just wanted to mull it over after a full night's rest.

But rest wouldn't come, so Megan did what she always did when her mind refused to shut up: she took a bath. She stripped off her pajamas and filled the tub with hot water, hot enough for her skin to barely tolerate, and dumped in some of the epsom salts bubble bath she'd first bought to soothe her sore legs from walking all day and later just kept around because it was practical. Then, she lit two candles, the generic kind since the official Yankee Candle brand was too expensive for her to justify purchasing, and turned off the bathroom lights.

It was almost midnight. The house was quiet, and would probably stay quiet because Matt would spend the whole night playing video games. She had time to process in the way she liked, and so she sank into the steaming bubbles, hissing as her cold skin contacted the water. She couldn't quite submerge all the way in this bathtub; even though she was slim, her legs were too long, and her knees poked up out of the bubbles like an iceberg. She was able to get her whole torso beneath the water, though, the bubbles brushing her chin, a few bits of foam sticking to her hair. In the dark, only the flickering candle light to illuminate the room, she ran through what she had just agreed to and what in the world she was going to do next.

She had to be practical, of course. She needed to figure out the exact mileage between Crystal River, Florida, and the Chateau Frontenac in Quebec. Then she needed to get her car serviced. It was a Toyota Camry, so it was going to last forever, very unlike whatever ridiculous vanity car Scarlett had bought back in high school and then tried to keep limping along nearly a decade later. She was so irresponsible sometimes. Scarlett always blew her money on dumb purchases, when Megan was likely to save and be smart and start a responsible bank account and a Roth IRA. Megan could afford to fly to Quebec if she wanted to. Scarlett could not.

Maybe if she hadn't blown all her money on fancy-ass private college, Scarlett could have afforded it. What was she doing freelancing, anyway? The University of South Florida wasn't good enough for Scarlett. A mean little inner voice wondered how she'd even gotten into a private college; it wasn't like her grades were anything special. As soon as she thought it, though, she winced and pulled the words back. She might be jealous, but she wasn't mean. That wasn't like her.

Jealous. She rolled that thought around while she gathered handfuls of bubbly foam and piled them on her knees, only to watch the bubbles slide back down her skin again. Was she really jealous of Scarlett? Certain things, sure. Her amazing body, with those incredible curves that landed everyone Scarlett ever wanted: guys, girls, even people who didn't fit into either of those categories. Scarlett was the first bisexual person Megan had ever known, the first person to be out in their middle school—middle school, for crying out loud! She had always known who she was.

And Megan? Megan didn't know shit about herself for

most of her life. She hadn't figured out that she wasn't straight until college. She'd been through three relationships before figuring out how to ask for what she wanted in bed, and even then, she was better at doing it herself than getting a partner to do it for her. That was good, because she kind of hated dating. Nobody gave Megan a second glance. Megan was average, and average meant nobody noticed you. Average meant blending in.

Nothing about Scarlett was average, and she was never someone to blend in.

In high school, Scarlett's vivaciousness had lit up Megan's life. She was only too happy to follow along, carried in Scarlett's orbit or drawn like a moth to a flame. But she'd been burned. Scarlett's friendship had meant the world to Megan, but Megan's friendship had been easily tossed aside for a better college, a world of broken promises and a sudden unwillingness to speak to her best friend again. Scarlett had moved up in the world. Megan had done nothing.

But now, Scarlett was out of money, and she needed Megan's help, and she wanted Megan to drive her to Quebec. And Megan had…had what? Had volunteered to pay for it, even. God, had she been suckered again? Was Scarlett using her as a way to get to Canada? A little nugget of sickness settled into her stomach. This trip was a terrible idea.

But.

But.

Megan had had twenty-five years to accumulate goals and dreams for herself, and she had a scrapbook filled with the places she wanted to travel to and the goals she wanted to achieve, and she wasn't going to make the first step on her own. She never made the first step on her own. Even now, even on the other side of their friendship in this morass of weird discomfort between them, Scarlett was pushing her to take the first step.

Megan looked up at the ceiling, where the flames cast long shadows. She was going to have to stay in a car with this woman for a week. Maybe more than a week. What in the hell had she gotten herself into?

Even after her bath, she couldn't settle. She wandered around the house for a while, cleaned some things, and then tried to read a book. That's where Matt found her when he rolled in a little after one, key fumbling in the lock, crashing inside with no attempt to be quiet. "Hey!" He grinned, stumbling a little as he came inside. "You still up?"

"Yeah." Megan closed her book. "Are you drunk?"

"A little." He rubbed his face. "What the fuck do you care?"

"Did you drive?"

"No, I didn't drive. Dan drove me home." Matt yawned. "That reminds me. Can you drive me to his place tomorrow to get my car?"

Megan stared up at him. What a fucking asshole. She sighed. "Sure. You get me the rent yet?"

"Oh right! Remind me tomorrow. It's one in the goddamn morning." He went to the fridge and grabbed a Gatorade. "Can you get more Gatorade next time you get groceries?"

"Write it on the list." Megan tried to focus on the book again, but her unease was still unsettling her.

A few envelopes fell onto her lap from above, making

her jump. "I got the mail," Matt said. "You actually got something that's not a bill."

Megan held the heavy envelope and knew immediately what it was. She pulled out Juliet's invitation and turned it to catch the light. The navy blue card stock was decorated with golden stars, the fancy golden script proclaiming, Together with their parents, Mr. Gabriel Bouchard and Miss Juliet Letourneau request the honor of your presence at their wedding...

"What's that?" Matt flopped down on the couch next to her, shoving her feet out of the way.

"It's a wedding invitation." She was going to have to tell him at some point. "It's in Quebec."

Matt snorted. "You want me to throw it out?"

Megan pressed it to her chest. "No. I'm going."

Matt stopped, bottle halfway to his mouth, and slowly lowered it again. "You're what?"

"I'm going to the wedding." Megan hated how her voice trembled even when she tried to sound confident. "It's in a few weeks."

"You're not going." He laughed and took another sip. "You don't go anywhere. You don't even have a passport."

"Yes, I do." He didn't know her at all.

"Why? Waste of money, if you ask me." He kicked his feet up onto the coffee table. "Look, no offense, Meg, but you're not the traveling kind. Some people are adventurous, and some people aren't. You're not." He patted her shin. "Nothing wrong with that."

"I said I'm going, and I'm going." Megan flared in anger,

all her frustration and confusion suddenly directed at him. "I'm driving up there with Scarlett."

"Scarlett who?"

"Scarlett Andrews."

Matt scrunched up his nose like he was trying to remember her. "Did I ever sleep with that one?"

Revulsion ran through Megan at the mere thought of it. "God, I hope not." Shit, what if he had?

"What got into you tonight? That time of the month?" Matt got to his feet, shaking his head. "Ugh. Whatever. I'm going to bed."

He left her there on the couch and wandered into his room at the other end of the house. Megan watched him go, annoyed and for some reason embarrassed. Embarrassed by what? Maybe her past, maybe what she had and hadn't done with her life. She'd been a little uncertain about her decision, but now, she needed to go to prove Matt wrong. She needed to do something to move forward.

She grabbed a pen and the RSVP card. Matt could say what he wanted. She was going to Quebec.

Don't miss Hairpin Curves *by Elia Winters, Available now wherever Carina Press ebooks are sold.*
www.CarinaPress.com

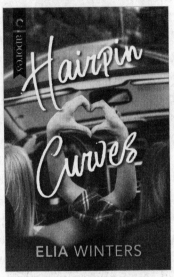
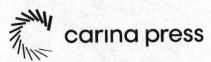

IF YOU ENJOYED THIS BOOK
WE THINK YOU WILL ALSO LOVE

Carina Adores is home to highly romantic contemporary love stories featuring beloved romance tropes, where LGBTQ+ characters find their happily-ever-afters.

1 NEW BOOK AVAILABLE EVERY MONTH!